THE TANNHAUSER GATE

THE TANNHAUSER GATE

A HOPE FOR TOMORROW

by

Willum Morsie

Pesky Publishing Ltd

First edition, 2024

ISBN 978-1-0687533-2-9

Published by Pesky Publishing Ltd

PREFACE

ALL good stories have a story themselves. This book started off as a small story amongst friends before being adapted into, at present, four books, with this forming book one.

At some point in 2010 a group of university friends got together and built a universe with complex interplay, unique characters and a plot to keep you guessing. Almost a quindecade after the first words were put to page the first book has finally been completed.

The book was then written, tweaked and tuned by Willum Morsie before finally ending up here, in your hands.

Morsie would like to thank all those who helped shape this story. Whether that was just by listening to the raw ideas or shaping them with input. Morsie would also like to thank those university friends that helped start this idea. While we were once one big *dysfunctional family* most of those relationships have now drifted apart. But this story keeps one part of that family alive.

Lastly, Morsie would like to thank Pesky Publishing Ltd. This story had been consigned to the annals of history, dust growing more than the words. Until one chance interaction with Pesky Publishing Ltd revived the story and the want to get it finished.

All that is left is for you to enjoy this story.

Contents

Chapter I

Lying on her front, with the soft, blue grass beneath her and the bright stars above, a thin, dark-haired girl of five sang an ancient Christian hymn and drew diagrams for devices that contemporary science said were impossible.

This was the Republic, second largest and at least third most powerful spatial power in the galaxy. But the girl neither knew nor cared about inter-stellar politics as she began the third verse of *O, for a Thousand Tongues to Sing* and scrawled a mathematical equation in symbols none but she ever used or understood.

A short distance away, the orphanage matron stared down a government official with the uniquely disapproving stare of nuns, teachers and grand-mothers alone. In this case, it helped that the matron was all three.

"I don't think I've been told the full story of this project, Mr Weams," the matron stated, each word a weapon that was loaded, but not yet fired. "It seems to me that you haven't thought through the fates of these children enough."

Mr Weams smiled. "I assure you, the happiness of the children is among the prime concerns of the *Tomorrow's Hope* Project," he replied. "You've seen the facts and figures. On-board food, education, entertainment. The ship's library contains everything from modern classics such as A Dance in the Moons to ancient earth classics by Victor Hugo and even ancient reference books like the OED. We have a choice with these kids, matron. We can keep them cooped up in here. No future prospects to speak of. No real hope. Or we can let them go free, out there, to glitter in the dark alongside the stars."

It was a good line, the matron had to concede. Clearly thought up in a boardroom of salespeople with the sole purpose of making something so horrid sound like an excellent idea.

It was true, in its way. The orphanage relied on donations and volunteers, and neither of those things had been growing as fast as the number of orphans. The *Tomorrow's Hope* Project seemed like the perfect solution for everyone. An unwanted dream come true, or an undesirable answered prayer.

"These kids whom you've selected for the project," the matron started and paused to look around, "I have to question the judgement." She gestured to the little girl on the grass, who ignored her, entirely wrapped up in her own sketches. "I love these kids like I loved my own, Mr Weams, but most of the ones you've picked are the unusual ones. The ones with the delicate minds, or those we struggle to teach, because they get too wrapped up in scribblings that can't be understood. I want to know who made these choices."

"No need to worry, matron," Mr Weams cheerfully assured her. "The selection process has been investigated and signed off by the highest authority there is."

The matron raised her eyebrows feigning shock and chuckled, "Goodness. That's funny. The sisters and I talk with Him three times a day at the least, and He never signed anything for us."

Mr Weams, refusing to be put off, countered, "My apologies, matron. I refer, of course, to the highest human power. Save the Republic President, of course."

He presented a small tablet computer, above which a logo floated in hologram form. The matron raised her eyebrows in real shock.

"Is this a joke?" she demanded. Mr Weams, still cheerful, shook his head.

The matron recognised the symbol, but only because her previous employers had taught her of it. The symbol of the highest authority. The assembly that sat in judgement over everything in the Republic, they said. Not everyone even believed in its existence.

"The Tannhauser Gate," the matron breathed.

"The very same," nodded Mr Weams. "Our senior sponsorship partners. They care as deeply as we do about the fate of the children. And no one's welfare is beyond the control of the Gate."

The matron glared thoughtfully at the floating symbol, and then turned to leave. The girl on the grass stopped her singing and watched as the matron stopped short. There was another child on the matron's other side, grasping the woman's hand in a tiny one of his own. His bright red mop of hair poking out from behind the matron's skirt. The child hadn't moved when the matron went to walk away. Instead, he chose to focus his awkward, unguarded gaze on the government representative.

"Hoiser," said the tiny redhead, taking both the matron and Mr Weams by surprise. The girl on the grass tilted her head and laid aside her pen.

"Tann-hoiser Gate," said the boy, blinking at Mr Weams, who blinked back, and quietly turned his tablet away from the matron so that he could tap, unseen, at the screen.

"Is this child destined for the project, matron?"

"Yes," replied the matron, frowning. "His parents requested it when they left him."

"Good. Good," smiled Mr Weams, tucking away the tablet and shaking the matron by the hand. "All is arranged, then. You won't hear from us again until the day of transportation. Good day, matron. Good day."

The girl on the grass was intrigued by the matron's expression. Ever since the words 'Tannhauser Gate', her expression had been unsure. The matron was almost never unsure. She always told the orphans that everything happened for a reason. The Tannhauser Gate had to be something very special to get to the matron. Strange, then, that of all people, a little boy of about two had seemed to recognise the name.

It wasn't long before the girl on the blue grass was struck by a new idea, and remembered the last verse of *O, for a Thousand Tongues*, and so went back to drawing and singing, the name of the Tannhauser Gate already forgotten. Above, the sky darkened, and the stars shone all the brighter for it.

This was the Republic. Big, and powerful. And as a result, full of secrets. Big, powerful secrets, that glittered away, unsaid, on dark nights.

Like stars.

Chapter II

IT HAD BEEN TEN YEARS SINCE the President of the Republic had been 'delighted to inform the galaxy that poverty in the cities of the Republic was a thing of the past'. This wasn't technically a lie. The income for anyone who could afford to live inside a Republic city was well above the poverty line. And for those who didn't fancy living in the shiny apartment blocks of the cities themselves, there were stately houses with spacious grounds surrounding each now poverty-free city inside Republic Space. The fact that some pretentious town planner with a poor grasp of French history had decided to name the idyllic, English-speaking suburbs the 'Banlieues' was unfortunate. That said they were elegant and refined and the cities themselves were sparkling and glorious, so no one really minded. In fact, anyone who happened to land their spaceship in one of the Republic's in-city docking ports would assume the place was a real-life utopia.

Unfortunately, not everything was as ideal as it first appeared. If the tourists were to venture further afield, maybe if they headed down the wrong alleyway or got lost down a side street, they would see a much darker and more unpleasant colony.

This sprawling warren of shacks, known as 'The Outer Slums', had started as a small settlement but had expanded to engulf the non-city portions of the planet. It became home to the ever-increasing number of people who had nowhere else to go. Other planets followed suit and soon a Republic wide cleanse of the cities was underway. Having been forced out of their homes and towns, and not being one of the impoverished, parentless

5

children given a new life with the *Tomorrow's Hope* Project, the 'undesirables' swarmed out of the Banlieues and into the slums where they adapted or died. Or, in many cases, adapted and still died because disease-ridden cesspools of poverty and sin are serious threats to the longevity of even the most resilient individuals. Inevitably, the slum folk became beggars, thieves and pickpockets.

And then, ten years ago, the Outer Slums had been crossed off the map. They officially no longer existed to the city dwellers, or to the rest of the Republic controlled universe. No one wanted to know, and no one wanted to help. And if anyone ever did discover the depravity behind the affluence, someone or something made sure they kept quiet about it. The Outer Slums were the lowest of the low. No one could redeem themselves from there. Or so the authorities made sure.

Elios Bennett was on a mission. He'd been skulking in his usual haunt for hours, hoping to get lucky, waiting for a stray tourist to mug or a fellow thief to borrow a favour from. He needed money, or rather, he needed what money could be traded for. Folk need the stuff you can buy with money, but Elios knew cold cash is pretty useless on its own. In fact, Elios had considered often, enough coins could fill a sock and make a pretty decent flail, but in the Outer Slums the only people with that much wealth were the better off drug dealers and gang leaders. He knew from firsthand experience; they'd rather carry jimmy-hooks and knuckle-crackers and so would have no need for a coin sock. Besides, as Elios would inevitably think, rocks could be weaponised just as easily. They were cheaper and heavier, and less likely to get you mugged compared to walking around with an entire sockful of cash.

All of this was theoretical to Elios, of course, who had never owned a pair of socks in his life. His damp feet were protruding from the tattered remnants of two paper bags that he'd found in a refuse site behind Madame's. A hybrid bakery and brothel next door to a drug den where Elios spent much of his time. The Madame, who baked the bread and looked after the poor wretches who found themselves in her service, had discovered from a young age that customers were always hungry after indulging the kind of entertainment her girls offered.

Elios hated the place. The stench of sweat and cheap perfume from the brothel upstairs and clouds of sweat and smoke from the drug den next door seeped into the bread, making it inedible to anyone who wasn't famished.

Right now, having been refused entry into the drug den due to lack of funds, Elios was leaning against a pillar across the street from Madame's with his space monkey, Moncello, perched on his shoulder. Both monkey and master were shaking uncontrollably, and not just from the chill of the spitting rain. Elios needed **The Drug** and, having been barred from the drug den, the only way to get **The Drug** now was to buy it from one of the dealers. As so often was the case for slum dwellers, Elios found his options blocked by the bitter wall of poverty. Theoretically, he could break into the Banlieues and steal **The Drug** from one of the legal chemists, but that took time and effort, not to mention, it was very risky. Especially when a person's judgement was impaired by withdrawal.

Elios was getting desperate; he knew that it wouldn't be long before the sweats would start and then the anger. Elios didn't want to think about what would come after that. The last time he'd been that far gone, things hadn't turned out well. Not for him, and certainly not for that poor sod who got in his way. The details were a bit hazy, but Elios knew he had woken up with **The Drug** leaves scattered around him and blood on his shirt and hands. He couldn't let things come to that.

Across the road a couple of young employees came out of Madame's front door and lit a couple of smokes. Moncello's sensitive nose twitched in disgust and Elios patted his wet back comfortingly. The smokes were drugs, certainly, and theoretically no less addictive than the type Elios needed, but they weren't **The Drug**. And Elios needed **The Drug** soon.

One of the employees called to Elios, inviting him over for a good time, but Elios was too overcome by his burning need for **The Drug** to answer. The person shrugged unconcerned and finished their smoke before they and their companion headed back indoors.

Suddenly the space monkey on Elios's shoulder uttered a soft squeak and cocked his head to one side.

"What's wrong, Moncello?" Elios asked, hastily checking around him. "Do you hear somethi—" He broke off mid-sentence, frozen to the spot, listening intently.

A course sniffing and shuffling sound was coming into focus.

A horrid sinking feeling attacked his stomach. That faint snuffling told him all he needed to know; only one creature in the whole of the Outer Slums made a noise like that. Huge, fanged, pink-eyed sniffer moles were deaf and blind, but their sense of smell was second to none. Some of the hardened street thugs used them to intimidate the common slum dwellers and sniff out rival criminals who had ventured into their territory.

Elios swore under his breath and retreated into the shadows. He wasn't important enough to be considered a threat, but he still didn't want to get in the way of one of those beasts, and he wasn't particularly anxious to meet the mole's owner. Anyone with enough cash to afford a sniffer mole had to be influential in the slums. The most powerful and influential mole owners stayed because they could make a profit rather than because they had nowhere else to go. Elios knew of several dealers who actually lived in the Banlieues and commuted to the Outer Slums each day to sell their wares. Many of them even had families. In fact, Elios's favourite supplier of **The Drug**, a middle-aged man named Percy who would sometimes throw in an extra leaf or two for Moncello, was leading an entire double life. He'd told his fiancée that he was a policeman from New Brussels who had emigrated to this part of the galaxy to look for work.

The snuffling grew louder, and Elios and Moncello watched as a large quivering snout poked out from behind one of the abandoned shops that lined the alley. The snout was followed by two huge fangs and Elios felt a wave of panic rush through him as the rest of the mole appeared. He wanted to run but he was frozen to the spot. He even had to remind himself to breathe.

The chain around the sniffer mole's neck clanked menacingly as its owner tugged at it. Elios vaguely recognised this particular mole's owner. The man had been an acquaintance of Elios's late mother and had sometimes helped her find work in the slums. In return, she had offered the man her services free of charge.

Elios had no desire to be found, especially not by one of his mother's old clients, and began to wonder if it was maybe a good thing that he'd been free of **The Drug** for the last couple of days. Combined with the dirt covering his body, there was very little to distinguish Elios's smell from that of his surroundings, and, despite their impeccable noses, sniffer moles were by no means infallible. On top of all that, it wasn't as if the mole was actually looking for Elios. If only the streets weren't so narrow, he thought.

Its claws clacking on the muddy cobbles, the mole and the gangster passed within two feet of where Elios and Moncello were hiding, completely unaware that they were being watched, and disappeared down one of the side alleys. As soon as he was sure they were gone, Elios emerged from his hiding place and fled in the opposite direction.

To an outsider, the twisting labyrinth of the Outer Slums was a treacherous and confusing place. The snaking alleyways wriggled back on themselves, tricking and teasing the unfortunate newcomer. As if getting lost in this hellhole weren't enough to worry about, the uneven cobbles and loose bricks and slates were perilous death traps to anyone who lowered their guard for an instant.

Elios had lived in the Outer Slums for as long as he could remember and knew all of the shortcuts and back alleys that allowed him to avoid the more dangerous patches, but he still kept his fist clenched around the switchblade in his pocket. He kept the knife for protection, at least that's what he kept telling himself. Elios didn't like to dwell on the other uses the knife could be put to, especially when he was so desperate for **The Drug**.

He hadn't gone far when he tripped over a bundle of old clothes that someone had left in the alley. Cussing under his breath, Elios realised that he'd ripped the already very thin elbow of his jacket. He glanced at the pile of clothes; they were no better than rags but there might be a replacement coat in there, it couldn't hurt to look. Elios approached the bundle and a taloned, veined claw shot out and grabbed hold of his ankle. The bundle shifted threateningly and, as Elios tried to shake free, Moncello tensed, ready to pounce if his master gave the signal.

"Spare a couple of credits for a poor, starving woman?" the bundle croaked, and Elios stopped struggling for long enough to see the rotting face of one of thousands of beggar-crones that infested the slums. Her shrunken features were framed by wisps of grey hair and giant, pustulating pox-boils suggested what her career may have been at some point in her life. The beggar tried to smile. Elios almost felt sorry for her.

With an extra vigorous kick, Elios's boot caught the hag's chin, causing her to release his leg with a muffled grunt. Elios backed away as the crone nursed her bruised face.

Moncello made a strangled clicking noise in the back of his throat and signalled for Elios to look up. Glancing in the direction that Moncello was gesturing, Elios saw the hull of a huge cargo ship flying low overhead. It had obviously been trading in the Banlieues and, from Moncello's excited squeaks, Elios could tell that there could be plenty leaves of **The Drug** on board. How Moncello was able to know a ship may be carrying **The Drug** from several kilometres away through the airtight hull of said ship, Elios didn't know. But he did know that Moncello hadn't been wrong before and there was no time to question the situation further. The cargo ship would soon be out of the range of his transporter. Usually, he would only go after inbound ships, as he would be guaranteed return to the slums, but desperation made it clear that he had to have **The Drug** now.

"Sorry, lady," he grinned impishly at the old crone who was struggling to drag herself across the narrow street towards him. Opening up a small round device, he turned the dial, held his breath and closed his eyes. Then he, the space monkey, and the small device disappeared.

Elios found himself in a blue-lit room, full of sealed ceramic crates. The clinically sterile smell was overwhelming. As his lungs swelled in gratitude after the nauseating journey, they inhaled in the cool, menthol sharp air and Elios's vision blacked over.

Don't faint, he willed himself. His trembling hands reached out, groping for a crate to sit on until his eyesight returned. It's never fun to space bounce, even when you're used to it, and this clean air wasn't helping matters. If he'd had a proper teleporter, one of those high-tech ones with a tingle at each end and blissful unconsciousness in the middle, then maybe right now he'd be steadier. But the transporter he did own was a piece of junk. He'd won it in a craps game from a poor desperate who was later disappeared by the mole owners for failing to pay up. It was short-range, determined by how long you could hold your breath, and the travel method, which allowed him to bounce across the slits of space, made even the most hardened transport users feel space sick. The only advantage to owning such a horrid transporter was that no one expected it, so Elios could bypass security systems that would have picked up the residual emissions from regular, comfy teleporters without much difficulty.

Eventually his eyes regained focus and Elios watched as Moncello scampered off, searching out the scent of **The Drug**. Space monkeys have the second-best sense of smell in the universe and Moncello had been trained to sniff out **The Drug** since before Elios could remember. Within a few minutes Moncello was stood on top of a crate with a leaf of **The Drug** in his mouth. Elios grinned wryly, he knew Moncello was probably addicted to **The Drug** as well, by now. As Elios removed the leaf from Moncello's mouth, the monkey began to squeak in happiness.

"Shh!" Elios hushed him. He could hear footsteps just outside. "D'you want to get us caught?" Moncello cringed back at his master's harsh tone, and Elios sighed. "Sorry," he whispered, gesturing to his shoulder. "I guess I'm further gone than I thought."

Moncello silently jumped up on the shoulder and started to groom the side of Elios's head for nits, occasionally finding one and eating it. Elios left him to it, his mind now wholly absorbed by **The Drug**. He reached into his coat and pulled out a small, brass unlocking-device. Sticking his tongue out of the side of his mouth with concentration, he placed the device on top of the crate Moncello had jumped from, and it silently began to bore a hole through it. Elios stood watching it with increasing apprehension. It wasn't state of the art technology by any means; Elios had stolen it from an old inventor whom he had drugged to the point of delirium. By the time the man had woken up, Elios was long gone.

The device made a small click and Elios picked it up and looked through the hole it had made. Moncello had done his job well; the crate was packed full of **The Drug**. Sticking his hands in the hole, Elios pulled out handful after handful of leaves and stuffed them into his pockets. He knew better than to take any of **The Drug** now, when he could easily be caught.

Suddenly a voice behind Elios called out, "Freeze!"

Elios jumped at the command and spun round. Standing in front of him were two stern-looking men. Both had, what he assumed to be, guns pointed at him.

"Moncello," Elios growled through his teeth. "We've been over this. You're s'posed to let me know the security goons are here before they've got their shooters out." The monkey blinked blankly at him, and Elios sighed. Weighing up his options, he decided to risk it. He reached in his pocket for his transporter but before he even had time to turn the dial, one of the men pulled the trigger. Moncello let out a small screech and jumped in the line of fire.

The space monkey fell to the floor with a thud, but he had bought Elios the time he needed. Turning the dial and scooping up Moncello, Elios took a deep breath, you never know how much oxygen there is in any certain slit, but he couldn't resist taunting the two men.

"Sayonara, suckers!" Elios saluted them. Then he bounced. Elios felt so pleased with himself he hardly noticed the huge band of light zooming towards him. Until he hit it.

Light concaved around him, like a trampoline around a boulder. Elios just had time to wonder how light could be rubbery before he felt himself hurtling back in the direction he had come from. His leg hit something hard and there was a crash of crates as Elios stumbled backwards. He was still in the hold.

Elios gawped groggily up at the two men who had discovered him. They weren't looking angry now. One of them, the one pointing the weapon at Elios's head, was actually grinning.

"I think it would be more appropriate to say, Jya a mata," he said with an amused tolerance.

"That means see you later," the other added, for their captive's benefit. "It's foreign."

The grinning gunman pulled the trigger and there was a rippling of air as a bolt of energy shot towards Elios with an electric *tzap*. A short, sharp shock, a high-pitched ringing in his ears, it took a second for Elios to realise that he had been shot before he fell into blackness.

Chapter III

Tomorrow's Hope Outwith Known Space

For a long time, engineers and transport-related scientists had been split down the middle, half of them concentrating on improving the generation ships that could vastly increase humanity's reach in the universe, the other half focusing on creating the faster-than-light travel that would render these generation ships obsolete. It had taken an extraordinarily devious mind to come up with the idea of putting both ideas together.

Tomorrow's Hope had been the fourth FTL Generation Ship, or FTLGS as they were commonly known, ever constructed, and only the third functional ship, at least by humankind. The first had essentially been to test the idea, and had been almost uncannily fraught with failure. The second had been to refine the idea and get one that would actually work properly. The third had been the first one with a clear purpose and design. By the time the fourth ship came around, people had started to come up with less ethical uses for the concept.

The government had identified a problem. It wasn't a new problem, but it was a resilient one. There had always been people who were deemed a drain on society. Some people just seemed destined to be more trouble than they were worth. People who had nothing to contribute to the progress or maintenance of society, and likely never would. Every year for as far back as anyone cared to recall, it had cost the rest of humanity a vast amount just to keep these people alive. State benefits, soup kitchens, hostels, and the one that had been inexplicably growing in recent years: orphanages.

The orphan designated Blue-46-O4-1000 had never much listened in any of his classes. He picked up enough to vaguely get by, but nothing more. He knew the vague basics of evolution, for example. Survival of the fittest, species changing over time as certain traits get weeded out, everyone becoming better at surviving and screwing over their own predators and prey. It had struck him at the time that humanity, in this context, made no sense to him. From this point of view, rather than the emotional, feeling creatures humans had become, they should, in his mind, have turned into armoured tigers by now.

It had taken him almost a year to realise that the armoured tiger was still there, only becoming apparent in extreme circumstances when one's own survival relied on an ability to ignore one's own humanity. It had then taken him only a few weeks to realise that some of the humans in the universe had come out as armoured tigers. People for whom efficiency and ease of survival overrode every emotion and every trace of compassion.

The people who had come up with *Tomorrow's Hope* had been armoured tigers. They had seen an issue and found a solution, at the expense of their own humanity. There were too many orphanages in the galaxy, they said. Too many drains on the economy. Some of the orphans would grow up to make a positive change on the galaxy. Others, however, would not. To save money, time, effort and space, they needed to be got rid of. Government-condoned mass murder was generally too frowned upon to be a viable option. There was, however, a new FTLGS under construction, built by an organisation that wanted to hitch a ride on the success of the third one. It made perfect sense to send orphans on a generation ship. They would be young with no family to miss. No one would argue if you sent a vast number of orphans away, especially if you got a good spin-doctor to make it look like they were going to a better life. Once on the ship, there was no need to come good on any of the promises made. The ship doesn't need to be capable of sustaining them all. It doesn't need to be capable of sustaining itself. It doesn't even need to be going anywhere specific. Once it's out of range and out of mind, no one will care what happens to the people on board.

But then someone had produced a better idea, one that solved another problem at the same time. Up until this point in history, no one had ever been able to, for example, find out the exact extent of human endurance by experiment, because experimenting on unwilling humans was considered abominable. Now, however, there was about to be a vast number of orphans who essentially did not exist. Who knew what issues could appear in later years that could be resolved faster if only someone could experiment on some humans without anyone knowing?

So, *Tomorrow's Hope* had been fitted with a secure communication line, via an equally secure system and linked to, if anything, an even more secure Inter-Galactic Communication Station. All its systems had been made remotely controllable from this station. A separate area had been made for a few dedicated people to keep an eye on things at the deep space end. These people knew that they were on a one-way trip to nowhere. They were willing to give up their lives for the good of the human race as a whole. *Tomorrow's Hope* had been made capable of sustaining everyone on it for a few decades. That, they estimated, was how long it would take them to get their hands on another generation ship and a new boatload of useless orphans.

Blue-46-O4-1000 didn't know any of this, he didn't know any more than he needed to get by. What he did know was that his parents had abandoned him at an early age, requesting that he be sent away from the galaxy on an FTLGS. And that this ship was run by people he hated, and who seemed to hate him. He wanted to get off, if only that were possible. He also knew that something called the Tannhäuser Gate was important, and he wanted to find out why.

None of the rooms in *Tomorrow's Hope*, or more commonly just, The *Hope*, were pretty. At least, none of the rooms the unimportant inhabitants were allowed inside. They had doubtless been pretty to begin with. Most of the older orphans could at least dimly remember fresh, sparkling, optimistic decor when they first got on. Maintenance, however, was not a high priority on The *Hope*. It wasn't even on the priority list. Maintenance required resources which cost money, and the more money the ship cost, the less efficient the franchise became. It was agreed, however, that the classrooms were among the least pleasant communal areas, because nobody cared enough to clean them.

Blue-46-O4-1000 sat on a broken chair, scribbling in the plain notebook he had resting on a chipped desk that had once been a light silvery blue. The desk, now black, after thirteen years of students deciding that writing witty or not-so-witty messages on their desks was a good way to occupy their time. The education video droned on in the background, but Blue-46-O4-1000 wasn't listening. He was writing determinedly in his notebook, as he had done almost every class for as far back as he could remember. The same words, over and over. In different fonts, or different sizes, and sometimes written at different angles. Sometimes underlined or circled. But always the same words. The words that had been in his head, without explanation, for as long as he could remember.

Tannhäuser Gate.

It never mattered how he wrote it, or how long he stared at it. It never meant anything to him. He had learned that gate on its own meant a lot of things. An opening, an ambush, a political scandal, a set hour for return, an openable barrier, or even a chess move. Tannhäuser, as far as he could find, meant nothing. It may have once been a name, probably German, but none of the research he had done with the ship's limited electronic library could tell him more than that.

"Tannhauser," announced the educational video, and Blue-46-O4-1000's head shot up, eyes open and alert, ears straining to hear more. He strained to dredge up the previous sentence which his brain was already halfway to discarding. "...forgotten completely like the prose of Breslin or the poetry of Tannhauser." That was as much as he could recall. And then it moved on to something unrelated. No explanation or expansion on Tannhauser. But Blue-46-O4-1000 didn't mind that much. He had been writing out and staring at words for his whole life with little or no progress. Now he had something new to go on.

Without conscious thought, he corrected the narrator under his breath, "Tannhäuser." As his hand moved to a new page of the notebook and scrawled excitedly, Tannhäuser was a poet.

Blue-46-O4-1000 returned to his room in what, for the first time he could remember, could arguably be called a light mood. He jerked his head to get the unkempt red hair out of his eyes, ignoring the tiny protesting voice that kept telling him it needed washed and cut. He was humming along to a tune in his head that he couldn't place but didn't care. Tannhäuser was a poet. He had made progress, proving the name wasn't just in his head.

He passed the other doors nearby to his own, all locked. He was used to that. Isolation was familiar to him. The words in his head left him little time for people, and no one was willing to make the effort to interact with him unless it was in a more distinctly damaging sense. He barely spoke to other people at all nowadays, preferring to criticise them to himself under his breath. It was therefore a shock when a female voice started singing along to the tune he was humming. He stopped and turned.

Room Blue-46-O1-2460 had its door open. There was a dark-haired girl inside, a few years older than him. Blue-46-O4-1000 recognised her, but he had never spoken to her before. She was thin, weak and pale like all the children on board, and still bore the marks from a recent discipline session. Her eyes were bright, and she was smiling, he was sure he could see or sense some inner strength beyond the just-about-surviving exterior.

"*Oh, for a Thousand Tongues to Sing,*" she smiled. She had stopped singing shortly after he'd stopped humming. Her singing voice had been clear and reasonably good, but when she spoke it became clear that this was held together by conscious effort. Without that effort, her voice was hoarse and soft, and somehow cracked. "The matron at the orphanage used to sing me that. I only ever remember fragments, but I love the tune."

Matron would whistle it, Blue-46-O4-1000 realised. That was where he'd heard it before. She would whistle it in the corridors all the time. Giving the air that she was happy. Something that was missing on the ship, as no one on the ship was happy.

"Val-Jean," the girl said, touching her hand gently to her own chest. "Call me Val." Blue-46-O4-1000 felt himself blushing, and without knowing why he felt oddly like he wished she hadn't said that.

"I don't have a name," he admitted. "No one's ever given me one. No one's ever really spoken to me enough to need one." Part of him was screaming to get away from there, to run back to the relative safety of his own nearby room.

"What's your room number?" Val asked, swallowing back a burst of pain in her throat she obviously couldn't hide. "That's where most people I know got theirs."

He stayed, for some reason, at least long enough to answer. "Blue-46-04-1000," he recited. Val's smile broke into a laugh, which then shattered harshly into a coarse cough.

"You're joking!" she whimpered sheepishly through the pain. "That's it then. Tongues. 04-1000. Tongues."

***

Since that day, Tongues had always made an effort to see Val at least once a day. It worried him that she always seemed to have been disciplined more than anyone else. He couldn't work out why, but then reasons were never needed and rarely given.

Eventually he asked her about it, after her legs gave under her when she opened her door for him one day. His arms instinctively rose to catch her, and she flinched away mid-fall, seizing the edge of the door in a panic. They were frozen for a second, his hands centimetres from her waist, her eyes staring in fear. Then the moment was over, and she dragged herself up with an apologetic smile, and walked awkwardly, painfully to her bed.

"What do they do to you?" he asked, running his gaze over her bruised arms. She looked away for a second, before returning to her usual smile.

"They like to discipline me," she shrugged. "I think they're trying to make me stop being so happy all the time." Tongues wasn't sure he understood that.

"Why are you so happy all the time?" he asked. Val seemed to consider the question. Eventually she went to a drawer and opened it. Tongues followed just behind and peered over her shoulder. The drawer was full of bits of junk, as far as Tongues could tell, some of it connected together.

"I have a way off," Val explained. "I haven't tested it yet, I haven't even worked out how to test it, but with what I've got here, I can get away from this place. I," The door slammed open, cutting her off.

Tongues and Val swung their heads around. Two huge, smirking boys, a few years older than Tongues, barged in. Tongues thought he could identify them as Blue-46-B4-1000 and Blue-01-B4-1000. Or as they preferred to be known, Seborga and Police. All B4 rooms were inhabited by people who worked for the ship's authorities. No one knew why. That was just the way of things. Police was basically in charge of all B4s in the Blue secto, if he was accompanying Seborga, it was either something very important or he was getting something out of it.

"Surprise discipline session!" Seborga announced with glee. Police, the comparatively smarter of the two, dragged Tongues forcibly away and bent his head back painfully by the hair.

"Somebody trying to steal our rights here?" he sneered. "Somebody trying to discipline Val without authority? That's not very nice, you know. We might need to keep you around for afterwards."

Seborga had noticed the drawer that Val was trying to shut. "Here!" he cried. "What's she got that she don't want us to see?"

"Doesn't want," Tongues corrected instinctively, and Police stamped on his ankle causing him to scream. Seborga hurled Val inelegantly across the room and hauled the drawer open. He stared in incomprehension and opened his mouth to question.

The question never came. He seemed instead to leap off of his feet and hurl himself into the wall, his body jerking as a blue-white energy crackled across it. Police stopped torturing Tongues and turned to stare. "What the," he managed to exclaim, before he followed suit with a subtle *whumpf*, throwing him over Tongues and bouncing off the door.

Val stood up, one slightly shaking hand still grasping a little plastic and metal contraption. The metal was still glowing with residual energy as she ran to the drawer, pulling out the contents and fleeing the room, snatching Tongues on the way past.

"That, what is that, some kind of tactical flintlock?" he said, staring at the thing in Val's hand. They reached room Blue-46-04-1000 and Tongues threw the door open.

"It's something I made up in case I needed to take someone down in a hurry," Val explained. "It stuns people, sort of. They'll probably get up again," she paused almost as if she was concerned, "eventually. I think."

They collapsed, Val onto Tongues's bed, Tongues onto a chair. "I'm going to have to leave," she panted. "Today. They've seen what I can do. I was safe as long as they still just thought I was mad." She looked down, and her eye caught one of Tongues's notebooks and she flipped it open.

"What?" she muttered, flipping through the pages, sheet after sheet of Tannhäuser Gate. "Tongues," she paused, as if reading a new line, "what's Tannhäuser Gate?"

"I don't know," Tongues admitted. "Well, gate can be an opening or a mountain pass or a door or an ambush or a judicial assembly, or directly as in gateward meaning straight there, or gateshodel which is a crossroads that goes in many directions," he excitedly stopped, no one had asked him about this before, so he scrambled to find what to say, "And Tannhäuser was a poet, apparently. But I don't know what the phrase means. It's just always been in my head. Since," he shrugged, "pretty much forever. Here. I've got more." He picked up the rest of his notebooks from the desk and opened the one on top. Val stared.

"Tongues," she said slowly, flicking through the notebook, "this is big. Why didn't you tell me before? Messages in your head, words you don't even understand," she looked up. "I think, I think someone somewhere wants you to do something," she said seriously. Tongues just stared back blankly.

"What do you mean?" he asked.

"I don't really know," admitted Val. "But, it's like," she stopped to consider her next words, "the one person with a way off happens to meet the one person on this ship with something weird in his head. The matron always told me that things happen for a reason. It was a long time ago, but," she froze, as if waiting for a thought to catch up, "I don't remember it all, ok? But it was definitely important. I think," She paused, looking

Tongues in the eye. "I can remember the Tannhauser Gate causing matron to freeze when talking to The *Hope* person. I don't know why it's important, but it must be," she continued rambling, ignoring Tongues correcting Tannhäuser, "I think you need to get off this ship."

"Behind this door is the communication system," Val explained, as the pair stood facing an imposing metal barrier. "What they have back there is basically a box, a big box," she held her hand out extending the word big, "and held in place in the box is this mobile point in space. Bear with me," she took a breath that may or may not have been to disguise a sigh, and Tongues wondered dimly exactly how blank he looked right now. "Think of space like a sheet that gets folded," Val continued. Tongues continued to stare, but she pressed on anyway. "So there are two points that are really far apart, but have been made to touch each other. And that means they can send communications through that point, and the box picks it up. Basically. In a manner of speaking."

"So," Tongues lingered, "we do, what?" he asked, raising an eyebrow causing Val to sigh.

"What I have here," she brandished the apparent junk she was carrying, "can," she paused, "kind of rewire the box, so that it pulls the point," she paused again, clearly fighting back some kind of pain before she finished, "bigger."

"That makes no sense," Tongues said, his face contorting in thought.

"No, it doesn't," sighed Val. "But if I told you the exact truth I'd have to explain every other concept. So I won't." Tongues didn't bother pretending to understand any of that.

"So what do we do?" he asked, making a peddling motion with his hands between the pair of them. Val smiled.

"For that we need to go a bit further down the hall."

A short distance away, she stopped and grasped a screw in the corner of a panel on the wall. It came out without even needing twisted. The other three screws followed suit.

"I can't believe they didn't even notice me vandalising their screws," Val said as she reached into the gap behind the panel and pulled out some preexposed wires. "That's not just laziness, that's idiocy. Give me a second to wire these things up."

The parts of the ship pertaining to its communication with the galaxy they had left were the only bits outside of the Adult Area that were regularly maintained and constantly monitored. The doors could only be opened and the security systems disabled if expressly ordered to do so by one of the Adults running the vessel. Which was why it was particularly unexpected when they did open and disable, nicely in order, without any particular Adult being responsible.

Several floors up, in a section of the ship that none of the children were ever allowed in, all of the Adults were simultaneously alerted to this fact, and swiftly called up the details on their personal monitors. Back several floors below, Val's addition to the systems carried out its primary purpose, widening a single point of space-time, or rather, two single points of space-time, into an area large enough to fit a human being through. The energy made to pour into the system was incredible. Every non-vital system, barring FTL, not connected directly to the communications immediately failed due to lack of energy. Lights turned off, air conditioning stopped, lessons ceased in mid-lecture, electronic doors temporarily turned into walls.

Most of those systems that were connected to the communications were overloaded by an unexpected backlash and either burnt themselves out or outright exploded, including the personal monitors of almost every Adult on the ship. The systems themselves would either be automatically repaired or switched to backup versions. There were no backups for the humans. Some of them would survive long enough for their injuries to heal, some of them would not, but none of them were left in much of a position to be disciplining anyone for a while.

"That's interesting," Val noted as she and Tongues trotted through the dark. "I might need to fix some of that. I think some of the parts that just died were quite important." They came to a solid metal wall. Val felt around for a small hatch. "This was put in just in case they needed to do vital maintenance to the inside of this thing. It's supposed to be locked by at least seven different bits of technology. I don't think any of them are working properly right now." The hatch opened.

There was an oppressive blackness inside, somehow so dark that it made the absolute darkness the ship was currently in bright by comparison. Brilliant white lightning lanced irregularly through the black, an eerie kind of white that gave the impression it was made by mixing frequencies not of visible light but of some other spectrum entirely that human eyes were not used to seeing. Tongues stared, wondering dimly whether or not he should be terrified. Val stared as well, probably for different reasons, and then turned to Tongues.

"I don't know how long it'll last. You should probably go immediately."

"Ca—," Tongues started, stumbling on the word, "can't you come with me?" Val shook her head, and then realised Tongues couldn't see her.

"Nope. It's only just capable of fitting one small person through. As soon as solid matter goes through it, it'll stop. Burn itself out, sort of thing. And there's not enough energy available to do it again, even if my adjustments haven't outright died from the stress. This is goodbye, I'm afraid."

"Are you," Tongues stuttered, "Do I," he tried again, "Are—"

"Shut up and go, Tongues." Tongues looked at the blackness again. He swallowed.

"OK," he said.

Val's hug nearly knocked him off his feet. After a second, it softened into a gentle hold, "Goodbye, Tongues."

Tongues hesitated, and then gingerly reciprocated, "Goodbye Val."

"Do good things," Val instructed as they broke apart. "Go," She whispered. Tongues turned, braced himself, and pulled himself through the hatch.

CHAPTER IV

THE *ELISMERE* REPUBLIC SPACE

I T WAS A LONG RUN HOME from Metropolis for the *Elismere*, generally made all the longer for the fact that she never took anything but
a circuitous route. Even travelling at faster-than-light speeds through hyper, long-distance travel took time. And when you were taking deliberately
longer routes because you wanted to pay attention to some of the less public
activities of certain powerful groups within the Republic, it took longer.

Picking up a thankfully still-unconscious stowaway on Metropolis made
a bit of a difference, and in some ways was a happy change in normal schedule. Knowing that some of the newer security systems worked properly, as
well as that the ship's security teams were as fast reacting, was always nice.

Currently the *Elismere* was running silent on one of the less commonly
used bands of hyper. It made no difference to her speed, bands didn't work
like that, but it was one of the more commonly used divisions of the hyper dimension for high security transmissions within the Republic. If she
hadn't been, she never could have intercepted the signal that would change
everything. Most of the crew were asleep, recovering from the more rigor-
ous parts of the run. The command staff were pairing off on bridge duty
to give them the rest they required. That rest was about to be disrupted.

"Jen, I just picked something up on the very edge of our detection
sphere." Jennifer Alberson turned from her favoured position at the piloting station as her brother spoke. "It's weird."

:Define weird, Adrian. Normal weird or you weird?: Jenny's reply
wouldn't be heard by others for when alone with her brother she preferred

to use their natural mental talent to speak. And Adrian was quite happy to oblige her preference.

:It's a transmission coming from a station that shouldn't be where it is. The message header identifies the sender as a Stationmaster Imleros of IGC 0765. That's all I can get without stripping the code and cracking the contents, but I can tell you just from looking at the header that it's got an Amythest bypass.: Adrian shook his head, sweeping blond hair out of his green eyes to focus on the problem in front of him. *:Whatever is in this message, it's important. I've only seen this sort of encryption a handful of times, and the degree of compression on the burst is almost beyond what our systems can catch. The sender went to a great deal of trouble to try and stop this getting detected.:* He smiled at his sister. *:Good thing we happened to be here, isn't it?:*

:Can you break the encryption?: Jenny asked, concentration clear in her mental voice.

:We've got the new cryptography software from Marzena loaded,: Adrian replied easily, as if that answered everything. That it did was beside the point. *:And we've also got EVI.:* He gestured faintly at the ceiling, referring to the *Elismere's* Virtual Intelligence. Jenny shot him an arch look, prompting a laugh. *:Yes sis, I can crack it.:* She considered that for a few more seconds and then nodded sharply.

:Do it.:

:Done.: He tapped a control at his station and smiled faintly as the illegal, depending on which star nation you were in, decryption system the crew had found for him on Marzena went to work. The gibberish in front of him blurred before fading away to reveal rapidly scrolling text, and his eyes sharpened as he read. *:Jenny, you're going to want to see this. Sending to your panel.:* His mental voice was suddenly very cold, and Jenny glanced around from her station. There were very few things that could do that to her brother. Then she looked back at the text in front of her, and just like that, his tone made sense. The message was simple, but that very simplicity emphasised the callousness of the sender:

To whom it may concern,

We have a leak from the *Tomorrow's Hope* Project. A subject has somehow managed to come through the FSC connection

between *IGC 0765* and *Tomorrow's Hope*. **We are currently moving to obtain the subject, who is thought to be one of the expendables of the project's crew. BioScans are attached to this message. Please dispatch a purge unit.**

Stationmaster Vels Imleros

Her eyes widened as she pulled up the biological scans of the referenced subject before hardening, and she was altering course before her mind could even begin to catch up.

The *Elismere* shifted in her steady trek through hyper, drive coming to full power as her trajectory lined up on the transmission pathway from the *IGC 0765*, and lights started to flicker to life across the vessel.

:Wake the crew. I don't know what's going on here, but I'm not leaving a child with people that call him expendable. And this might even give us an opening. Remember who helped build Tomorrow's Hope.:

Adrian's fierce affirmative through their link was all the reply she needed. They could both remember their parents talking about *Tomorrow's Hope* and how it was almost certainly linked to the Gate. A generation ship of that scale couldn't have been completed without some major governmental support, and from everything Adrian and Jenny managed to find, their mutual obsession had supplied that support. He tapped a few controls, and the *Elismere's* General Quarters signal pulsed to life, waking the entire ship in a matter of moments. And his voice was waiting as they jerked from their rest.

"This is Adrian; we've intercepted a transmission from an InterGal-Comm station that is not on the books and are moving to investigate. I need all systems ready to blind their sensor net when we hit normal space. And we're going to need to be ready for a boarding action. Move it, people."

The bridge lift hissed open and the rest of the command crew spilled out. Jack spoke first.

"Why is it that whenever the two of you are on the bridge alone, something happens?" His face was serious, but his tone held a welcome edge of humour. He made his way to his chair, letting the rest of the command staff get to their stations. "What have we got?"

"Adrian, roll it," Jenny said tersely.

"We intercepted an outer-band transmission with high military encryption from an Inter-Galactic Communications station, that shouldn't exist according to the records. That piqued my interest, given where we are, so I looked deeper and found an Amethyst-level bypass in the transmission. Whoever sent this needed it to get to wherever it was meant to go, and fast."

The rest of the staff nodded, an Amethyst bypass was normally only used by the military, or extremely powerful members of the government, and gave the transmission holding it complete priority over all other messages, including emergency broadcasts. "I told Jenny and she agreed that we should crack it. This is what we found."

He brought up the message and the BioScan that had come with it on holo. "Whoever these people are, they know the truth of what's happening on the *Tomorrow's Hope*, and from the tone of it, it's very different, and a whole lot uglier, from what the Republic says is happening. I also ran the scan through our database, and something popped out. That kid, whoever he is, is one of us. I'm not sure exactly which family he comes from yet, but he's far enough down the generation chain that he might have the same trigger Jen and I do. And quite besides that, there is no way in hell that I'm leaving a child in the hands of people who write messages like that about them. Not when we have the chance to get him out."

Jack held up his hands as Jenny started to add her agreement to that statement.

"Jen, stop. I agree." His eyes, only moments ago laughing, were now very cold. And the words that followed were very deliberate. "I want to make sure that no one gets killed during the boarding action. And I think we want to keep their computer core intact."

"Agreed. But if this is what we think it is, then it's probably going to bring the Gate down on us for good. Nothing we do afterwards will stop that once we start it," Emily Vaneli noted softly. "Are we absolutely sure we want to do this?"

"Ems, if I didn't know you were just doing that to be the voice of reason," Jenny's voice was thick with emotion.

"I know, Jen, I know. And I recognise a need when I see one. But the possible consequences needed to be voiced." She looked over at the last member of the command crew, "Glen, your thoughts?"

"Do it."

Jack nodded. "That's it then. Adrian, do you have any idea how long it'll take for a response to get out here compared to us?"

"I'm not sure, but if everything works perfectly in handling and the receivers dispatch one of their faster vessels,""he ticked his tongue off his teeth, "they would get there maybe an hour after us at our current velocity. I can't be sure about that thou," His tone took on an edge of mock desperation as Jack turned to his sister. "Jack, I'm sure we don't need the," he pleaded.

"Jenny, I am authorising use of the FTL boosters regardless of your brother's," Jack paused for effect and smirked, "protests." Her face lit up with an almost childlike grin.

"I thought you might say that," She tapped two keys on her control screens. "So, I set them up for activation when I put us on course for the station." She opened a shipwide channel. "All hands, brace for booster activation. Approximate ETA is two hours." Her smile turned to a smirk as she glanced at Adrian and cut the channel. "Hold on."

Two panels slid back on the *Elismere's* hull, just below her wings, to reveal a bank of what looked for all the world like the business ends of old-fashioned chemical rockets, coming to riotous life as their camouflage slid away. Jets of radiation blasted out from them as they activated, stretching out along the sides of the ship's gently tapered stern and she shuddered for a moment as the shockwaves released by the boosters shook her frame. Then she began to accelerate, boosters pushing her steadily beyond the power of her drive and dangerously close to her structural limits, as she raced towards the station that called to her crew.

CHAPTER V

FOR AN INSTANT that felt like it lasted an eternity, Tongues seemed to be left void of all sensation save an extreme case of vertigo and an inexplicable and unplaceable itch. Every micron of his being seemed to be simultaneously everywhere and nowhere. He could see nothing, not even the darkness. He could hear nothing, not even the silence.

And then the world returned in an instantaneous detonation of colour, sound, temperature and pressure. Tongues could have sworn his internal organs all lurched sideways and hauled him into the wall. He was vaguely aware of delicate looking equipment that surrounded him in every direction. He vomited, and briefly pondered how anyone was going to be able to clean the damaged equipment. Without warning the thought was out of his head as he vomited again. Attempting to stand up straight he could feel all of his senses acclimatising, light seemed less bright, smells less strong, and his skin stopped burning.

He seemed to be in an even larger version of that box Val had spoken about. The inside of said box was lined with equipment, none of which Tongues recognised. There was a muffled sound, vaguely reminiscent of the alarms that would go off on board *Tomorrow's Hope*. Those alarms would go off from time to time, when someone had broken into an off-limits room or attempted to set a small part of the ship on fire, or occasionally simply because the system was faulty. It struck Tongues that being locked in a metal box with alarms going off outside was probably not an ideal position.

He stumbled along the wall, searching for a way out, while trying to rapidly habituate himself to the subtle differences of this new environment. There was a distinct lack of a low rumbling that he had grown use to on *Tomorrow's Hope*, but more eerily, he was sure he could feel the difference of no longer traveling at superluminal velocities. Eventually he came across a maintenance hatch, not unlike the one he had recently gone through aboard *Tomorrow's Hope*. This one was at least large enough to walk through. It opened on his first attempt. Clearly, no one had been planning for anyone to be trying to break out of this box.

A man in a simple white and grey uniform, with an expression Tongues only recognised as the frustration often shown by the adults on The *Hope*, was staring at him when he emerged. In his peripheral vision he could see several other similarly dressed people panicking loudly at an irritable look-ing woman. Tongues assumed she must be to some extent in charge given she wore a higher quality version of the same uniform. He froze unsure if anyone had noticed him yet.

The man screamed a warning that sounded incoherent to Tongues. Every other head in the room whipped around to focus on him. Tongues ran, flinging up his arms as he barrelled into the still shouting man, pushing him to the floor. He almost tripped on the man's falling body, staggered into the frame of the open doorway opposite, rebounded into the other side of the same frame, before regaining his balance and fleeing. He could already feel a stitch manifesting around his lower torso as the unwelcome noise of efficient running footsteps politely tapped his brain on its metaphorical shoulder. On *Tomorrow's Hope* there was no point in running from the adults, you would never get away, but something in Tongues's mind willed him on now.

Tongues's pursuers caught up with him around the third corner. He knew they were faster than him, and he had probably only made it this far by the force of his own sheer terror, but he couldn't come up with any other options. He heard the sound's of the people getting closer and closer. It was close enough to make out distinct words and feel the spit of those words. It was almost close enough to grab him.

His mind panicked. No conscious decision-making ability existed, and his mind was filled by one huge mental scream at the inevitability of his current fate. Somewhere amid this chaos, his muscles appeared to take control with their own course of action. As is often the case in these situations, it was a course of action that really didn't make much sense. Tongues turned to face his pursuers.

As a consequence of not making sense, the sudden change in direction caught the man immediately behind Tongues off-guard. The two collided and Tongues, being the lighter by far, bounced off, pushed himself off the wall almost by accident, and hurtled diagonally past a second man. The third was equally unprepared but managed to twist and snatch at the back of Tongues's T-shirt before he could desperately weave around him. Tongues screamed and tripped causing the material to slip free as he stumbled. The fourth man had stopped running and spread himself out, blocking the corridor with his bulk, arms out waiting to catch the boy's shape moving erratically towards him. Tongues couldn't fight against either the gravity pulling him to the floor or the momentum pulling him to the man. So, with haphazard logic, he averaged things out and threw himself at the man's feet.

He rolled, or bounced, or both, he wasn't sure. Most of his joints seemed to get knocked against either a floor or a leg or, in the case of one elbow, his own face. He had no time to consider the unlikely nature of this anatomical feat. He had managed to get one hand under himself and press against the floor, and the adrenaline still surging through his body forced that arm to straighten, throwing his entire body back to vaguely upright.

Before he could congratulate himself on this small victory, part of his mind calmed down enough to alert him to the fact that the men behind him had also turned around. He began to run again, but before he could get back to the end of this corridor, another two shapes appeared, blocking his only other possible exit, both bearing items which Tongues's addled brain could figure out would probably turn out to be offensive weapons. Out of an entirely justifiable desire to get away from the weapons, he tried to turn again.

His attention was brought to a door next to him as it opened automatically. That was rather convenient, he thought, as his mind tried to get his feet to switch direction once again.

He continued through this newfound direction, all too aware of the feeling of air moving very quickly behind him and a sound of gunfire that immediately followed. Someone back in the corridor started shouting at someone else rather than in the direction of him. He couldn't make out what was said as the door closed behind him. It appeared, he noticed, to be a communal bathroom, that had a second exit. He assumed the exit on the other side of the room lead to another corridor. He slowed down for just long enough to let the depressingly faded, probably once bright coloured door open for him.

Someone was waiting for him on the other side. Tongues noticed strong arms lunging at him and jumped backwards. The large man on the other side of the door started to come through it. The door Tongues had just come through opened at the same time.

With flight out of options, fight took over. Tongues bit the man, as hard as he could, pouring all of his fear and desperation through his jaw into the outstretched hand. The large man recoiled in shock, and struggled to keep his balance for just long enough that Tongues was able to barrel past, out into the corridor.

There were likely more people in the corridor. Tongues could hear more approaching footsteps. He selected what seemed to be the safest direction and resumed running.

His breath was now coming raggedly and irregularly. Fire seared through every muscle and tendon he had. He could no longer feel his legs, although he was pretty sure they were still moving because it was the only explanation for the walls blurring past him. Somehow, his own semi-delirium allowed him to distance himself from the pain, pushing himself onwards. Another corner, and he was faced with a heavy-duty emergency door. It was closing.

He whimpered, and dived.

The door clipped his ankle as he tumbled through it, causing pain to shoot up his shin. He yelped. More footsteps sounded, and he scrambled up, wincing. Something uncomfortably reminiscent of the energy that had hit Police on The *Hope*, smashed into the door above his head as his leg temporarily gave way. Somebody ahead swore. Tongues whimpered again and began to run in the first direction his legs took him.

This was a large open area, different to the repetitive, claustrophobia inducing corridors. The floor he was currently running on formed a sort of mezzanine around a big central column that extended at least a couple of floors below. Looking down at the opposite wall, he could see similar mezzanines lower down. Each had at least one access point that would open into the empty air. Occupying the central space were vehicles hovering in place, clearly designed to be roughly stacked on top of each other in columns and rows. There were a lot of obvious gaps where some had been removed.

Tongues didn't really know much about anti-gravity. He knew it was possible to achieve and easier to simulate. Seeing a stack of cars floating on top of each other still unnerved him. He mentally hesitated, without actually ceasing to run.

Another shot snapped him roughly back to his present situation. He was still being chased. His pursuers had now got him surrounded, coming at him from all directions, herding him towards the barrier at the edge of the mezzanine. At least one of them had a weapon. Stealing a look over his shoulder, he could see others now producing weaponry of their own. Probably shorter-range weapons that could stun him from nearby. He looked back. The edge was charging closer by the instant. He had nowhere else to go. There was a car a short distance from the edge and slightly below.

Tongues could feel an internal voice scream loudly that this was insane.

A horrified scream escaped Tongues's lips as he sprang. The low barrier passed centimetres underneath his feet, followed by an uncomfortable falling sensation. People were shouting, but he wasn't paying attention to the words. He began to fall.

Pain jolted through his body as it hit the top of the car. He waited until his vision returned and tried to push himself up. His hand slipped off into open space causing him to roll.

Several shots slammed into the body of the car as Tongues tumbled off it. He fell the height of two empty spaces where cars were presumably meant to be, before crashing onto the car below. He looked upwards to see whether the people shooting at him could still reach. Three of them were already aiming.

Gritting his teeth, he pushed himself to his feet and ran up and across the roof of the car. The marksmen fired. Tongues was briefly aware of an increasingly ominous high-pitched buzzing crackle. He could feel the sudden heat radiating from the metal bodywork. His foot came down hard on the edge of the car, and he lifted off.

With a deafening bang a ball of heat and light burst from the car, lifting Tongues further into the air and propelling him onto another car further along the row. For a second or two, everything was black. Then everything was vaguely grey as his vision began to return. Briefly everything was some unidentifiable colour that Tongues was pretty sure didn't exist outside of his own head. Before finally his vision cleared.

He was dimly aware of a series of crashes from somewhere nearby. He raised his head. The car he'd been on was gone, and the noise was coming from somewhere below. He crawled to the edge of the car and got himself at an angle where he could see.

The car he'd been on was largely blackened, parts of the metal bodywork twisted, and none of its functions seemed to be working. Or at least, whatever had been keeping it in the air didn't work anymore, because it was currently plummeting through the layers, taking out any other cars directly below. The vertical domino effect was almost hypnotic. There were a lot of people shouting back up on the mezzanine he'd started on.

There was another vehicle moving downwards as well. This one, however, was not falling. It was descending towards him. Tongues turned and noticed there was another mezzanine just below him only a couple of cars away. He could probably make it there in time. He stood up causing pain to shoot through his body.

He sniffed back a tear as he took a running jump at the next car. He hit and began to slide off. Just as he cleared the bottom of the car, he managed to grab something to swing himself to fall on the car below. The pain only masked by anger, he pushed himself up. There was nothing but open space between this car and the mezzanine.

The vehicle that had been coming after him came into view, floating so that it was at roughly his head height. It slowly, calmly descended, until he could see in the window. There was a female guard inside, glaring at him. Tongues jumped, slamming into the car so that enough of him was on the top to get something of a purchase. His rushing, scrabbling feet found a foothold on the door handle and propelled him onto the roof.

The car accelerated, trying to throw him off, but Tongues had already jumped. The mezzanine barrier passed beneath him by a hair. He hit comparatively solid ground.

The vehicle turned. The window was now open. The guard aimed her weapon at him, a similar one to that which had caused the burst of electricity that had taken out the first vehicle. Tongues was running again before he was fully on his feet, heading for the door.

A few floors below, the collapsing column of cars had finally hit the ground. Many of them were badly damaged. At least one had started to smoke. Sensors picked this fact up and immediately activated an emergency suppression system to stop any fire from spreading to the rest of the vehicles. Presumably as part of the fire safety system the door was now unlocked. It opened allowing Tongues to flee.

Before he could celebrate that the door was open, Tongues could hear the distinct sound of a shot being fired. Even while the sound was still building the door slammed shut behind him. He considered if this was part of the fire suppression system. Realising there was an odd smell in the air he turned to look through the window of the door in time to see the energy bolt hit the viewport at eye level. The bolt did not stop, it ricocheted. While waiting for the realisation that the bolt did not hit him, his mind rushed to find an explanation for why this particular energy shot did not dissipate like the rest. His mind did not have chance to half-bake a response before he heard a scolding voice through the door, exclaiming shots should not be fired at metal while the room was flooded with fire suppression gas.

Tongues watched as the lightning crackled throughout the car park, leaping from vehicle to vehicle. Each one it touched eventually shorted out and fell. In some cases, they fell several stories.

His body ached. Every muscle was exhausted. But now he had a distraction. So maybe he could find somewhere to hide.

He rounded a few corners before finding an unassuming door unlike the automated doors throughout. This one had a simple door handle. He grabbed the handle, threw himself into the small space and slammed the door behind him. Finally, he collapsed onto a pile of supply boxes.

Tongues was sprawled, exhausted and aching, in what appeared to be a broom closet. Every so often footsteps came uncomfortably close, but he couldn't bring himself to do anything about it for some time.

He snapped out of his semi-conscious stupor when an alarm that had previously been going off stopped. He looked around. The room was small and filled with boxes, mostly containing what he assumed was likely cleaning equipment. Thankfully, no one deemed this room important enough to warrant having a camera inside. There was only one door, through which was another of those corridors he'd become somewhat averse to by this point.

Ruling out the door he had come through and seeing no vents, he looked up. The roof of the room was made of tiles of some sort, one of them was visibly broken. There was a space above it which looked large enough for the slightly emaciated teenager to fit into. If he dragged some of the boxes around for a bit, he was pretty sure he could climb up there.

Someone ran right past the door to the room. Tongues carefully stood up and got to work, as quietly as he could.

When at last he got to the broken tile, he shoved it up into the space beyond. It was a tighter fit than he'd assumed, especially when you took into account all the little metal girders and wires. It was, however, still about enough for him to fit. He crawled inside replacing the tile.

It struck him that the tile hadn't been particularly thick, and he was currently crawling over more of them. Either he was even lighter than he thought, or the tiles were deceptively strong, or else he could be in trouble if he stayed in place too long. That was not a comforting thought.

He could still hear the sounds of footsteps and the occasional shout, muffled from below, as he crawled through the hidden spaces like a rodent. Some parts were too tight or too cluttered for him to conceivably crawl through, but that didn't matter much as he didn't really know where he was going anyway. He didn't even know where he was. The only place he'd ever had the option of calling his home was an unknown number of light-years away and rapidly gaining distance at such a speed that he could never hope to so much as see it again. He was used to being alone and friendless in a place he didn't much like, but right now he was alone and friendless in a world he didn't even know. And everybody was trying to kidnap him. He had no plan, and he no longer even had somebody with him smart enough to think of one. He was reduced to hiding between the floors of whatever hellish construction he was currently inside.

Tongues's limbs gave way and he collapsed, weeping, onto his front.

A sudden, unexplained shockwave plucked him from his position and tossed him carelessly into a girder, knee first. He howled.

Then a roof tile a short distance away was thrown aside and was replaced by a small woman with a gun. Tongues blurted out a half-formed scream and part scrambled, part slithered away. The guard couldn't fire too far in this confined space, he reasoned. She'd hit something else, surely.

Tongues wasn't looking where he was putting his limbs. His body lurched downwards as his arm fell through the gap of a missing tile. His face crashed against the edge of the gap and his shoulder got jammed half-out. He could hear someone moving behind him, possibly the woman had managed to squeeze in after him, or someone else nearby was removing another tile. With his mind racing he struggled harder.

Without warning, the entire roof was shaken by another shockwave and Tongues came free, slipping further in the process. He was too far gone now to get back up. He could see the floor of the corridor, an almost sickening distance downwards. He'd fallen further already today. But he wasn't sure how much more his body could take. His fingers seized anything they could and heaved, but there was no conceivable way he could lift himself with only his own strength. All he could do was hold on for another few minutes. So he did. The fiery pain gradually worked its way up his fingers and through his hand. He screwed up his eyes, forcing himself to breathe through the pain. It had reached the stage where the digits themselves were essentially numb, the problem being that all the tendons and muscles linked to them were no longer simply protesting but had now begun failing.

His concentration was briefly distracted by an efficient but irritated voice radiating out of nowhere.

*

The *Elismere* came tumbling out of hyper, already well within her target's sensor nets thanks to her emission control systems, more commonly referred to as Baffles, being fully online. As she down-synched into normal space, her shield looped grabbing a section of hyper, and then as she came fully into normal space, released it in a massive pulse of disruptive radiation. On the viewscreen the lights of the station flickered, and then went dark.

"Bring us up to their docking rings and lock us in. Hopefully they're still chasing their 'subject' and we can get in before their generators cycle back up."

"Way ahead of you, Jack," Jenny replied as she spun the *Elismere* one hundred and eighty degrees, doing nothing to reduce the ship's momentum until the hull was barely fifty metres from the station. The ship's thrusters fired, and she decelerated sharply, spots of grey marring her crew's vision as her inertial compensators fought to keep them conscious. Then she slid to a stop, thrusters flaring again to shove her onto the docking ring. "Ringlock attained. Adrian, get on that override."

"I can do it easier if I'm down ther—"

Jack leaned forward, nodding sharply. "Fine. And take Jen with you, I know you both too well to try and stop you." The siblings lunged up almost as one and crossed the bridge within seconds. "Just don't kill anyo—," The lift door hissed shut, cutting off the end of Jack's statement. For once, Adrian's expression was a match for the cold and lethal one on his sister's face as she checked her pistol. They stepped out of the lift, almost running over one of the members of the boarding party in their haste. Neither noticed.

Adrian crouched beside the airlock's control panel and fiddled with the controls for a few seconds before pulling a small, cylindrical device from one of his pockets. He connected the cylinder lengthwise across the control panel and bared his teeth as lights began to flash, the plug-in unit bypassing the security lockouts.

"Five seconds, get ready." He leaned in against the wall on one side of the door and Jen moved beside him, motioning for one of the boarding crew to take up position on the other side of the doorway. The device beeped once and every button on the airlock control flashed before going out. Jen checked every member of her team by eye and then nodded to her brother. He hit a button on the panel and the airlock door hissed with the suppressed sigh of hydraulics before springing open. Jen peeked around the wall, scanning the entrance corridor and then nodded.

"All right; Adrian, take Kim and her team and get everything you can from their computer core. Pal, Adena, your teams are on retrieval duty with me. We've got a rough position from EVI's sensors; we just need to track him down. There seems to be a lot of activity in the area around him though, so we're going in hard."

"Got it," Paldaros replied, Adena simply nodding as Adrian set off down the corridor with Kim's team. Jen paused, blinking slowly as the others moved off.

"Lady, let the harm I do this day be just. And stay my hand if it would not," she whispered, tracing a sceptre in the air before her. Then she lifted out of the crouch she had been holding and set off in a light jog to catch up with the teams she was meant to be leading.

"Calling all personnel, I repeat, all personnel, do you copy? This is Stationmaster Imleros. The majority of our systems have been disabled and we are currently being boarded by the crew of an unidentified vessel. Internal sensors are only partially online, but we appear to have teams heading for the subject and the computer core. I am initiating purge protocols. Capture teams, if it looks like the subject is going to be captured by these intruders, ensure that he is not able to pass any information on to them."

Jenny growled as the message filtered through her comm, and she waved her teams forward. They had managed to make it most of the way to their target, but now the station forces had finally realised they were no longer alone.

Don't complain Jen, she thought to herself, Adrian did take the computer core before they were able to initiate even the simplest of data protection protocols. He should be done by the time we get this kid out. It's going to be a bit more difficult with them knowing we're here and all, but unfortunately for them we have a few tricks that I doubt they'll expect.

"All right, people," she subvocalised, via an implant in her throat. This worked by analysing the vibrations of her voicebox and bouncing the message to her compatriots, "they know we're here and we probably don't have much time. Adena, I've uploaded a bypass around their position to your display. We'll start pushing and then you hit them from behind. Remember, keep your weapons on stun. Regardless of what these bastards have been keeping hidden, we want them held accountable for it. Killing them won't do that. And I think Jack would prefer it if we didn't get murder tacked on to the list of charges we've started amassing here."

She looked over her team, making sure they knew she was serious before nodding, and then tapped a button on her wristband. "Adrian, kill section lights and gravity." Her entire team mag-locked themselves to the deck as artificial gravity in the section went down with the lights, plunging it into darkness. Jen tapped another control to activate the night-vision layer of her contact lenses, checked the charge on her pistol again, and advanced into the darkness.

***

As Tongues held tight he registered a new voice that appeared to be coming from everywhere, "Calling all personnel, I repeat, all personnel, do you copy? This is Stationmaster Imleros. The majority of our systems," he was no longer able to hear over the pain in his hands.

He couldn't hold on any longer. His eyes sprang open, rolling wildly. It was no longer a case of resisting pain. It was now strength, pure and simple, and that was something Tongues simply did not have. He screwed his eyes shut tightly and dropped.

About halfway to the ground, Tongues felt a sudden strange sensation, as if he was falling slower, or at least not accelerating. He could remember vague lessons concerning terminal velocity, at which humans falling would stop getting faster and seem to float in a beautiful, deadly freefall. He was pretty sure there was nothing in the lecture about that velocity being as low as he was going now.

He hit the ground with his arms, and instinctively pressed against it.

He bounced, leaving the floor behind, and rising back up into the air. His eyes opened in shock. The lights had all gone off, and the corridor was black. Something caught his foot, and he flicked it away. A flash of light from somewhere confirmed it had been the ceiling.

He spun gently in the air, staring blankly at the darkness as it rotated about him. For a brief moment he questioned if he had gone blind, or if his body had finally succumbed to the pain. The momentary tranquillity was shattered by the delayed pain of hitting the ceiling with his foot. This was nowhere near as strange as the sensation of being instantly transported through two distinct but linked points in space, it was still pretty discomforting. He vomited, and assuming it was following the same rules of gravity he was, he pictured it staying as one irregular mass of vile globules, floating off down the corridor under their own momentum. One of the more exhausted parts of his mind dimly alerted him that he should try to stop doing that.

More footsteps. More people. Tongues wanted to cry, except that he didn't even have the energy for that.

There was a shout, then a faint blast of sound. Tongues couldn't even bring himself to care. There were a few more blasts, followed by an odd sensation, as if the air was rippling around him. Some of the harsher blasts of noise he recognised from the guards' weapons, and the corridor was briefly lit by a series of flashes. The sounds continued for a short while, and then the flashes stopped.

Tongues didn't know what was happening. He no longer knew a lot of things, such as which way was up and whether he was still alive.

Something, which may or may not have been a human had taken hold of him as a face seemed to have appeared in his vision. Did that mean the lights were on again? Did it even really matter?

He may have managed a small moan, he didn't recall. The person said something. Tongues never consciously got to hear what was said, as his mind gave in to the influence of his exhausted body. But the words rang in his ears as he drifted away from consciousness, and the idea behind them spread through his dreams like a gentle warmth.

"You're safe."

*

"Adrian, we have him. Set the system as we discussed and get the hell out of there," Jen snapped into her comm. Lights came back on in the section, gravity dropping the stunned station security personnel down onto the decking and Jen's team began to fall back through the corridor at a run.

On the other side of the station, Adrian tapped a few keys on the main computer panel, locking every high-level system interface on the station. A higher-level command code would probably be able to fix things, he just hoped that whomever the Gate would be sending had high enough clearance.

He nodded to Kim and pulled the module he had attached to the station's computer core free. Knowing that they probably wouldn't have the time for him to crack the inner encryptions, he had brought along a high-compression vampire module. He had a feeling that a great deal of his rest shifts were going to be taken up by the data on that module, but that was OK. They had the data, and from Jen's tone what was in there could end up being very important. But for now, they had to get out. Kim's team spread out around him, moving quickly through the corridors back towards the docking ring, alert for any sign of station personnel. They found none.

Jen's group likewise met no resistance as they withdrew with their job done. As they came within sight of the airlock, Jen tapped a sequence on her wristband to start the undock process and the fifteen men and woman of the retrieval group flung themselves through the conduit between the station and the *Elismere*.

"Pal, get him to medical," Jen snapped as she and Adrian vanished behind the lift doors once again.

Jen slid into her piloting couch, stretching her hands out over the interface, and sighed blissfully as she connected with the piloting systems. She felt more than saw the airlock connection unlocking, and the *Elismere's* port thrusters fired in the same instant, sending the ship hurtling away from the station.

Metal screamed under the onslaught of superheated plasma as it hammered into the station's docking ring, deforming the connection the *Elismere* had used, and a sizeable portion of the ring around it.

The ship shuddered as the powerful thruster system launched her away from the station and Jen's hands flowed through a lightning-fast and well-practised sequence once again. Her hyper field bloomed out around her, caressing the very edge of the station before pulling back as EVI completed the appropriate equations and the *Elismere* vanished into hyper.

Another shockwave slammed over the station as she vanished, forcing the few members of the installation's crew who were still conscious to the ground as the hyper distortion washed over them. Already overstressed metal groaned beneath the power of that wave, cracks splaying through delicate ceramics, and for a moment the conscious members of the crew thought they were dead. But then the wave passed, sweeping out past the station, in the process doing even more damage to the already defunct sensor net, and dissipating into the blackness of space.

Chapter VI

When Elios Bennett came round, he was in a small metal cell. One wall contained a door, and a glass window where people could come and check on the prisoner without fearing for their own safety. Considering the technology on the ship that Elios had experienced so far, the window was probably indestructible and he didn't even bother trying the door. On the other side of the glass was a hygienically white corridor with pristine white walls merged into immaculate white floors. In the cell opposite him a small cage hung from the ceiling, and in the bottom of the cage, still stunned from the shot he guessed, lay Moncello. Elios assumed Moncello was still alive, as even these spacers couldn't be sick enough to keep the corpse of a dead pet.

Rubbing his neck, Elios noticed a small, glowing band of light circling his wrist. He tried to tug it off, but his hand passed right through it. Shrugging it off as unimportant, Elios reached for **The Drug** in his pocket, then stopped. He looked down. His coat was gone, in fact he was wearing an entirely new set of clothes. There was nothing particularly special about them. A pair of black trousers and a brown jacket, the first outfit he'd ever had on that wasn't several sizes too large. But **The Drug** was not there.

Elios cussed under his breath. He already had the shakes, so there wasn't much time before he started sweating and then things could get ugly. Hoping against hope that the people on the ship would come before it got to that stage, Elios sat down on the hard floor and hugged his knees, trying to focus on something, anything, to keep his mind off **The Drug**.

Elios looked up as the door slid open and a young, blonde woman stepped through, followed by a similarly straw-haired, slenderly built man. Each wore flowing, well-tailored street clothes that had obviously been designed so that they didn't hinder movement, and each had a holstered pistol fastened on their belts. Both the hair and similar grass-green eyes told Elios that they were probably related. They positioned themselves between the door and their captive, their posture unthreatening. The woman, moved forward and crouched in front of him before pulling out a small device and waving it at him. She muttered a curse as she looked over the readout.

"Adrian, he's going into withdrawal, and I don't know how much longer he can hold against the secondary stages. Do you know how Ems is doing with that chemical breakdown?" Her calm soprano was warped slightly by a caring fear that, Elios realised with some amazement, was directed at him. The man who was obviously too young to be the woman's father, he must be her brother, Elios thought, moved forward as well to get a good look at the portable display. His face tightened slightly, and he shook his head.

"Ems is good, but not even a miracle would find a solution in the time that he has left." The man indicated Elios. "Either we compound the addiction a little bit more or we kill him." His sister sighed and then nodded.

"Fine. I don't like it, but if the only alternative is death, you know which one I'll pick." She pulled a small bag from an inside pocket of her jacket and laid it on the floor in front of Elios before she and her brother withdrew from the cell.

As soon as the door closed, Elios scurried towards the bag. Any other time, he would probably have been suspicious of the strange woman and her quiet brother. As it was, his physical need for **The Drug** was overriding all rational thought. He opened the bag and pulled out one of **The Drug** leaves. Putting it in his mouth, he immediately felt an overwhelming sense of relief. His limbs went heavy, his eyes unfocused and his head lolled to one side slowly. And now for the hallucinations, he thought to himself. He chuckled as he corrected himself, like he would each time taking **The Drug**. Hallucination, not hallucinations, it was always the same one.

A huge, three-pronged gateway loomed in front of his vision. Each prong, in the form of glowing pillars, curved round and met at a point at the top.

They seemed to be made of stones that had been heated to extreme temperatures so that they gave off a warm golden light, and down the outside of the pillars were strange pictoglyphs. Even with his small knowledge of writing, and being in a drug-induced hallucination, Elios instinctively knew that this was not English, nor any other common language in the universe. He was sure it only existed inside his head. Elios could feel that these symbols were something different. Something horrifying and fascinating and wonderful and terrible all at the same time. But what was even more mesmerising and foreboding was the swirling darkness that lay just inside the gateway. What was it hiding within that fog? Elios didn't know. All he could do was observe. He couldn't see past it. He couldn't reach it and he couldn't escape it. It was just there, implanted in his mind, like a memory of a dream. Such a gate could not exist in reality, Elios would reassure himself while also wishing it existed, it just couldn't. The familiar desiderium overcame him as he faded out from the hallucination as he thought to himself, at least it existed here.

Chapter VII

IGC 0765

"Captain, the *GBS Sanitarian* has docked without clearance," a rather rushed junior officer addressed his nearby superior.

"Thank you, leave them to me. Back to work." The Night Captain walked around the corner towards the buckled docking ring on the side of the communication station while running through scenarios in his head. Given all that had happened so far on his shift, he was not looking forward to nosy military guests.

"Welcome aboard, Captain Singer," he said sarcastically, "a courtesy call to warn us of your docking would have been nice, but since you're here." He paused, nodding at his guest, "Currently the Station Captain can't be found, but I am Night Captain John Michel and I hope I can be of service."

"Where the hell are they?" Came a calm but firm demand. A short plump woman stepped through the entrance to the *IGC 0765*. The woman did not show any form of hesitation or wait for an invitation to enter the presence of the IGC's acting Captain.

"Your reputation does not do you justice, you might want to be more specific about who you are looking for," Captain John acknowledged the woman, his voice coming down in volume as he could see the face of the woman who, although standing a head shorter than him, was beaming redder and redder with every word he said.

"Well, let's see, shall we? A full-sized communication station was taken down by a simple interstellar cargo ship. Come on, Captain, do the maths, does that sound likely to you?" Captain Singer slowly widened her gaze so the captain could see her eyes more fully.

The Night Captain could see the black of Captain Singer's eyes slowly change in colour towards a deep blood red. "Well no," he started, trying to determine if the colour change was due to legitimate anger, "it's not likely," The Night Captain went to continue but was quickly cut off by Singer.

"Does anyone here actually know what happened?" Singer demanded, addressing all members of personnel who seemed to be hovering around the area. After a brief pause, she continued, "I'll take that to be a no. I want a download of the full sensory systems database in the next five minutes," Captain Singer finished, every word said with a hard beat but without raising her voice.

"Sorry, Captain, our sensors were down. We don't know what happened." Night Captain John lowered his gaze. He was taller than her, but she had already managed to drive him to quivering. Singer set off walking without warning.

"Stop quivering like a little girl, it's off-putting. Are your sensors back online?" Singer questioned, swinging around to face the Night Captain who was trying desperately to hold himself together.

"Well," The man started to quiver again just as Captain Singer cut in.

"Well what?" she said in an uncannily cool fashion. "You have had, what," she glanced at her wrist, "about seventeen hours since the attack? That should have been more than ample time to repair the grid."

"We are several hours from the nearest resource centre," the Night Captain tried to defend himself, with his head still bowed, his eye started to glisten.

Noticing the formation of the moisture on his eyes Singer rolled her own and sighed, "I'm not going to kill you, so you can stop your worrying. What did they do to disable the system?" She paused for an answer and noticed a prod was needed. "I need information. Was it an EM Pulse? Subwave energy gun? Or, let me guess, subwave pulse gun?" The Captain of the *Sanitarian*, still keeping her voice at a slow, constant and steady level, turned to walk as she spoke. Knowing his place, the Night Captain followed at her heel.

"We don't know, they disabled our sensors and computer grid before we could check what equipment they had. We did get a scan of them, but we were unable to see the report," the man started to speak again but was once again cut off by Singer.

"Take me to your Sensornet," Singer said, and when the man did not move, she exclaimed, "Now!" Singer moved to the side and gestured to the other end of the corridor.

"Sorry," he replied hesitantly, "ma'am, but I don't think there is anything left you can do." The man's head lifted slightly as if hoping that the woman might take the hint and leave, but then he caught glimpse of her eyes once again.

Singer's eyes weren't like a normal person's, hers had black irises, and the pupils changed colour as her mood varied. At this moment of time, they seemed to be settling even further on deep red. This curious trait was thanks to a little bit of crossbreeding between her family and a Terineti tribe during their initial expansion into space.

"Did I ask you to tell me what I can do?" Singer's voice rose slightly with every word. "No? Well then take me to the Sensornet." There was a pause and John did not move, she jerked her head to the corridor end and snapped once again, "Now!"

"That I couldn't even if I wanted to, ma'am. Captain." The Night Captain looked up and finally managed to lock eyes with her. Singer broke the gaze by flicking her head to the side, this both revealed the length of her willowy hair and let her eyes return to neutral black.

She reached into the innermost pocket of her coat, specifically choosing to use her right arm so as to emphasise the presence of the four stars pinned to her lower sleeve. She pulled a small device from her pocket and flicked it on with a faint smirk. "I think this will help you make the right decision." She said smugly, as a small symbol popped into the air above the device.

The symbol seemed to trigger something within the Night Captain's mind, a sort of innate fear of it and what it stood for. "Oh, sorry, ma'am, I didn't know. I thought you were just military. Please forgive me. Right this way." Just so he could remove his eyes from the symbol, he turned rapidly and started down the nearest corridor without waiting for his guest.

Before heading off with the man she had clearly frightened, Captain Singer turned to address the group of the crew that had been following them. "Tetriana, go and seal off the bridge and, if you can, find the captain. Also see if you can find more information on what the hell actually happened here." Finishing her commands, Captain Singer turned on the spot and made after her guide.

A tall, muscular woman with shoulder length light blue hair and an expressionless face came marching in military style. She was wearing black military grade trousers and a light purple upper body garment. Decorating her left arm were four neatly placed golden stars. She stopped after entering the space station and, with her hands clasped behind her back, stood to attention.

"Yes, Captain," she acknowledged as Singer rounded a corner out of Tetriana's sight. She turned on her left heel and headed down the corridor in the opposite direction to her captain.

Captain Singer extended her right arm to remove the four stars, and as she did she placed them, one by one, into a small plastic box she had produced from one of her inside jacket pockets. She then replaced the now occupied box back into the pocket. Out of a separate pocket she removed four Velcro bands with embroidered stars centred on them and strapped them around her right arm. In an almost annoyed sigh she mumbled, "Got to keep up with technicalities."

While Singer was a captain, she was not the captain of this vessel. Under republic rule it was courteous to remove one's own insignia and replace it with representational bands when on another's vessel. Singer did not agree with this, viewing it as a demotion of sorts.

She and John walked down many corridors, each lit slightly duller and slightly less appealing to the eye.

The pair passed rooms with names such as 'Computer Coolant Control Room', 'Turret Programming Suite' and 'Life Support Maintenance Room'. Nearing the end of the corridor, Captain Singer found herself being led up to a black door with a small, tarnished sign reading 'Sensor Systems Mainframe'.

John stopped and assessed the door, and then turned on his heels to allow Singer to open it.

She leaned past him and activated the door's control panel. The door barely opened to which John looked towards Singer, who seemed to have expected this.

"You might want to stand back," Singer suggested calmly to John gesturing back down the corridor. Just as he moved out of the way, Singer covered her face with her arm, raised a leg, kicked the door with the power of a small horse, and flinched backwards as if expecting something to happen. Nothing bar the sound of the door falling to the floor came from the now hollow black void in front of her.

"What was that all about?" asked John, looking rather confused while moving towards the doorway.

Singer almost instinctively grabbed John's arm and pulled him away from the door. "As once told to me by the great late Captain Quisby, 'you can never trust a closed door', and just because it is now open does not mean you should now trust it."

"Late? What got him?" John asked shaking her off him.

"Booby trapped docking port," Singer said, half laughing. She reached into her pocket, pulled out a small energy pistol and held it readily out in front of her. She crept through the door, lifted her free hand off the gun and hit a small panel on the inside of the door. All at once the room was completely visible and she swung her gun violently from left to right and back again before lowering it to her side. "Even now you cannot trust the room." She looked suspiciously around, again scanning every inch of it for any sign of disturbance.

John thought to himself that the legends of Singer were likely over sold. Singer appeared to him to be a little unstable.

Singer tapped a console that protruded from a wall and instantaneously a small square display projected itself above the console screen. In large red lettering it read:

"Error code eo.033252336xxx"

"Group connection error"

"Grid fault"

She tapped a few controls, attempting to access a diagnostic, and then hit the screen with the side of her hand several times until it cleared.

"Error code ie-404"

"Group connection error"

"Grid not found"

Singer pulled a small handheld device out of her right-hand external pocket and entered the Error code. Without delay the handheld device returned a message:

"Main grid computer connection fault"

Singer returned the personal computer to her pocket, reached under the control console and peeled away a panel that was on its underside. Behind the panel there was an array of buttons. She hit the smallest of the buttons and in response the room echoed with a synthesised voice:

"Authorisation code required." Singer rolled her eyes and reached to a small cluster of buttons that seemed to resemble a keypad. Without looking, she entered a combination of keys. All at once the lights on the dials, the display and all the other flashing lights in the room went black. Then, one by one, all the lights came back on, while the display finally started back up. It now read:

"Re-establishing connection with mainframe computer."

Both Singer and John stood looking curiously at the screen waiting. While Singer did not have direct experience with an IGC core, she assumed such a large computer would likely take longer than her personal console to start up. After several minutes the screen refreshed, showing all the individual settings for the sensory systems and, in bold black writing printed at the bottom:

"Connection established – *IGC 0765* sensory system online."

"If in doubt," Singer began chuckling, before being cut off curtly by John.

"I know, turn it off and on again, that has been relevant since Sol 1970s," he finished, humourless.

"It could be worse, you could have been asked to find the Any Key." Singer chuckled, undeterred by John's short tone.

*

Tetriana's tall, muscular frame moved in an almost hovering fashion as she walked off down a corridor, looking for some detail that could help her reach her goal. While she walked, several of the space station's crewmembers shot glances of poorly veiled disgust towards her and even made deliberate moves aside, but this did not seem to alter her pace.

The glances of disgust and hatred likely stemmed from her long, shimmering midnight blue hair. Tetriana, like Captain Singer, was part-Terineti. Unlike her captain, she was half-Terineti and so the signs were more obvious. Some people in the Republic had never gotten over the freeing and integration of the Terineti and, as such, being one carried a disadvantage.

In Terineti culture blue is considered the most boring colour. When expressing blue, most Terineti are likely resting or do not have any real feeling for the current situation. In Tetriana's case this was down to honing her control of her emotions. It is impossible for a Terineti to express a colour opposite to their emotions, but they can change their emotions to express a colour. With this in the Terineti culture, came the ideal of absolute candour, because it is very difficult to be so exposed with one's emotions without also being utterly candid.

Even with her apparent disadvantage, Tetriana had managed to achieve a lot in the Republic military. Down her left were the obvious, glinting four stars, which showed that she had attained the rank of Captain. Onlookers would know instantly that she did not captain her own vessel by the lack of stars on her right. Unlike Singer, Tetriana was not required to change her pins for bands when boarding another's ship. Lastly the red stripe along her purple uniform top signified she was the ship's Head of Security.

Before boarding Tetriana had read the IGC plans, but like a lot of non-existent stations the Republic oversaw, the plans were more than a little out of date. To her, dealing with the bureaucrats' ineptitude was just part of the job. As she continued marching, the sign for the Mess Hall guided her towards a perfect gathering point for station staff and this seemed like a suitable place to start her hunt for the station captain.

As she entered the Mess, she paused to look around for the distinctive captains' colour among the sea of smog grey unranked uniforms of the unimportant. He was clearly not here. Tetriana went to move when a sharp metallic voice called out and stopped her, "*IGC 0765* sensory system online."

She took no time in answering to the voice in a rather self-important way, "*IGC 0765*, locate the station captain."

The computer lagged for a moment before replying with, "The acting captain of the *IGC 0765* is currently situated in LD1 Maintenance Corridor."

Tetriana straightened up, noticed the use of the word acting in the computer's response, and replied, "*IGC 0765*, locate Captain Vels Imleros." There was some debate in relevant groups as to whether or not ship and station computers were capable of deliberately misunderstanding requests. Kids are taught from a young age that they need to be exact when dealing with machines. The often-cited fable is one of a captain instructing his computer to make the ship a little duller. The ship replied by turning the engines off and leaving the crew stranded for three days.

After a shorter lag, the computer replied "Captain Vels Imleros of the *IGC 0765* Can be located in Outer-ring, Section Twelve."

"*IGC 0765*, be more specific," Tetriana demanded. As she knew, the outer rings where large areas and a single section is just the distance between two airtight doors.

"System error; start-up incomplete, individual room sensors offline. Ask again when sensor start-up has completed." Tetriana caught herself before her eyes rolled, dealing with incompetent computers was also just part of the job. As the name suggests, the Outer-ring surrounds the vessel. On most stations this would be central to the station relative to the plain where gravity was being generated. Knowing that the Mess was on the central deck and therefore the Outer-ring would be surrounding her, Tetriana set off through the nearest exit. Exiting the Mess, Tetriana thought it best to find some form of transport to get to her destination and so followed the signs to the Hover Vehicle Port.

The door opened and a plume of black smoke rolled out, releasing the faint smell of an electrical fire. Tetriana marched in and looked towards the void where stacks of hovercraft were supposed to be. Even with this setback, her expression did not change. She merely walked up to the edge of the mezzanine and peered over to assess what had happened. When she had gathered enough information about the situation, she continued her search as if she had never entered.

The hover port doors closed silently behind her as she looked around for another sign to point her towards the station captain. At the furthest end of the corridor from her current position, Tetriana could see a sign pointing towards the 'Outer-ring Sections 8-20' and so she headed off, marching with purpose.

Tetriana paused at the entrance sign to Outer-ring Sections 8-20. After scanning the available destinations pointed out on the sign, she lifted an eyebrow while reading 'Outer-ring Sections 14-17' and 'Outer-ring Sections 18-20', as they were both highlighted with big red lights reading 'not accessible'. Next to the line 'Outer-ring Sections 10-13' was an amber light reading 'status unknown'.

Tetriana remembered that, while docking, the *GBS Sanitarian* picked up damage to the outer structures of the station. She headed off in the direction of Outer-ring Sections 10-13. If the *IGC 0765* sensors were able to pick up the captain's signal there must be some power to Section 12 and therefore it must be accessible in some way, she concluded.

After entering the outer rings of the station, Tetriana headed for a door marked 'Outer-ring Section 12' and waited for the doors to move apart and grant her access. The doors did not move.

"*IGC 0765*, open doors to Outer-ring Section twelve," she commanded the computer of the IGC with the same level of respect she would show to a human. Although that respect would probably have been more acceptable to a computer.

"Unable to comply," a dull soft metallic voice replied.

"Clarify," Tetriana snapped back.

"Doors to Outer-ring Section twelve are out of order."

There was no clear structural damage that Tetriana could see to the door, and there had to be atmosphere behind the door as there was a slim gap with no escaping sounds. With great ease Tetriana pulled the doors open.

She started through the corridor in her military march until she noticed a man stumbling around a few metres away. As she neared the person, she could make out the captain's uniform meaning it had to be none other than Stationmaster Captain Vels Imleros of the *IGC 0765*. He seemed to be struggling to get to his feet, all the while mumbling incoherently.

Tetriana stopped just short of Captain Vels and stood to address him in the manner in which she was taught to address people of power in non-military vessels. "Vels Imleros, I presume."

"Boarded... where... when... ugh—" Vels began rambling.

"I am Captain Tetriana, Head of Security aboard the *GBS Sanitarian*, here to investigate," She paused to see if the rambling fool had started to listen.

"Oh... no... they didn't... they wouldn't—" the rambling continued.

Realising she was getting nowhere, Tetriana leaned down, placed one military-hardened arm around the waist of the Captain and, in one swift movement threw him over her shoulder and turned on the spot. This reaction seemed to knock the Captain for six, as he passed out over her shoulder.

She started back the way she had entered the outer rings and then, when it was visible, she followed a thick, deep-yellow line that was engraved on the floor, which, under most common practice, would lead to the command centre of a space station. On her journey, Tetriana received quite a few strange looks from the crew of the space station. Her marching speed never changed, even when approaching doors. The doors always seemed to be open to the right distance by the time she had reached them, and she would pass elegantly through them. She had marched through several sections of the space station and passed quite a few people by the time she had reached a big set of doors with the logo of the IGC branded into the centre of them.

These doors, being quite large for both security and decorative reasons, were slower at opening, giving Tetriana time to adjust her poise, the little she required to, so she would seem more commanding. Just as the doors stopped in their place she started towards the centre of the room, ignoring the other people who were currently occupying the command centre and who seemed to have taken a disliking to seeing their captain over some stranger's shoulder. Vels made a slight groan as Tetriana placed him gently into the captain's seat, but this sign of consciousness was short lived as he slumped over, out cold.

Without noticing the attention she had drawn to herself, Tetriana moved to the centre of the room and straightened her back, although to an onlooker her back wouldn't really appear to straighten, in the same way as you can't really straighten a Roman road. After she was satisfied with the situation she was in, Tetriana cleared her throat.

"Everyone out!" she exclaimed, moving her hands into a clasp behind her back.

A few of the lower officers got up from their stations and left the room, giving a quiet 'Yes, ma'am' or 'Right away' as they left, but not everyone.

"Under whose authority?" A short, plump man, wearing what any military person would recognise as a lieutenant's uniform stood up from his seat to address the woman who had given him a command. His tone was one of confrontation rather than inquisitive.

"That is irrelevant." Tetriana moved her hands into a clasp towards the man, making clearly visible the number of stars she was wearing on her left arm. "You will all now please leave this room in an orderly fashion or you will be removed by force. Do I make myself clear?"

Several more people stood up and said 'Yes, ma'am' as they walked past her.

When everyone who wanted to leave had done so, Tetriana was left looking upon three security officers who had chosen to stay behind. The tallest of the three officers, a rather muscular, heavyset man, walked towards her, but she stood stoically in her spot. When the man was no more than an arm's length away, he lifted a fist and sent it hurtling towards Tetriana. Just as his face changed to accommodate the expected meeting with solid matter, the man realised that what he had hit was the palm of Tetriana's hand, and with this interaction her hair became a dark red.

Without a word, she began to twist the man's wrist until her own hand could no longer turn at the wrist. His arm made several unspeakable noises.

The other two still in the room moved forward to help their friend, but flinched backwards as Tetriana released his hand. All three left, the two uninjured men supporting their larger friend who was now cradling his limp hand.

Tetriana reached up, grabbed the lobe of her left ear, and said clearly, "Tetriana to Captain Singer."

Singer replied directly into her ear: "Captain Singer here."

"Captain and bridge secured; preparing to take station control," she responded with a very flat tone. This was all in a day's work for Tetriana, she enjoyed her job, though would never tell anyone as much.

"Thank you, that was quick, we are on our way, lockdown the station." Singer trailed off clearly distracted by something at her end.

Tetriana grabbed at her lobe again killing the connection then announced, "*IGC 0765*, command mode!" She waited for a soft bell sound before continuing, "Gate lockdown, ship-based authentication, *GBS Sanitarian*, Captain Tetriana reporting to Ship's Captain Singer." With the last word the lights of the command station moved from a subdued working level to fully powered.

The station responded, "Understood, lockdown in progress, Gate override accepted."

Tetriana didn't flinch when the Stations true captain mumbled behind her, "Gate, no, no, Gate, why, Gate." Before dropping from consciousness again.

A few moments later, Captain Singer marched through the doors and up in front of Tetriana. Behind Captain Singer followed Night Captain John and several *GBS Sanitarian* crewmembers.

"What the hell happened here?" Captain Singer exclaimed to Tetriana while looking down at the blood on the carpet.

"Apologies, Captain. There were some crewmembers who didn't understand the meaning of the words please leave," Tetriana said as she stepped down from the raised platform on which the captain's seat sat. When on a bridge or command station, the highest-ranking officer must never be stood lower than a subordinate. Tetriana stepped down in order to signify the handing of control over to Captain Singer.

"And here I thought you were always the courteous one," Captain Singer replied in an overly sarcastic tone before stepping onto the raised platform to take Tetriana's place. In this instance Singer was completing the ceremonial dance accepting the handover of power and showing superiority to all in the room. Both Singer and Tetriana enjoyed this show, both for their own reasons. Tetriana strongly believed in keeping to traditions as a code to maintain. Whereas, Singer, liked showing dominance over anyone below her.

Captain Vels started to come to again, and without opening his eyes he mumbled, almost continuing from where he left off before passing out, "They couldn't... they didn't... they wouldn't send—" He sighed as he opened his eyes.

"Hello," Captain Singer said, allowing a full-sized grin to cover her face and forcing the pupils of her eyes back to black as they tried to approach a rose pink.

"Singer?" Vels enquired, sighing.

Vels started to lose consciousness once again. Singer rolled his head around a couple of times and patted him on the cheek, but he remained limp. Her pupils started to go blood red as she shouted, "That's Captain Singer to you! Have you been drinking on the job, Captain Imleros?"

He tried to mumble something in reply but the words were slurred.

Captain Singer's pupils had completely gone red as she produced a pistol, toyed with some settings and raised it to his head before sighing, "I will deal with you later." She pulled the trigger. The Night Captain flinched and the semiconscious body of Vels slumped in his chair.

Singer swung round violently to address her crew, who had entered with her and had taken up positions around the room. "I want a download of every sensor system in this place to the *Sanitarian*, anything you can find I want a download of. I want to know what the hell happened here and where the hell they went." She swung around violently once more to address Tetriana directly. "Report!?"

"The main Hovercraft Bay is non-operational, segments of the outer ring are out of order, most of the internal sensors are still down and there is one crewmember with a broken wrist. That, I take responsibility for. Captain," Tetriana responded keeping a steady beat and not looking down to meet her captain's eyes. She unclasped her hands, placed them at her sides and gave a nod to her captain.

Content with this response Singer turned on the spot and began addressing other crewmembers. Without warning, she pointed directly towards an unsuspecting young-looking man. "Ensign, what do we know so far?"

A shiver passed down the ensign's back as he stopped working and swung around on his chair. "The Fold Space Communications system picked up a very large transmission shortly before the sensor blackout. It wasn't saved into the FSC memory, Captain, so I can't get a copy of it. And it doesn't seem to have a sender at all, it just appeared." The ensign turned back around on his chair and went back to work.

"Things don't just appear, Ensign. And you don't turn away from your workstation unless you have been instructed to. Back to work," Captain Singer snapped and continued finding her next victim. She moved slightly and pointed to a similarly young-looking woman sitting at the security desk who was frantically hitting the screen in several points at the same time. "Lieutenant, security details?"

Without turning away from her workstation, she spoke rapidly, "During the large transmission the internal sensory system picked up a new unknown biological mass on the station." The Lieutenant ran through the report on her screen, following the timeline shown by the computer. "It was humanoid in structure," she said scanning further down the report, "showing as a child from the *Tomorrow's Hope* Project. The genetic scanner has matched it to the child by the designation of Blue-46-04-1000." The woman took in a deep breath, turned round to her captain, looked her in the eye and asked, "What is so important about the *Tomorrow's Hope* Project? Captain."

"If I told you that, Lieutenant Kolbe, I would have to kill you, and myself. They probably wouldn't even tell me what it is. They just sent us out here to find out what happened and write a report on our findings." Singer lifted her head to address the whole room. "So, any information you can come up with and download to our ship is greatly needed." She turned on her feet once more to face a muscular woman sitting behind the external sensory station. "What did the external sensors pick up? Ensign."

The woman looked up at her captain, stopped working and began to stutter. "A sh-sh-ship c-c-came out of hyper."

Singer rolled her eyes and snapped, "Stuttering, st-st-stop it."

"So-sorry, Captain, they came out of hyper quite close to the station. The sensors picked up a trading vessel with a mix of low-grade weaponry, and shields as expected for the class. After that the sensors went offline. It was only after the sensors went down that the structural damage occurred," the ensign paused and just as she was about to continue was interrupted.

"Captain Singer, I have found something that might interest you." Singer rushed over to another ensign and looked over her shoulder.

"What is it, Ensign?" She replied swiftly.

"Well, I have just run a complete search of the station with the internal sensors and Blue-46-04-1000 appears to be no longer on board." The ensign lifted her gaze to meet those of her captain. "Do you think the child escaped on the ship, or even that the ship had planned to pick the child up?"

"I don't know, Ensign, and we are not here to jump to conclusions. Check to see if there are any files on the child in the space station's database." Singer turned around violently on the spot again to face Tetriana. "What are your thoughts on this?"

"The Captain was stumbling around in the outer rings. Also there are several sections of the outer rings that have been rendered useless; the computer has blocked them off. The sensors in parts of the outer rings are probably offline due to the damage, so the child could be there," Tetriana answered then nodded. "Captain."

Singer walked towards the internal sensors panel. "Ensign, find out what you can about the broken outer rings and if there is anyone in them, use the

Sanitarian's sensors if you have to, and," she turned to address the room, "someone find out what happened in the hovercraft bay." She finally walked up to the captain of the space station, lifted his head up and slapped him lightly on one of his unshaven cheeks. "Wake up." Vels slowly started to come around. Singer continued to slap him until he had completely come to.

"What! Where am I? What are you doing on my space station?" the Captain jumped to a start and was completely conscious now. "What happened!" Vels demanded as he realised that he was not where he expected to be.

Singer was taken aback by Vels's attitude. "I will be asking the questions," she grunted. "What happened here? Because it seems like, to me, you have been drinking on the job," Singer said sternly while standing, looking down at him on his chair, this, was a novelty to her as she was smaller than most people.

"Of course I haven't! Singer, you know I have not worked for twenty-five years to become a captain and stationmaster to then start drinking. What gave you that idea?" The captain straightened up in his chair, which gave him the perfect view of Singer's eyes as her pupils switched from red to pink.

"I said I will ask the questions. What were you doing stumbling around the outer rings?" Singer asked with a soft lilt in her voice.

"I was chasing down a small, emaciated boy. The last thing I remember was running towards the scene through the outer ring, when the artificial gravity and life support systems went offline. Then it all went black," Vels paused, rubbing his head, "I must have lost consciousness. Would you, please, like to tell me what is going on?" He finished.

Singer reached into an inside pocket of her uniform with one hand and started to remove something from it. Seeing this Vels breathed sharply, then commanded, "You will not wield a weapon on my control deck."

Singer looked up, instantly taking umbrage at this comment. "If I wanted to wield a weapon on board, I would. However, luckily for you, it is not a weapon. But it is as good as one." Her pupils darkened to a red and this caused Vels to tense up in his seat, anticipating what she was going to remove from her pocket. She produced the same device she had used to establish her authority over the Night Captain. Vels let out a deep sigh and let himself slump in the seat again. Then she flicked it on and a small symbol sprang into being between them.

"Oh. I didn't know, sorry."

"That is OK; this is not the first time I have had to show it," Singer smiled, her pupils turning a slight pinkish red, her voice becoming softer again. Tetriana let out a forced cough forcing Singer to blink and adjust her pupils to black.

Singer turned to Tetriana with a clear sense of announce in her expression. "Please collect as much information from here as possible, then wipe their system. I will deal with Captain Vels personally."

She went to turn around to talk to Vels when he snorted, "Deal with me, will you?" in a curiously sarcastic tone, as if he either didn't know that no one talks to Captain Singer like that, or that he somehow already knew her personally.

"Yes, Captain," Tetriana replied, as both commanders left the bridge side by side. She thought this odd as Singer would only walk beside someone she considered at the same level as her, and Vels, being a Stationmaster Captain who had failed at his duties, would normally be walking behind her, far behind her. For that matter, there were very few people that Singer ever considered at the same level as herself.

Now Tetriana was finally the highest-ranked person in the room, she walked over to the captain's seat and lowered herself elegantly into it. She sat straight with both her hands on the armrests. "I want all the information possible on Captain Vels Imleros," She said, leaning slightly forward and then back again. She looked comfortable in the chair, so comfortable that her hair went a clear ocean blue, the colour of serenity in her culture, it was like she belonged. "Where he was born? Where he was trained? Anything."

Almost all at once the rest of the crew announced, "Yes ma'am." The overall atmosphere of the room shifted from when Singer was in command. Everyone appearing to be a little more relaxed.

After several minutes of fast typing, one ensign spun around on his seat and said, "He was born on the planet Ferreus-Vita and at the age of seventeen went to train on the cadet school Evigilo, but left shortly afterwards for committing a minor trading offence. He then went and studied on the Securus Vicis School for Communications Systems and Command Training. After four years he graduated and started working here, and has been ever since."

Tetriana raised an eyebrow. Her hair had now returned to its normal shade of midnight blue. She stood up, marched to the console and said, "Ensign, stand." She took the Ensign's seat and started to type rapidly without looking at her hands, the years of working on ships showing in her swift movement. After about a minute she stopped typing, her eyebrow lifted again and she whispered, "I knew it."

The ensign looked at Tetriana, confused. "Knew what, ma'am?"

"Nothing, Ensign, carry on with your work, good job," she said, lifting herself off the seat and moving to the middle of the room, standing tall and announcing, "Keep up with your work. I will return shortly. Until then I am placing Lieutenant Kolbe in command." She clasped her hands behind her back and turned towards the door, then marched off the command deck.

Tetriana walked some distance before she could hear her captain's voice from around a corner, but it wasn't her captain's usual tone. It was softer and kinder. Her voice was also answered by a soft version of Captain Vels's voice. Tetriana stopped at the corner to listen.

"I can't, Vels, it's been too long, and I'm on a mission that has been handed to me from the highest authority." Singer's tone was very soft and tender, like a young, childish version of herself.

"But, Bethany, can't you stop just a little while? Not even long enough to catch up? It has been nearly twenty-five years and I think we have a lot of catching up to do," the other voice whimpered back to her like a newborn pup whose mum has just left the bed.

"I know it's been twenty-five years, and it broke my heart that the commander found a reason to kick you out of Evigilo. So I think it's the best that we don't do anything. If we just act like we don't know each other. It got you into trouble last time we did something." Her voice was even softer now. "I don't think I can bear seeing anything like that happen again."

"How would they find out? They are hours away from here at best," the man whimpered.

"Ships may take hours to get here. But it only takes a couple of jiffies for a transmission to get to your head office or worse," her voice seemed to stutter at the thought of this situation making its way back to her superiors. "But if you are really intent on talking to me on a personal level, come aboard the *Sanitarian* tonight after your shift and don't let anyone see you." Singer seemed to verbally straighten herself up and regained her professional voice. "Now, I need to get back and check on my crew and you need to tell your crew that this station is part of an investigation and that they have to comply with everything we say." Tetriana could make out the footsteps of her captain walking towards her, so she rounded the corner and straightened up before Singer gave her a nod which Tetriana understood to be the, what are you doing here, nod.

In answer to her captain's not-question, she remarked, "We have downloaded and analysed nearly all of the information on this station. At this rate we will be able to leave here earlier than expected. About six hours earlier."

"I doubt that, there are probably thousands of loose ends to look at," Singer snapped as she and Tetriana started to march back towards the command deck. As they did so, Singer surveyed Tetriana for any sign that she had been listening to her conversation with Vels. Her first impression was that she had not heard a thing.

"As the sensors were knocked offline just after the unknown vessel came out of hyper, the time to go through the information will be greatly decreased. Those personnel who managed to get close to the intruders could not give useful descriptions. There should be no reason to stay docked for more than a few hours." There was a small pause in their conversation as Tetriana took a breath and then continued, "Unless you learned something from Captain Vels."

Tetriana's emphasis of the word learned seemed odd to Singer, "What's that supposed to mean?" she said, turning her head towards Tetriana as they marched, giving her a cold scowl. "I'll have you know that," she tried to continue before being cut off by Tetriana.

"Did you find anything out from Captain Vels?" Tetriana inquired directly.

"Nothing useful, no," Singer said distractedly in a slightly girly voice, and then snapped out of it again. "He hardly wanted to talk at all. So I let him go and get on with his duties."

Tetriana and her captain approached the oversized doors to the Command Deck when, against her own better judgement, she turned to block Singer from entering. "I know your history with Captain Vels. Born on the same planet, dated for quite some time and then he was expelled to prevent your relationship. Take this as a warning from your Head of Security. If it looks like your emotions will jeopardise our mission or prevent it from running smoothly in any way, I will request that you stand down as captain," Tetriana said in a strong commanding voice, not showing any fear. Her hair didn't even show signs of changing colour.

"Are you threatening me?" Singer almost screamed. "ARE YOU THREATENING ME?" she roared, and as she did so her pupils went deep blood red.

"I am not threatening you, Captain Singer. I do not threaten. I am merely following the rules. As you should be," Tetriana said calmly. "Rule 13E Part 15 of the Galactic Council Captaincy Code states: 'There shall be no personal contact of any kind, aboard the ship or not, during a mission'," Tetriana finished keeping her calm, cool and collected voice, her hair still unchanged.

"Are you telling me, your captain, how to follow rules?" Singer burst out again. "If I find out you are trying to tell me how to follow rules, so help me I will court-martial your ass as quick as possible, do I make myself clear?" Singer moved to open the door but found her way blocked by another hand.

"I doubt that. As you of all people should know, Rule 19F Part 27 of the Galactic Council Captaincy Code states: 'A court martial cannot and will not be held against a person or officer when he/she is being charged for abiding by the rules'," Tetriana said, her voice still very calm as she removed her hand from blocking Singer and gestured for her to open the door.

"Just remember who wears the stars on her right arm in this ship. Captain Tetriana." Singer brandished the bands on her right arm. She could feel her control of the situation slip away filling her with anger.

"We are not currently on your ship, Captain. Aboard the IGC we are equals by rank and the authority of command, here and now, belongs to Night Captain John Michel." Tetriana knew this was only a technicality, and that, Singer ultimately was her captain. All the same, she did not want to see her captain jeopardise any mission.

Captain Singer stormed past Tetriana and through the doorway onto the command deck, Tetriana followed. People rushed back to the consoles and started to work rapidly. She turned to face Tetriana and breathed deeply. "You are relieved of duty until your next shift. Get back to the ship. I will deal with you later." With every word she spoke Tetriana's hair moved from its midnight blue to red.

Tetriana acknowledged her Captain's petty decision to intentionally scold her in sight of her peers. With a "Yes, Captain!" she marched back out the double doors she had barely entered towards the *GBS Sanitarian*.

Captain Singer stormed towards one of the consoles at the far end of the command deck and stood to attention behind its user. "Ensign, have you had any luck in finding out what happened to the outer rings?"

"I have managed to patch the *Sanitarian* sensors," the ensign started.

"Captain, there is an encrypted message for you," a quiet voice came from the other side of the command deck. Without hesitation the Captain walked towards the voice. Singer glared at the man who had spoken until he seemed to get the hint and stood up to allow her to sit.

"Ensign, don't stand behind me," Singer snapped.

At once the ensign said, "Yes, ma'am. of course, ma'am," and moved to the other side of the console.

Captain Singer sighed while she started to type on the screen, and then stopped to read. Her finger followed sentences on the screen, and as she read them her pupils went slightly green. When she had finished she stood up and commanded, "We have a new mission. Finalise any downloads and return to the *Sanitarian*." There was no pause before she left the bridge in a rush. She headed down a few corridors and found a door branded with the name Stationmaster Captain Vels. She opened it quietly and spoke softly. "Vels, are you there?"

Singer stepped into the room and looked around for where Vels was standing. The room was pretty bare, as would be expected for the captain of a space station so far from civilisation. There were only a couple of defining features. On a desk across the room from Singer there were two framed pictures. The first was of a young Singer standing with a young Vels in formal clothing. She could remember the picture being taken during their end of year dance, the last time they had spent any personal time together. The second looked like a printout of some article entitled 'Bethany Singer Receives Honorary Captaincy'. When she noticed the picture under the title she let out a little grunt. She hated having her picture taken and that had definitely been one of the worst.

"I'll be right with you," Vels replied. His breathing was heavy and there was a distinct trace of sobbing in his voice.

Vels walked out from behind a corner facing away from Singer and towards his desk. He placed both hands flat on the desk and leaned onto them. "How can I help you?" he mumbled, raising a hand from the desk to wipe a single tear from his eye.

"I have been thinking about what you said and," Singer started, her voice getting higher in pitch. Her pupils moved from their neutral black to a neon pink and her heart rate picked up.

"As have I," Vels replied, his voice lowering slightly and becoming less mumbled, "and, you know what? You were right." His voice became weak again, but he managed to hold it together, "I think it would be a horrible idea if we got together." Pre-empting a tear appearing, Vels raised his hands and covered his eyes. "I think as soon as you have the chance you should leave the space station." He forced the last line out before giving up on holding tears back.

Singer moved further into the room in a state of confusion. Her eyes shot back to their neutral black and she cleared her throat. This wasn't going the way she had anticipated. "What do you mean, Vels?"

"Captain Imleros, please," he corrected, "It won't work. It didn't before so why would it now? Just please leave," he began to mumble again and his crying slowly became uncontrollable.

Holding back tears herself, Singer's pupils became a soft ocean blue. She turned and exited the room. As the door closed behind her she stopped to think, but hearing the muffled wailing of the man she had once loved through the door forced her into motion.

She raised her hand to her left earlobe and announced aloud, "Singer to Kolbe. Have the crew completed all tasks and are they back aboard the *Sanitarian*?"

"Kolbe here. Yes, Captain, all crew and personnel are back aboard." The juniors voice replied in her ear.

"Good!" she exclaimed before once again pressing down on her earlobe. "Crew of the *Sanitarian*, this is Captain Singer, prepare for departure. We leave in ten minutes."

When Singer arrived at the docking ring to her ship she was met by the Night Captain. Without acknowledging him, she barked, "That is us departing. I hope I never have to come here again."

"That makes two of us," the Night Captain said, as the doors to the *Sanitarian* closed between him and Captain Singer. Her eyes went blood red as she shot the Night Captain a glare, and the *Sanitarian* broke off from the *IGC 0765*. The resulting sound, like a pair of large suction cups being pried off of glass, made the Night Captain smile, as if proving to him that the *Sanitarian* had at last gone and could now be forgotten. The Night Captain turned on the spot and whistled as he walked off down the corridor.

Chapter VIII

The *Elismere*, Republic Space

WHILST THE BRIDGE on the *Elismere* could be used as a briefing area, when the command staff wanted to explain things to the rest of the crew, they used one of the observation decks. They weren't actually observation decks in the traditional sense as holo-projectors had replaced windows, but they served a similar purpose. Due to the holograms and large seating area, it was also easier to do briefings there.

A small space had been cleared at one end of the room, and Jack moved up through the crowd, greeting various members of the crew with a word or handclasp. The other command staff were scattered across the room, conversing. The entire gathering felt more like a dinner party than a briefing about the ship's current state of affairs.

Finally, Jack reached the open space and cleared his throat. The hum of conversation throughout the room dropped into silence.

"So you've all been aware of our recent actions over the past few days, especially the addition of two people to our current crew complement. My thanks to those who went onto *IGC 0765* to retrieve the younger of our guests. The data that we managed to retrieve from the computer core, that which Adrian has decrypted thus far, is shaping up to be an invaluable addition to our current collection," he said. "However, we are now presented with a dilemma. Things seem to be starting to accelerate again. We know that there has to be a ship after us at this point. With the attention we may have now garnered we must plan for the potential that it catches us. I know, it goes against just about everything we've done up to this point, but if we run straight for the Federation, that'll elicit a response that we can't evade. Therefore we are going to take a more circuitous route." There was a ripple of sound around the room as he said that, but he continued steadily. "The Gate knows that the Federation has been trying to get access to something like what we have for centuries. If we act like covert ops, then they'll send everything they have after us. A Shadowship might be able to evade all that, but we couldn't."

"So," a holographic map of the Republic sprang into the air beside him, "we're going to head down this way." He gestured at the display and a line grew from their current position on the map, curving out around star systems and stations. It was a slow, complicated course. But it, eventually, brought them within twelve hours of the Federation border. "I know it's slow, and I wish we could move faster. But even this is going to stretch our ability to slip under the radar. We're hoping that we'll not run into what-ever they sent after us until somewhere around here," he indicated a small box surrounding the last third of their course. "If we do meet it, it is more than likely, we're going to have to destroy it. And that will alert the Gate to our being more than we appear. By that point however, we should be close enough to the Barrier to run straight for it. After having blown up a Republic ship, it'll make sense. And if we're lucky, they'll classify us as some BDC mercs doing a daredevil tour." He smiled slightly at that, similar reactions spreading across the room.

The Bisolar Democratic Coalition was the name given to the binary star system colonised by Switzerland during the hyper boom. It was tiny on the scale of star nations, but lay at a nexus between four of the spatial superpow-ers. It also produced some of the finest mercenaries in known space. The BDC still maintained the neutrality of their parent state, and most of their mercs were tied down on permanent contract with the Misaligned Worlds, the star nation that had grown out of the old Terran Confederation and that still contained the ancient homeworld, Earth. But not all of them were. And baiting the Gate had become something of a thrill sport for a rather large portion of them. The *Elismere* were pretty sure they had been desig-nated as a Swiss daredevil tour at least four times in their thirty-year history. That was something to be proud of.

"Hopefully we'll be able to break for the Border and actually get there before they mobilise any other assets. EVI's run several simulations, and so far the outcome looks pretty good."

"That is to say," the *Elismere's* Virtual Intelligence interjected into the conversation, "that the chance of our reaching the Barrier intact, following this course and without random variables, is seventy-two percent. A direct burn for the border lowers that probability to less than twenty."

"Thank you, EVI," Jack said, nodding at the ceiling. "So you've heard the plan. Any questions or suggestions?"

"I have one." A tall, muscled man spoke up from the back. "Find us some courier contracts that run into the Federation. That way we have a reason for heading in the direction we're heading." Jack nodded.

"Good idea, Od. We're going to be operating under the *Zephyra* ID on this run, so that would also make sense. Emily?"

"I'll find us some things to move," the redhead smirked. "I've got a few contacts that I haven't used in a while down this way. They should be able to find us something."

"Anything else?" Jack asked. There wasn't, and after a few moments of silence, he nodded. "Then we're good. Let's do this."

Chapter IX

The ATMOSPHERE ON THE bridge of the *Sanitarian* was one of a relaxed nature. That was until the automatic doors to the bridge parted, revealing a rather stressed looking Captain Singer. The room fell silent. She threw a fleeting look around the room, her pupils on the cusp of crimson, while she made her way to the optimum position to command.

When she had reached the centre of the room, without pausing, she began to bark, "New mission. We are in pursuit of a vessel known as the *Quosmod*." She gave a sigh before continuing. "Its last known coordinates are listed in the dock, and they are believed to still be in the vicinity. As the nature of our mission is classified, the *Quosmod* are unaware we are intercepting. We are not after the *Quosmod* itself, we are after a single crewmember. We are not at liberty to divulge the reason for arrest." Singer turned and began to walk towards a door off to one side of the bridge. "If anyone needs me, I will be in my quarters. But let me be very clear, no one will need me!" Just as she passed through the opening door, she gave one last command, "Captain Tetriana, you have the bridge." She finished talking in unison with the door closing.

Tetriana, who was currently stood at the security workstation, nodded at the command and lifted her hand to activate her communications device. "Captain Tetriana to Lieutenant Commander Kolbe, respond."

A soft and rather childlike voice replied in Tetriana's ear, "Kolbe here."

"Lieutenant Commander, report to the bridge and man the security station," Tetriana commanded. Tetriana never spoke on familiar terms over comms when on duty and especially never when she was in command, you never knew who was listening.

Kolbe's reply was just as quick but this time there was a distinct hint of excitement, "On my way." To the crew on the bridge it would have appeared that Tetriana had stood motionless as if in a trance as she waited for the sentence to be correctly punctuated with, "Captain."

Having confirmed her replacement at the security station, Tetriana stepped out from behind the console and walked towards the position Captain Singer occupied a few moments earlier.

The *GBS Sanitarian* was commissioned as a standard military-class battlecruiser with some major modifications. As part of the negotiations for her job, Singer had made some aesthetic demands. The bridge observation screen stood at nearly double in size compared to the standard model and even had the capability of displaying three-dimensional holograms. Her bridge was primarily beech with smoky oak for finishes, which Singer considered a vast improvement from the standard tinfoil grey. Most prized of all by the Captain was the tall chair that sat in the centre of the bridge upon a small platform. The chair itself had the Singer coat of arms embroidered into the fabric almost as if it was to mark her territory. This was clearly Captain Singer's ship, and no one could deny it. Tetriana had just been given command to control it, she basked for a moment in the privilege of her situation.

Tetriana made her way to the centre of the bridge where she lowered herself into Captain Singer's chair with an air of importance. She had always wanted to captain her own vessel and planned to do so at some point in her career. In one quick, steady motion, she swivelled the seat around to face the front of the ship, leaned forward and announced, "Communications! Find us the *Quosmod*."

Without hesitation, the ensign behind the communications console began to work with a quiet "Yes, ma'am." He was dressed like any military communications ensign would be a black uniform, bar a brown patch across the shoulders, and his rank displayed with a single gold star on his left arm and a single band embroidered into his right.

Tetriana swung the seat anticlockwise to face the woman working at the sensors station. The woman was also adorned with the Republic black uniform but the colour across her shoulders was a yellowed green and down her left and right arms there were two stars and two bands respectively. Tetriana straightened her back and barked, "Lieutenant!"

With no pause the woman stopped what she was doing and looked straight up at her commanding officer to address her. "Yes, ma'am?"

In a lowered voice, Tetriana said, "Keep a lock on Singer. Tell me if anything suspicious appears." The Lieutenant acknowledged her superior's command with a puzzled look and a nod. On any other ship this would have warranted a question around command conduct, but, as the crew were used to not questioning Singer's directions, they had learned not to question any command directions.

The doors to the bridge opened and a slender young woman walked through. Tetriana adjusted her seat so that it was facing the person who was currently taking up Tetriana's original position on the bridge.

"Thank you for joining us, Lieutenant," Tetriana paused slightly and moved from a commanding voice into a more informal voice, which to a normal person would still be considered rather commanding, "Sorry, Lieutenant Commander Kolbe." Kolbe and Tetriana exchanged a smile before she continued. "The promotion was definitely overdue. How does the new title feel?" Tetriana was consciously preventing her hair from shifting colour. While the crew of the *Sanitarian* were not as prejudiced as others against Terineti, Tetriana had always been trained that allowing her Terineti side to show her emotions was unprofessional.

Kolbe's uniform was the same black as everyone else. Her band colour was purple showing she worked in security. She had three stars on her left arm with two bands embroidered around her right. Moving her long hair from her face she looked at her commanding officer. "Not bad for a twenty-three year old," she chuckled. "Although by my age you had been a Lieutenant Commander for, what, almost two years." She flicked her hair once more and started to work away on the console.

A smile grew on Tetriana's face, she could feel her hair drifting from its neutral purple, but as she swung around on the chair once more the smile faded to the stoic look that had been there before and her hair snapped back. She slid further back into the chair and commanded, "Ensign, Captain Singer requested I get a ship-wide diagnostic finished and handed to her in four hours. She is only looking for the basics. Engine, shields, computer and weapon status."

A voice from behind her replied instantly, "For you, Captain, I'll have it in two."

She gave a quick smile and acknowledged, "Now that is what I like to hear on my bridge." To get back on task she turned towards the communications officer, "Ensign, any luck in finding the *Quosmod*?"

"No, ma'am, but their last docking. Was yesterday. At a trading facility called. *Profession-Constituo*," he replied slowly, pausing every couple of words while working on the console in front of him.

"Very well. Lieutenant Markus, set in a course for the *Profession-Constituo*," she ordered, focusing her attention on the helmsman. "How long will it take us to get there?" she enquired.

After a couple of seconds Markus called out, "About two hours, ma'am."

It had been an uneventful journey so far. Tetriana sat watch on the bridge ready to react whenever the need would arise. While going through the republic captains guide in her head she was caught off guard by a sharp voice, "Captain, you asked to be informed of scan results," the lieutenant behind the sensors console was staring towards Tetriana.

Spinning the seat around to face the lieutenant, Tetriana replied, "What have you found, Lieutenant?" She was certain she already knew what her subordinate was going to say, but she had learned that, as a captain, it is often better to let your staff tell you than assume.

"There is an outgoing communications link open from the captain's quarters," the lieutenant asserted.

Tetriana turned to the ensign behind the communications desk and with cool urgency said, "Where is that link addressed to?"

"Sorry, Captain, I can't scan that. It's asking for a level ten security code," the Ensign behind the communications desk replied and stopped working to look up.

"For the captain's eyes only," Tetriana remarked with a small smirk and a sense of sarcasm in her voice. She got up from her perch and marched towards the communications console. "Well, there have to be some benefits of being a Captain."

Tetriana began to work on the console when Kolbe giggled. "You should try 'Singer-Alpha-One', it always worked in the old sci-fis."

For a short moment the air of the bridge felt jovial, before Tetriana let out a small grunt of amusement and the bridge returned to its working silence as she continued typing away. Just as she finished working, the console flashed up a small information box. She paused for a couple of seconds to read the box, then lifted her head and began to march out from behind the desk, throwing a finger down on the console and turning it black.

"Lieutenant Commander Kolbe, take the bridge," she commanded with a neutral tone as she headed towards the small door Captain Singer had left through nearly an hour ago.

The doors closed behind Tetriana as she walked into the Captain's quarters. Singer was sitting behind her desk talking to her computer. She looked up, her pupils rose pink, to see Tetriana walking towards her. Singer looked back down at her screen and said, "I have to go take care of some business." While mid-sentence, Singer shut her computer screen and looked back to address her guest who was now standing right across the desk from her, staring her down. Singer's pupils made a speedy transition to black but clearly through blood red on the way.

"Can I help you?" Singer spoke calmly, with an inquisitive tone. "I believe I was clear about interruptions on the bridge, was I not?" She continued with the tone of a parent scolding a child.

"Yes, you can," Tetriana replied with such speed that she caught her captain unawares and clearly ignoring her quip about interruptions. "Why was there an open communications link between here and the *IGC 0765*?"

Singer raised an eyebrow to make the rapid reddening of her pupils more obvious. When she knew she had her security officer's attention, she calmly gave her rebuttal, "Is it of any importance to you?"

"If it has any possibility of harming this ship's mission, just remember where that mission came from, then, yes, it is of importance to me. Or more accurately, it is of importance to them!" Tetriana hardened her tone to emphasise the party they both knew of but could not openly speak about. She continued to stare down her commanding officer ignoring the clear attempts at intimidation.

There was a pause in the room, and a chill filled in the air, both Singer and Tetriana inwardly acknowledged that a ship was rarely this quiet. Singer adjusted herself in her seat and began, "There were a couple of loose ends to clear up on the IGC and so I contacted them,"

She was abruptly cut off by a very direct return, "You do not honestly think I am stupid?" Confused whether this was a rhetorical question, Singer raised an eyebrow but chose not to answer. "So, I am guessing the crewmembers you needed were all in Captain Vels's private quarters? And this conversation just so happened to need additional advanced security?"

The short figure of the captain rose steadily from her seat and leaned over her desk on her hands raising her gaze from her hands to her subordinate. "Do I need to remind you who your captain is, and what sort of powers she holds over you?" Singer rebutted with clear spite in her voice.

Without flinching, Tetriana joined Singer leaning over the desk and lowly whispered towards her, "Do I need to remind you what will happen to you if any harm were to come to me? Angelyne would have much more than your job removed."

"Don't pretend he'd protect you. I know you don't talk to your father anymore," Singer began before Tetriana lifted a hand from the desk to cut her off.

"That doesn't stop him being overly protec—," Tetriana was cut off mid-sentence by a loud beeping.

A very official voice came over the communications system, "Captains to the bridge, we have a situation."

Tetriana pushed herself upright and stepped away from the desk, waiting for her superior to walk out towards the bridge. She knew her captain was in the right mood to kill the next person that would cross her in the wrong way.

Singer nodded and walked past Tetriana. Tetriana fell in to heal and closely followed Singer out onto the bridge.

The two captains simultaneously demanded, "Lieutenant Commander, report!"

Singer threw a look at Tetriana, which she understood to mean, this is my bridge. She walked past her enraged captain towards the security station.

"We hit a hyper disruption charge and fell out of our band back to normal space. Three ships were waiting for us in normal space, and they are holding us for fuel, Captain." Lieutenant Commander Kolbe reported.

Singer sighed deeply and straightened up her uniform before pointing towards the communications desk exclaiming, "Open a link!"

There was a short pause before she continued, "This is Captain Singer of the *GBS Sanitarian*, can I speak to the captain of the lead vessel?" she forced her most polite voice, but her crew could tell this could end in an off the books disappearance.

"He is speaking to you," a cold wheezing voice replied.

"Can I ask you what it is you want?" Captain Singer replied, holding her polite voice.

"Listen up, woman, I have no time to play games, we need fuel and I understand you use the same fuel as us. You will give us fuel, or you will be destroyed," the voice demanded. "And in case you haven't noticed, there are three of us and only one of you."

"Woman?!" Singer repeated with a shout, and then signalled to close the link. Her pupils reddened with anger. There were a few sure ways to get an angry response out of Singer, sexism was one. "Tactical options!"

"There is actually only one ship, the other two are clever creations of holographic and sensor masking. On top of that, the real ship is actually pretty weak, he is actually flying a Debelian-class freighter, so he poses no risk to us. One torpedo to the engine should do it, Captain." The tactical officer turned and waited for further commands.

"Reopen the link," Captain Singer ordered, calming herself down as her pupils returned to black. "We're not giving up our fuel, so be our guest and destroy us. Close the link." Singer spoke swiftly. "Raise shields and load one EAT torpedo into the torpedo bay."

Another major upgrade Singer had done to the ship was the overhauled weapons systems. EAT Torpedoes, or Energy Absorbing Torpedo Torpedoes, are high-class missiles that absorb almost all forms of energy as they head towards their target. When they hit, they release their designed pay-load and, on top of that, all the energy they have absorbed during their travel. It was possible to shield against them, but it was extremely difficult as conventional energy shielding was absorbed by the torpedo.

"Shields are up and torpedo is loaded and ready to be fired. Captain," a voice spoke from behind her. "He's charging his weapons, but he is also turning away from us."

The other captain seemed to understand his position and started turning away. The two fake vessels moved between the real one and the *Sanitarian* before disappearing to reveal a missile heading towards the ship as he had left a parting gift and fired upon the *Sanitarian*.

Singer froze and without moving started to mutter, "Mistake one, inter-rupting me. Mistake two, referring to me as woman as a clap down. Third and final mistake, firing upon my ship. Strike three, you're out. Fire the torpedo, Ensign."

A smooth ball of apparent nothingness shot from the *Sanitarian's* dorsal arrays, crossing the distance between the two vessels in the blink of an eye and angling in on the target.

As the torpedo hit its target, where the engine must have sat underneath, it discharged all the energy it had built up and then, when it had used all the built-up energy, the torpedo exploded. A great flash of light blinded the *Sanitarian* sensors. When the sensors adjusted to the explosion only minor debris was left where the ship had been.

"Report!" Singer demanded swiftly, showing a bit more motion as she turned to the sensor station.

"The ship has been completely destroyed," the lieutenant behind the sensors console replied.

"Good. Start bio clean-up," Singer grinned with a look akin to the fabled Cheshire cat. "Someone bring me up to speed on what's happening with finding the *Quosmod*." She headed towards the centre of the room and placed herself in her chair, then swung it around to face the rest of her crew on the bridge.

"We have not managed to locate the *Quosmod*, but we are on route to the last station it docked at to see if they have any useful information," Tetriana explained, stood to one side of the security console. When she had finished explaining she gave a friendly nod to the person already in position at the security console and clearly commanded, "You are excused, Kolbe."

Lieutenant Commander Kolbe walked out from station and, with a smile and a nod said, "Thank you."

Captain Singer spoke a little louder. "And what's our ETA?"

"Just over an hour, Captain," Lieutenant Markus stated.

"When we find the *Quosmod*, I will take a small landing team. Tetriana, you're with me. Round up some security personnel!" Singer exclaimed, sat very comfortable with one leg crossed over the other looking towards Tetriana.

"Right away, Captain," Tetriana accepted, and started working on the security console.

Chapter X

Now that his addiction had been quelled, Elios found he could relax a little more. To be fair, his new accommodation wasn't too bad, in fact, it was better than anywhere else he had ever spent a night. He had vague memories of the dark, mouldy one-roomed shack that he and his mother had shared when she was still alive. But those drug-addled memories were very hazy. After his mother died, and **The Drug** was no longer in constant supply, the memories were clearer, but this wasn't always a good thing. Maybe it would be easier to forget how the sharp winter nights had cut through his bony body so that he had to hug Moncello like a living, breathing, monkey-shaped hot water bottle. Or to wipe the memory of the traumatising nights he'd spent in the local jail. He was seldom kept in for more than one night at a time, normally because the cell was required for more hardened criminals than Elios would ever be, but he had seen his fair share of prison and was not anxious to go back in a hurry. Lying awake listening to the mad laughter or screams of the poor sods who had been stifled inside too long was a good deterrent.

Yes, he had definitely been in worse places than this, Elios decided. The door to the cell slid open again, and in stepped the two siblings who had given him **The Drug**. Elios eyed them distrustfully.

"Did you sleep well?" the woman asked gently. Taken aback by the odd question, Elios didn't really know what to say.

"What's it to you?" he replied suspiciously. He could feel his legs become tense with apprehension as he watched his captors at the door.

"That drug you take," the woman said. "It's strong, dangerous, and highly addictive." She shook her head.

"It also causes insomnia, eating disorders and paranoia," her brother added, and then almost to himself. "If there was any other way to cure the Calesvor Virus, it would have been banned decades ago." The man was visibly in thought, he returned his gaze to Elios shaking his head as if trying to get a stuck thought out.

"Insomni-what?" The big words were making Elios's head spin. Those living in the slum had no need for big complex words, they would rather communicate in short words, or even grunts if that would do.

"It means having difficulties sleeping," said the woman, kindly. "We were worried about you last night. Thrashing about, muttering,"

The woman didn't have chance to finish her line before Elios blurted, "Were you spying on me?"

"No," the man said, frowning slightly. The girl laid a hand on his folded arm, and his posture relaxed. "We were checking in on you from time to time to make sure you were still alive."

Yeah, right, pull the other one, Elios thought to himself, but couldn't bring himself to say it.

"But that doesn't matter right now," the woman said, breezily. "What matters is what we're going to do with you."

"Put me back home and pretend none of this ever happened?" Elios suggested insolently. Feeling equal measures of fear and frustration towards his captors.

"We can't do that," the man said. Elios thought he could see a hint of sympathy in the man's eyes, as though he wished they could.

"We ran into a tiny bit of trouble while we were picking up some cargo and have no intention of going back for a while," the woman explained.

"What's more," the man added, "we think you might be one of us." The two siblings waited for the words to sink in, but Elios appeared unreceptive. His mind still cloudy from **The Drug**, he was struggling to understand what was said.

Suddenly, he felt a thought connect in his brain, "One of you?" he scoffed. "No offense, but I ain't thinking so."

"The evidence is quite clear," the man explained. "We did a standard medical scan on you while you were unconscious. You came up with a positive DNA match with one of our colleagues, himself a relative of one of our old crew, who died twenty-two years ago."

"Well, then one of your colleagues slept with a hooker." Elios's face was deadpan.

"You would call your own mother a hooker?" the woman asked, her expression shuttered.

"Hooker, courtesan, lady of the night, call her what you like, she sold her body for money and that's the end of it." The siblings glanced at each other.

Elios could see that he had shocked them and felt a small victory for doing so. Up here gallivanting in their little spaceship, they probably had no idea what life was like for normal folks like him. Thinking through what he had just learned his mind fixed on the fact that his bleeding john-for-a-father had been a spacer! Hiring prostitutes for an evening was one of the perks of the spacers' consequence free lifestyle. It happened all the time. Most prostitutes had more sense than Elios's mother, and would not keep a pregnancy to a spacer. After all, at least the morning after drink was free for those living in the slums. The powers in charge didn't want the population growing uncontrollably.

Elios grimaced, these spacers holding him prisoner were no doubt just as naïve as the rest of their kind. They'd never understand something like the life of a slum dweller. Then he caught the edge of a sad smile on the woman's lips but before he could respond to it, the man spoke.

"We also believe we know why you're so addicted to those leaves," the man expertly steered the conversation away from prostitution.

"Because **The Drug's** very addictive?" Elios's voice was oozing with sarcasm.

"Partially," the woman admitted. "But your dependency is frighteningly high. You seem to require a fix every three days or so whereas, often, someone can survive up to three weeks without experiencing many negative symptoms."

"Well, go on then. Why am I so addicted to **The Drug**?" Elios said, rolling his eyes. His captors clearly thought they had found some marvel that they wished to share. A marvel he could not care any less about and at this point he wanted to appease them enough to get home.

"When you're tripping you often visualise a gate of some sort, don't you?" the man asked. Elios found his curiosity peeked, he nodded cautiously, unsure of where this was going. "Well, Jenny and I," the man gestured to his sister, "have this thing with our minds. We call it a trigger. It's quite hard to explain but basically, there's something in there that tells us that something called the Tannhauser Gate is really important."

"The Tannhauser Gate?" Elios asked becoming animated. He was suddenly interested. "What's it?"

"The Judicial Assembly that effectively controls the Republic, and that wields a great deal of power beyond, calls itself the Tannhauser Gate."

"Never heard of that," Elios said matter-of-factly. The frustration that was abated by his interest was growing again. He felt annoyed that these people could not answer a question that had haunted him for as long as he could think.

"No, you wouldn't have," the man told him, raising his eyebrows calmingly. "Hardly anyone has. That's what makes the Gate so difficult to keep tabs on. They keep to the shadows, subtly manipulating things to their own will without anyone realising. They're almost like a modern day Illuminati.".

"Illumi-what-what?" Elios could feel he was fully frustrated once again. He found it frustrating when he did not understand what people were talking about, something that would rarely happen back in the slums. He scowled his face.

"Illumina," the man paused, as if he'd suddenly changed his mind. "Doesn't matter, it's not important. What's important is that, for some reason, there are people out there who do know about the Gate and have been trying to figure out why their minds tell them it's significant."

"My condolences," Elios snorted insolently, unsure if he'd used the word condolences correctly and quickly wanting to move on in case he had not. "But I don't see what it's got to do with anything. My hallucinations show me an actual gate, one that you walk through to get to places, not some hyped up group of men in charge."

"We believe that's a consequence of how your trigger has manifested. When you're hallucinating, your subconscious mind tries to make sense of it and, because you know what a gate is and had never heard of the Judicial Assembly, you experience visions of an actual gate."

"You're crazy," Elios said simply. He could feel his limbs beginning to shake and a raising sense of anxiety. The woman, who the man had called Jenny, rolled her eyes.

"Look," she said. "The word Tannhauser obviously meant something to you."

"Well, yeah, but," Elios stuttered, his chest beginning to hurt as his heart pumped harder.

"And you'd never encountered it in the real world outside your hallucinations before now?" Jenny continued calmly.

"I guess not, but," Elios said, trying to keep his composure, his mind racing to find out where this line of conversation was going.

"Then I think you'd better come and see the captain." Jenny held out her hand to him, but Elios hung back.

"I, I don't think so," he said, shaking his head. "Not if you've told him I've got some kooky Tannhauser trigger in my head."

"Don't worry," Jenny insisted, her voice was calm, reassuring and controlling at the same time. "He won't judge you." Elios felt strangely inclined to believe her.

"I'm not going anywhere without Moncello!" He demanded, just realising he had forgotten about his pet monkey during this whole interaction.

"He's still out cold," the man answered, apologetically. "The standard stun setting required for a human is much greater than that for a monkey. I think it would be better if he was left for a day or so to recuperate." Elios wasn't happy about that, but he let himself be led out of the cell. Every fibre of his body pushing him to stay where he was. He couldn't explain why he was walking, but he decided to go with it.

As they headed along the white corridor, Jenny turned to him. "Most of the crew call the captain by his name, Jack, but we've been together for over thirty years and have earned that privilege. It would be best if you referred to him as Captain," she advised.

"Got it," Elios answered dryly. "Captain Jack it is!"

CHAPTER XI

THE *GBS SANITARIAN*, REPUBLIC SPACE

THE *SANITARIAN* ENTERED into communications range of an old-looking space station. While space stations could not rust in the traditional sense, the older a space station was the more solar radiation could discolour the surface. The older design of space stations would also give it away. The outer hull of this station was made from a dark alloy whereas most Republic stations constructed in the last fifty years used a light reflecting alloy to reduce radiation damage.

"The station is hailing us, Captain," the communications ensign announced. The bridge of the *Sanitarian* was once again tense. Singer sat centre to the room.

"Open the link," acknowledged Singer, barely lifting her head from a small personal device.

"This is Captain Leon of the *TRS Profession-Constituo*, how can we be of service to you today?" a cheerful voice announced from the audio system on the bridge of the *Sanitarian*. Singer pocketed her device and stood from her chair while stretching her neck to loosen it.

"Greetings, Captain, I am Captain Singer of the *GBS Sanitarian*. We are looking for information on a ship named *IGP Quosmod*, are you able to help us?" she replied, looking towards the ceiling addressing to the headless voice.

"It won't be hard to give you information on them. The amount they have done on board here, they are known by everyone," Leon replied chuckling through his words, "If you look at your comms station you should see the information coming in now." A faint beep sounded to Singers side. With that signal she walked towards the communication station and re-lieved the person behind it.

"Seven arrests, eleven confiscations, five warnings and one fine handed out. They certainly were busy, weren't they?" Singer gave an impressed smirk and a nod as she read off from the list she had just received.

"At the end of the list there is where they're now headed. Thank you for the visit, Captain. I hope I have been of assistance. See you in the future. Take care." Leon said signing out of the conversation.

"Thank you. And careful what you wish for," Singer said, closing the communications link. Singer appreciated efficiency, and she was happy that this interaction had been so smooth. "Take us to the *Quosmod*, Lieutenant," she commanded out loud sitting once again.

"Right away, Captain," the helmsman announced, hit the console a cou-ple of times and then, as the ship jolted forward continued, "ETA one hour, Captain."

"That's swift," Singer acknowledged, standing once again, "Away team, ready?" she half asked half commanded, turning to Tetriana who was work-ing away on the security console.

"Ready, Captain Singer," Tetriana responded. "Waiting to meet us in transporter room two."

Singer walked towards the door and nodded to Tetriana who walked out from behind the security console. "Lieutenant Commander Kolbe, take the bridge." With these words Tetriana and Singer left through the door to the bridge leaving Lieutenant Commander Kolbe to take up her position in Singer's chair.

As the two Captains made their way to their designated transporter room, Singer spoke to Tetriana, "We are here to arrest a man by the name of Lance-Corporal Timothy Angelos Luther Michael Xavier James Got-tfried Jean Freud." She began faux panting. "Wow that's a mouthful." Then turned her head towards Tetriana. "Arrest," she said once more, with a wink. "If you catch my drift?"

"I believe so, Captain," Tetriana responded, looking down towards her shorter superior as they marched. Singer only a foot ahead of Tetriana.

Chapter XII

The *IGP Quosmod*, Republic Space

As they came to a stop off the bow of the *IGP Quosmod*, the away team evaporated from the Sanitarian and reappeared in a well-lit open area of the *Quosmod*. There, waiting for them, was a small welcoming party led by the ship's captain. "Hi, I am Sergeant Captain Martine of the *IGP Quosmod*. I understand there is something important we must discuss today," The man stood at the head of the group stepped forward looking between Singer and Tetriana before reaching an open hand towards the latter, "Captain?"

"Singer." Captain Singer responded, stepping between Martine and Tetriana grabbing the offered hand in a tight handshake, "And yes, we do. I am looking for Lance-Corporal Timothy Angelos Luther Mi..." Captain Singer started but was cut off by the captain of the *Quosmod* who was waving his hands.

"Most people just call him Tim, and I know him. He is our best engineer and one of our best wardens. He is currently on the bridge running repairs on one of the helm consoles. Any particular reason you are looking for him?" Captain Martine questioned with a tone of worry in his voice furrowing his brow. "He isn't in any trouble, is he?"

"I am currently unable to divulge that information, but I will have a full report after the situation," Singer replied unreassuringly, appearing to be more concerned with a mark on her uniform she had found while removing her captains' stars. "Now, can you please lead me to your bridge?" The welcoming party stepped back and allowed Singer and her boarding crew to follow the ship's captain towards the bridge. Singer pulled at Tetriana's sleeve to get her attention and whispered something in her ear to which Tetriana replied with a nod.

Walking next to her captain, Tetriana jolted her arm, this simultaneously dislodged a gun from her right arm and unfurled it into her hand. She balanced the gun in her hand for a few seconds and then tapped on a small touch screen on its barrel. Finally, she jolted her arm again causing the gun to refold and recoil up her sleeve.

As the away team neared the bridge, they were met with two impressive doors with a large emblem engraved in the centre representing the 'Citizen Protection and Prevention of Crime Group.' There was a slight noise as the two doors parted revealing a pretty normal bridge for an Inter-Galactic Protection Vessel. Everything finished in grey plastic bar the hand rails, which were a finely polished metal, with the crew all working at their set locations and the captain's chair situated at the back, looking out onto the whole bridge.

Tetriana jolted her arm again, releasing the gun back into her hand. Singer looked up at her and said abruptly. "On you go."

Without hesitation Tetriana walked down to the front of the bridge where a tall, muscular man was lying under the helm controls desk working on the internal electronics. "Stand up!" she commanded, giving the man's foot a small nudge with her own. The man shuffled a little to move from beneath the helm and stand so he could see who had given the command. He was wearing a generic space warden uniform. Grey all-in-one suit with his name and rank clearly printed on the left side of his chest. Tetriana looked straight into his striking blue eyes, she could feel her hair starting to turn pink at the tips and corrected before any visible change had occurred. "Are you Lance-Corporal Timothy Angelos Luther Michael Xavier James Gottfried Jean Freud?"

"I am, and who might be asking?" the man replied with a joking tone, looking straight at Tetriana from an almost equal eye level.

"Never mind the pleasantries. Lance-Corporal Timothy Angelos Luther Michael Xavier James Gottfried Jean Freud, you are hereby sentenced to summary execution for treason against the Republic by aiding the enemy.

We are here to prevent your plans. You are afforded no last words." Tetriana declared, lifting the weapon from her side, and pointing at the chest of the man who moved back.

"What?" the man exclaimed as a single cyan flash left the end of the gun, knocking him to the ground in a heap. The only sign of the weapon's fire a small puff of steam leaving the spot where the energy had hit. Tetriana lowered the gun to her side, stood to attention and turned her head towards Singer with Captain Martine stood looking on in disbelief a minor tremble visible in his hands. Just as silence had fallen on the bridge a siren began sounding, singling the weapons fire.

"What was that?" Captain Martine exclaimed, "How did your weapon fire in a suppression zone?" His tone moved from shock to anger.

"Away team, return to the Sanitarian. That includes you, Tetriana," Singer commanded, ignoring Martine's protestations. "Captain Martine, eject the body into space in the normal fashion and write a death certificate, but don't write a report on this, one has already been submitted for you."

Instantly, Tetriana grabbed her ear lobe and announced, "Four to return. Singer to stay behind." Within seconds the entire away team, barring Singer, dissolve from existence. As Tetriana and the rest of the team left the bridge, Martine tried to protest again, "You cannot just barge in on my bridge and kill one of my crew?" he shrugged his arms signalling the room.

Singer reached into her inner pocket and removed a little device, it quickly lit a hovering symbol before it disappeared and was as quickly pocketed, "I can, and I have." Singer cooly replied, finally looking Martine in the eyes. "Do you understand me?" She finished briefly letting her eyes transition through a ready purple colour. Martine was unsure if this was as a result of the situation or the background siren noise stopping.

"Yes, ma'am." Captain Martine said under his breath, "Can I at least ask about the charges?" Captain Martine huffed, looking down at the dead body of one of his crew, still shaking in disbelief at what had just happened.

"I'm afraid not. It's all top secret," Singer replied, tapping her chest pocket before pushing her ear lobe. "You understand," she finished before announcing, "one to return." With these words, she dematerialised before Captain Martine's eyes.

"Fire the body out into space in a torpedo casing right away," Captain Martine said, still shaking, not able to move from the spot he was stood on. "And make way to the nearest IGP Head Quarters, I want to get to the bottom of this!"

Chapter XIII

The *GBS Sanitarian*, Republic Space

S INGER RE-MATERIALISED onto the glass plate of the *Sanitarian's* transporters and immediately headed off in the direction of the medical bay.

As she left the door to the transporter room, she shouted back to the person behind the transporter desk. "Standard Recovery, grab the body and send straight to the medical bay. Tetriana may have used a little more power than usual."

On any usual return to the ship, Singer would have asked to be transported directly to the bridge or her quarters. This time she opted to return like any other crewmember in order to relay her orders.

The person replied to the closing doors, "Aye, ma'am."

Chapter XIV

THE *ELISMERE* SLID into a secure docking hangar, umbilicals reaching out to lock her in position as her drive powered down. A graviton cradle held her invisibly in place, supporting the smooth contours of her hull. Her crew had gotten incredibly lucky, Emily's contacts had found them a courier contract from a trading station, the *R3 Siltis*, to Marzena, the Federation's primary trading world. And as the loading sequence for the contract kicked in, Adrian opened a shielded link to the *Siltis's* Virtual Intelligence interface.

The *R3 Siltis* was one of the hundreds of maintenance and resting facilities that now dotted the interstellar trade routes. *R3* was the intergalactic designation for the Rest, Refuel and Repair stations. The stations were a result of a somewhat pointed not-quite-insult from a Republic diplomat directed at the Camelot's Union. The Camelot's Union was a massive organisation that effectively ran space trade, they had only been around for about a hundred years.

A hundred and ten years ago, Emil Jarvis, the aforementioned Republic diplomat, effectively challenged the Union to be more than just a massive trading guild. In negotiations, he implied that if the Union was not willing to grant the Republic concession in trading fees, then certain critical shipments might suddenly become susceptible to pirating. He, and the Republic government, failed to take into account the staggering amounts of money that the Union brought in every year. That could have been down to the fact that most of it didn't go back into the economy except in private bank accounts. So, after Emil's challenge, and a not-inconsiderable level of agreement from the other stellar powers on the fact that they should at least do something with their wealth. The Union decided that, if the bureaucrats wanted them to actually do something with the ludicrous amounts of money they had tucked away, then they would do it properly. They decided to do it their way, and the bureaucrats would just have to put up with it.

Within a year, almost seven hundred *R3* stations like the *Siltis* had sprung up out of nowhere and small fleets of Camelot warships were patrolling the trade routes against any interference. Six months later, the Entente, one of the Republic's neighbouring powers, made the next mistake. Observing that groups that weren't nations couldn't really expect to have a fleet the size of the one the Union was theorised to have without becoming seen as threats to stability.

In response, the Union bought colonisation rights to a star system. A rather nice star system with not one but three habitable planets. A temperate, Earth-like binary and one of the most spectacular of all recorded paradise worlds. Having become quite sick of playing within the rules, but aware that they were at least somewhat necessary, the Union Directorate decided that if they couldn't have fun their way, they would have fun at the expense of the bureaucrats. They named the system Albion, the binary planet The Kingdoms, and their paradise world Excalibur.

They built nine cities on The Kingdoms, forming the primary population base of the system, and one city, Avalon, on Excalibur. It was around this point that they contacted the diplomatic branches of every major government and informed them that they now were a nation, and that their borders were closed to all but tourists and diplomats.

Excalibur, due to considerable efforts by the Union, was now the most well known of all the paradise worlds in existence, with Avalon one of the most visited locations in all of known space. Meaning that, at any point in time, the population of Avalon was mostly comprised of visitors, and anyone would be lucky if they saw someone who was actually part of the Union.

Six months of stalemate later, every star nation signed the Nimue Accords, a set of treaties that brought the unofficial don't touch status of the Union into agreed reality.

However, as a condition of the Accords, the Union relinquished all claim to the stations they had built, handing them over to the powers that controlled the sections of space they were in. This was the Union's last strike against the bureaucrats that had frustrated them for so long, dumping hundreds of already operating facilities into their laps. Many had Starcomms now, and they all acted as communication posts for the Union. They also acted as the primary maintenance stations for the Camelot fleet.

The *Siltis*, however, was special. Not because she was any different from the other *R3* stations in existence, the only major difference was the Starcomm installation, and that was becoming steadily more common on *R3* stations. No, the *Siltis* was special because the *Elismere* knew the Union passcode for its Starcomm. Any message they sent from there could never be traced, and never be found except by its intended recipient. To the rest of the universe, apart from the receiver, it would never have happened.

Another bone of contention between the Union and the more human-centric governments of the time. Every station in the network was run by a VI, and any attempt to remove it caused every system on the station apart from it to go haywire. After the last time the Entente had tried, which had ended with the VI fusing the galactic symbol for idiot, out of battle steel, onto every Entente registered vessel within its holds, people had pretty much given up. It just wasn't worth the trouble. Although it sort of rankled to leave another nations VI in control of a station you owned, the VI's managed the general maintenance and running of the facilities, proving their worth as better than the cost of removing them.

So, Adrian connected to the station, entered the code that Emily had acquired several years ago, and was promptly routed to the station's Starcomm controls. Emily had a few of these codes, most the results of trades with Camelot Warrants, the secretive group of elite agents that were the Union Directorate's troubleshooters. They had effectively complete access to all Union assets, and due to the nature of the relationship between the Tannhauser Gate and the Camelot's Union, which could be easily summed up as pistols at ten paces with starships, the *Elismere's* crew had had more interaction with them then most ever did. Quite profitable interaction on the whole, as this particular escapade showed. Being able to send shadow-messages through the Starcomm network was a godsend, even if the number of stations they could go through was highly limited. It was yet another one of the *Elismere's* hidden advantages in their shadow war with the Gate, the ability to send instantaneous and untraceable messages from outside the Federation Barrier to Federation Starcomms, allowing them to safely coordinate with their support there without fear of being caught. Even then though, they used code-worded messages. Today Adrian typed in two words that he had never really thought he'd ever be able to send.

Paradise Found.

That was the codeword for a breakthrough that could end the long-hidden war. And they had, if he wasn't mistaken, just found the mother of them. Two words, and yet they held such power. He tapped send, and the message vanished into the system. The *Siltis's* VI scrubbed all trace of its passage as it routed the data into the Starcomm queue, and it was gone before the *Elismere* undocked.

Paradise Found. Now it was up to them to make sure they didn't lose it.

Chapter XV

C APTAIN SINGER SAT FROZEN watching a green medical bed in a uniformly white room. She always hated visiting medical, the white of the walls and ceilings caused a sensation in her mind that she did not understand, and she did not want to. The medical staff moved around her pretending she was not there as much as she was pretending they did not exist. Singer closed her eyes briefly and thought to herself, 'I said to dispose of the body immediately, what is taking so long?'. She never understood the human propensity to grieve over a death and could not understand why other captains let people say goodbye to a dead body. Looking for distraction she pulled her palm device out of her inner pocket, staring back from the black screen she caught her reflected pupils show as a green-yellow. She felt an upsurge of anger and watched her pupils switch momentarily to red, then black as she unlocked her device.

The air in front of her began to crackle with static. She stood up as the naked tall figure of the man she had ordered Tetriana to shoot solidified into existence on the bed she had been watching. Medical staff descended on the bed like wasps on to a sweet substance. Some were checking his head, others were checking his torso, and one loudly proclaimed, "computer, deploy decency gown." The medical staff dispersed from the body leaving a woozy looking man sat slightly raised in a Republic issue medical gown.

"Welcome to my ship, the *GBS Sanitarian*, Lance-Corporal Timothy Angelos..." Singer started but was cut off by the man slowly and uneasily waiving a hand.

As he let his hand drop back to the bed he said, "Please, please, most call me Tim," the man said groggily, clearing his throat after speaking. He tried to sit up but fell back down again.

"Rest for now, Tim. I'm sure this has all been rather confusing. I'll answer all your questions when you get your strength back." The mans head lulled to the side and as if singer said the magic word, he was out cold.

Several hours later, Singer was in her quarters reading the monthly ship analysis reports checking for damage or any sign of wear and tear. She prided herself in a well maintained and kept ship, the slightest sign of wear, even a scratch on a console, and she would have the ship in for repair. Mid way through reading about the engine energy inverters, the chief medical officer spoke to her through her earpiece in his soft bedside voice, "The patient is sitting up and asking for you."

"I'll be right down," she replied out loud, closing the report down on her palm device as she stood up and started briskly walking towards the doorway to her quarters.

Entering medical, Singer made her way to the hazy energy screen that blocked view of the bay she had been visiting earlier. As she walked through the hazy veil, she was met by Tim now sat upright watching with interest the medical officer that was moving around him. The medical officer was prodding him here, taking readings from him there, moving Tim's arm one way, then the next, before he stepped back and said softly, "As healthy as he could be." Singer nodded to the officer, and he walked through the veil leaving her alone with Tim.

"How is our new recruit now?" Singer said walking up to the bed Tim was sitting on.

"Very good, thanks." Tim started, and cautiously added "Captain." His previous work did not have much to do with the Military directly, so he was guessing at the uniform the individual stood before him wore. "But I do have a lot of questions," he said, hurrying on, "Recruit? What am I a recruit for? The last thing I remember was being shot for charges I can barely remember, and how am I still alive?" Tim's face was a mix of confused and exhausted. Singer was just glad that he wasn't angry, usually the kinds of recruits she would have to collect would not respond as calmly to The Gate's process.

She cut Tim off before he could continue, "Ah, quick to get to the point. Well there is no point in, as they call it, beating around the bush," Singer chuckled, but noticed Tim did not share the humour and so continued, "Well. Welcome aboard the *GBS Sanitarian*. A ship that does not exist, meaning you do not exist. You have been recruited by the Tannhauser Gate to do whatever they tell you to with no questions asked. You are above the government, beyond the law and never can be questioned. You will receive your orders from the chief engineer, and you will work in engineering for the foreseeable future. Your start date will be when Medical Officer Loki determines you fit enough," she said as if well-rehearsed, before punctuating it with, "refusal is not an option. Any questions?"

"Just one," Tim said, figuring Singer's question was most likely rhetorical. "What does GBS stand for?"

Singer let out a laugh, then casually said, "Would you believe me if I said Grand Body Snatcher?" With that she turned on the spot and walked out of the medical bay chuckling to herself.

Tim smiled and relaxed on the bed waiting for further instructions. He knew there was no point in fighting this, when The Gate was mentioned, anyone with sense in the Republic, would know to just do as they are told.

Chapter XVI

Portalis, Republic Space

SEVERAL HUNDRED LIGHT-YEARS AWAY at the outskirts where the Republic met the Federation, Portalis, a small, semi-inhabited planet not much larger than Mercury, orbited a carbon star. One hemisphere of the planet was always completely shrouded in darkness, the other drenched in blood-red starlight. The Darkside, as it was known, was a damp, earthy wasteland inhabited almost exclusively by blind, fanged sniffer moles. The edges of the Lightside was a high-rise metropolis with business buildings, government offices and streamlined apartment blocks shooting into the crimson sky. The small planet was enveloped by a set of atmosphere generators that worked to replace the atmosphere constantly being removed by the star.

In one of the business buildings sat Mr Clive Wassell. A man above the government and beyond the law. He was one of seven senior Tannhauser Gate associates who made up its Gate Assembly. He also happened to be the only one with a human secretary.

The rest of the associates had androids to do the work that Tanya Heart was hired for, but Mr Wassell preferred a more personal connection with his employees. Tanya was effortlessly taking notes on her tablet knowing the notes would never be read by another human and would only be used if a Gate Assembly member needed to be held to account. She felt this was demeaning, a VI would be better suited to take notes. Each member had their own assistant take notes to make sure no-one was doctoring events. It at least gave her creative license to remove the regular inuendo from her superior. Indeed, she had just ignored the quip, "You only need one hand to take notes, the other may be better used under the table." These lines had ceased to shock her, and the lack of assembly members calling him out shocked her even less.

How, she wondered dimly, in a species that had left Earth for the stars over a thousand years ago, could so much sexual prejudice against women still exist? Tanya had read books about the suffragettes, who, over a millennium ago, had fought for and secured the rights for women to be treated as first-class citizens. But, since then, things seemed to have deteriorated. Even in the Gate itself, which was meant to be the pinnacle of Republic society, there was only one female Senior Associate.

Lady Abigail de Moivre was in her early seventies and had struggled no end to get a place on the committee. It had been her illustrious wealth that had finally tipped the balance in her favour but, although she was a spoilt, self-important vixen, she was the only member of the Senior Associates that Tanya had the tiniest morsel of respect for. The rest of the committee conjure images in her mind of an ancient earth story, Hoffman's mouse king. They were all vermin masquerading as royalty. And despite their inanimate secretaries, they were all as misogynistic as Clive, they were just more discrete about it than he was.

"As far as we can tell," William Carter, a large red-faced man with a thick jawline and clammy hands was saying, "an unidentified smuggler vessel disabled the sensor net, boarded *IGC 0765* and captured subject Blue-46-O4-1000."

"My department can deal with that," Kevin Marques, the only dark-skinned man on the committee, cut in. "One child and a small contraband boat will be no match for my fighters."

"At this point we have to assume that they also have a full download of the communication between *Tomorrow's Hope* and *IGC 0765*," Lady Abigail said regally. "Obviously we cannot allow the uncensored information to remain in these terrorists' hands. If it gets any farther it could ruin us. The methods employed on The *Hope* may be a tad upsetting for."

"Calm down, my dear," Sir Reginald Umpire, the old, wrinkly man at the head of the table drawled. He sat up further in his polished mahogany and electrum wheelchair and glared down the table. "It's only a small ship, it's unlikely that it will even possess any particle batteries."

"But, Sir," Carter began to protest.

"We have nothing to worry about," Sir Reginald insisted and added, gesturing to Marques. "It probably could be taken out by one standard fighter ship."

"Sir Reginald," Tanya's boss, Mr Wassell, interjected. Tanya could tell his excitement was rising by the lack of an inuendo comment to her. "Have you entertained the idea that this smuggler vessel may be more powerful than it appears? The crew did manage to disable an entire space station and steal an escaped subject right from under our noses without receiving any reported damages on their part."

"My people can deal with it!" Marques persisted, beads of sweat beginning to appear on his forehead. Tanya knew he needed to prove his worth on the committee before the next performance appraisal, which was drawing closer. His last evaluation had been less than satisfactory. And if his next performance evaluation was the same, the meeting notes would likely be called upon.

"Sir." Mr Wassell shot a spiteful glance at Marques, who narrowed his eyes. "Is it not better to be safe than sorry, to re-coin an old phrase? We do need to ensure we eliminate the perpetrators completely. In any case, what harm could it do to be over-prepared?"

"Very well," Sir Reginald was clearly irritated. "I believe there is a *Ninja* patrol in that area. Send out two *Ninjas* to find the smugglers. If the standard military option doesn't get them, give the assassins the order to fire, and don't let me hear another word about it."

"Sir," Mr Wassell nodded his respect, unable to keep the smugness out of his voice. "If you'll excuse me, fellow associates, I shall see to it tout d'suite." He rose majestically to his feet and left the room. As Tanya hurried after him, clenching and unclenching her writing hand, she noticed Marques making a rude hand gesture at Mr Wassell under the conference table.

Chapter XVII

CAPTAIN SINGER RE-ENTERED the bridge and marched right to her chair and announced, "Communications, open a channel to the rest of the ship." She lowered herself into her seat and cleared her throat to address her crew, "Crew of the *Sanitarian*. Our active orders have been updated we are now in pursuit of the ship that docked at the *IGC 0765*. Their crew are charged with stealing classified information, seizing a classified asset, and causing considerable damage to the facility. At this moment the vessels name is unknown. Current intelligence gathered thus far points us towards a small space station in the vicinity of our present location. We will be going to investigate the station for any clues to the ship's whereabouts." She paused, and appeared to begin addressing the bridge directly, "Standard station raid. Straight in, go for the bridge, download all information from their data storage and then off again." She nodded to the security station, then nodded to the comms station, and finally announced, "Captain Singer OUT."

Taking a deep breath, she sat back in her chair and turned it slightly to the left to face the helm desk. "Mark a heading to the *R3 Siltis* space station," she commanded, and then stood up from her chair. "Tetriana, you have the bridge. Call me when we arrive." The small door at the side of the bridge made the soft hush as it closed signalling Singer had left the bridge.

Tetriana moved out from behind the security desk announcing, "Take the desk, Lieutenant Commander Kolbe."

After she was sat where Singer had been moments before, Tetriana turned to the communications desk. "Make up a small away team. We will need technicians, security and sensor specialists."

The *Sanitarian* came to a stop at the space station. Captain Singer was standing at the docking ring, followed by Tetriana standing next to Tim, with a small crew standing behind them waiting for the *Sanitarian* to dock with the *Siltis*.

Tim turned to Tetriana and asked, "Is everyday as exciting as today?"

Tetriana turned and looked up at Tim, she tried to answer but was cut off when the ship shuddered as it begun docking procedure. Tim noticed a slight change in Tetriana's hair, as if a slight pink had briefly appeared.

An eerie hush signalled the *Sanitarian* coupling with the station. Before the docking doors had finished opening the small away team marched onto the space station. They left the docking room into a clear corridor lined with bluish grey plastic. As they rounded a corner they were confronted with a small team of armed men in half-black, half-blue uniforms.

"Identity and tags!" the leader of the armed team yelled, aiming his gun at Singer. Singer was a over a head shorter than the man suggesting that his outstretched aim would infact miss her if he were to shoot.

"Lower your gun sir, or feel it scratching your tonsils, and it won't be going down your throat," Singer retorted in a friendly but sinister tone. She brandished the right arm sleeve of her uniform coat to show the four stars pinned into the fabric.

"Excuse me?!" the man screamed at Singer, his face turning a deep shade of scarlet, his gun now aimed directly at her face. She moved to put her hand into her inner coat pocket when the man shouted, "Don't you even think about it!" His gun now trembling in his hand he continued "You have been warned!"

Singer let out a feigned sigh and rolled her eyes, "Tetriana, would you mind?" she said, moving to one side, giving a side glance at Tetriana who simply nodded back. While she would claim miscommunication, Singer had intentionally not sent a boarding request to the station controller. Internally she would justify it as not giving the staff of the station chance to cover up what she was looking for, but Tetriana knew it was really about displaying power.

Tetriana stepped forward with her arms at her side deliberately showing her clear palms. The guard switched his aim between Tetriana and Singer with the others in his party equally uncertain on who to aim. With a quick jolt of her arms, two guns appeared from up Tetriana's sleeves into her open palms. Before the officers had chance to respond, she aimed and fired, hitting none of them but still discharging exactly the right number of shots. She opened her hands and jolted her arms once more to return the guns to their position up her sleeves.

Singer stepped forward and looked at the security team's empty hands and smiled. "Now if you hadn't jumped the gun, as it were," she handed the man at the front of the group a device with a small emblem hovering above it, "you wouldn't be as close as you are to being executed for treason." Pushing past the now confused group of security staff, she ushered for her away team to follow towards the bridge.

"That was amazing," Tim whispered to Tetriana, leaning in closely so no one else would hear.

"That is my job," she retorted, refusing to look back at Tim. She could feel her hair colour changing and forced it back to its natural blue. Noticing this was not the first time her hair had almost given her away, she made a mental note to discuss removing Tim from all future away missions for the safety of the crew.

When they entered the bridge, Singer walked to the front of the room and was once again met by weapons pointed at her. She did not hesitate. "Leave the room now while you have the chance, or you won't be leaving it alive." She did not even blink but instead stood looking at the people on the bridge, changing her pupil colour rapidly from black to red. All at once the people in the room got up and walked out, leaving their weapons behind.

"You know what to do," Singer said to her away team clapping her hands together and sitting in the captain's seat of this station enjoying the spoils of her latest victim. She was internally counting down to her favourite moment of such drop-ins when the highest-ranking person on board tries to demand an explanation. One she did not have to officially give.

Right on cue, after a few minutes a well-dressed man marched in through the doors to the bridge and demanded, "What the hell is going on, on my bridge?"

Singer was taken aback not by the new person in the room rather by the pitch of the person's voice, which was rather high given his appearance. She stood up and brandished the device with the emblem, shoving it toward who she assumed to be the Stationmaster. The other captain, clearly displaying his stars, glanced at it, and scoffed. "And this gives you the right to fire upon my crew and forcefully take control of my bridge how?"

There was a pause and Singer raised an eyebrow. It wasn't uncommon to find someone who didn't recognise the emblem, or at least what it stood for, but it was really uncommon for a stationmaster not to. Generally, a stationmaster would have been at least told to turn a blind eye or outright told to fear seeing this in their job.

Contemplating what to do about it, singer raised both her eyebrows, rolled her eyes and sighed, "Well, there wasn't much resistance but if you're not happy with it, call up your superiors," she taunted the Stationmaster, who went straight to the comms desk and started to type furiously.

All of a sudden, a harsh male voice appeared. "What do you want, Stationmaster Barkly?"

"There is a rather annoying woman on board my station, who has carried out a control lockout on the pretext of the little doodle I have transmitted to you," the captain said in a smug voice looking towards Singer, who was busy checking her nails. "I am going to detain them in the brig, I'll need a lockout recovery team ASAP." he added, smiling to Singer.

There was a couple of seconds of metallic silence then the voice replied. "Barkly, you are hereby stripped of your rank as Stationmaster and relieved of duty. You should know that, what you call a, drawing is a no-questions-asked policy. Your replacement will be out within the next hour. Sorry for the inconvenience, Captain Singer."

"No problem, Vels," Singer spoke clearly. "Now, you, get off my bridge." She gestured with her hand to the ex-stationmaster. He looked at Singer and then turned on his feet and briskly walked off the bridge. "And that, people, is why we don't get questioned," Singer said, walking into the middle of the room, quietly giggling to herself.

"Singer," Vels began again, "you know what we were talking about earlier," he continued over the communications to the whole bridge. Singer's eyes started to turn red as she narrowed her gaze.

"Not now, Vels. Thank you for your help. I will be in touch if we need anything more. Singer out," Singer snapped, walking up to the communications desk, and hitting the close link button. "People, I need an estimate on the time of the data download." She sighed, walking briskly to the front of the room.

"About seven minutes, Cap'n," a voice called from near the centre of the bridge.

Singer headed for the doors of the bridge and turned to face the room again. "Tetriana, watch over this. When everything is done here, return to the *Sanitarian* and set coordinates for wherever the evidence takes us." She turned quickly on the spot, her short brown hair flicking behind her as she exited the room.

Tetriana walked over to the communications console Tim was working on and leaned down to look over his shoulder, the ends of her hair turning slightly pink again. "Are you busy?" she whispered into his ear.

Tim didn't look up from the panel continuing to work as he quietly replied, "Only as busy as you make me." Tetriana let out a slight smirk but quickly held herself back.

"Do you think you could get me Captain Singer's movements and keep an eye on her? I would like to know if she opens another connection to Vels," Tetriana said, leaning closer and whispering more quietly to Tim. She did not want the rest of the crew to know what they were up to. While most of the crew may have rathered Tetriana over Singer, she could not risk someone misjudging the situation and running to Singer. She knew that Tim likely had not had enough time to form allegiances in the crew.

"There you go," he said, almost immediately after she finished the sentence, and right enough there was a screen open on the console in front of them showing what Singer was currently doing. It showed the Captain getting to the end of a corridor on board the space station and then transporting from the station to the bridge of the *Sanitarian*. Tim and Tetriana watched the screen as she walked off the side of the bridge of the *Sanitarian* and into her private quarters.

Tetriana lifted her head. The away team aboard the space station buzzed around its bridge, like a well-oiled machine. Individual people, cogs doing their small jobs to complete the larger task. Tetriana moved her gaze back down onto the console as a red box appeared. "Communications link opened from the *Sanitarian* to the *IGC 0765*." She raised an eyebrow and looked closer at the panel, "Encrypted link level 10."

She looked up towards Tim with her crystal eyes, "Think you can get the receiving terminal name?"

Tim looked down towards the terminal to see what she was referring to, upon realising he looked up quickly and whispered, "Easily, it's surprising how many of these systems just give information away." In the republic, backdoors were required to all systems. Ostensibly so that law enforcement could keep citizens safe, and therefore it was widely known in any law enforcement position how to take advantage of them. Tim had his suspicion that the backdoors were likely part of a larger conspiracy by a government body to abuse power.

He started to type on the panel and, within a couple of seconds, white text on a black background covered the whole screen. The text streamed rapidly across the screen with occasional words reading as 'Firewall Breached,' and 'Connection Follow-up.' Then without warning, the text stopped moving and read one line in the middle of the panel:

"Connection Destination – *IGC 0765* / Captain Vels / Private Connection."

Without a thank you, or even a cursory glance at Tim, Tetriana turned and walked off to the side of the bridge. "Commander, take control, I will return shortly."

She ran the situation through her mind, what would she say or do when she got to Singer? She had warned her, so the logical choice would be to relieve the Captain of her duty. She stood with her back straight and announced, "One to return directly to the bridge," before disappearing from the spot she had been standing just seconds before. The Gate considered personal relationships a risk, and therefore would, and have in the past, retire captains for forming unsuitable relationships.

Almost instantly Tetriana rematerialized in the centre of the bridge, her hair a shimmering red colour. Ignoring all of the looks she received, she walked towards the metallic door decorated with several emblems, which Singer would be sitting behind. Without a sound, Tetriana glided into the room and stood just in the doorway where she could catch the faint sound of a conversation.

"Bethany, I can't do this anymore, please," the sound of a beseeching male voice carried to Tetriana.

"I can take a vacation or something, I can come and visit you," Singer was pleading with the console that had just come into Tetriana's view. She stood just behind a pillar in the entrance to the room so that Singer could not see her.

"You don't understand, it is not in my control as to why I can't see you and we all know in your line of work vacations are impossible," the voice grew a slight sense of courage. Singer's head fell towards the console as she started to blubber.

At this, Tetriana backed out of the room as quietly as she had entered. This was either because she could not stand the sight of emotions, or she couldn't bring herself to do what she should have done back at the IGC and relieve Singer of her duties. When she returned to the bridge, she walked up to the officer behind the transport controls and whispered into his ear, she then straightened her back and evaporated from the ship. Her hair flickered back from red to blue.

She came back into existence in the centre of the bridge of the *Siltis*. As soon as she had materialised, the Commander reported the completion of all tasks. On hearing this, Tetriana ordered the away team back to the *Sanitarian*.

Chapter XVIII

O N   T H E   E D G E S   O F   the Lightside of Portalis there were many business buildings, but the most impressive of these buildings was a 1215-floor monster, which loomed over the entire city, dwarfing all of the other skyscrapers in the process. The small planet size combined with the artificial atmosphere made this the perfect place to position such a large tower. It was the ominously named Judgement Tower and, on floor 49½, the Tannhauser Gate lurked.

Floor 49½ was a secret floor squished between the Department of Engineering Technology on floor 49 and the Akashic Library, which occupied floors 50, 51 and 52. There were no windows, but each office had a small artificial lighting system, which projected a window motif onto a screen to give the impression of looking outside as clearly as a window.

Tanya Heart gazed blankly out of one of the windowless windows as a cold, heavy hand pressed down on her shoulder and gripped it tightly. She wondered, as she had so many times before, if it might have been a bad idea to accept a job offer from a strange seventy-five-year-old man who worked for a company she hadn't known existed. It was true that he had been rather unusual, she hadn't particularly liked the way he kept invading her personal space, but he was also enigmatic and powerful and very rich. She found herself very intrigued by that.

And then there was the company's name, the Tannhauser Gate. Tanya had had a constant niggling sensation at the back of her mind since childhood, a desire to find out everything there was to know about something called the Tannhauser Gate. It wasn't until this job offer that she even knew what the Tannhauser Gate was.

At the beginning, her employer's antics were unpleasant but mostly harmless, a wandering hand under a conference table or a massage request after a long day, but that quickly changed. By the first time he actually hit her, she'd got herself in too deep by that point. No one expected her to understand any of the board meetings or private conversations, but she still couldn't be allowed to leave, even if she'd wanted to. Resigning meant not existing, and this was made clear to her in her first day on the job.

The worst part was she hadn't wanted to. This drive, or curse as her parents had called it, to learn about the Tannhäuser Gate was overpowering. It overpowered her judgement, her reservations and all of the qualms she should have had at that first encounter with Clive Wassell.

Clive Wassell, Tanya often thought to herself, even the name sounded slimy. A few days ago, Mr Wassell had sent out some *Ninja* assassin ships to track a light cargo vessel, which had apparently abducted a child. Some sort of test subject child known as Blue-46-O4-1000, if Tanya had understood correctly. She wasn't entirely sure why this child with a name like a barcode was so important to the Gate. But like most matters of this sort, she thought better to ignore it. It probably didn't matter to her anyway.

After embarrassing Kevin Marques at the last board meeting, Mr Wassell decided to rub salt in the wound having Tanya assigned to be his secretary. Ostensibly he said this was to help align the approach for tracking down the test subject. And so Tanya was expected to assist Marques for the afternoon.

She flinched as Marques knocked one of the bruises that hadn't quite subsided from the last time she'd been assigned to him.

"You want to be more careful," Marques smirked, running his finger over the bruise. "Blemishes are unbecoming on a young woman like you, you don't want Wassell to finally see sense and get rid of you, do you?"

She smiled sheepishly and flicked her blonde fringe out of her eyes. You mean that you don't want Wassell to get rid of me, she thought to herself. If only she had the guts to say that out loud, she thought. It was easier to keep her mouth shut, she wasn't hired to make intellectual conversation, or snide remarks. Actually, she wasn't hired to speak at all. She was hired to do what she was told.

The large screen, which covered one wall of Marques's office, sprang to life and a message in ominous red letters flickered up.

GBS *Sanitarian* REQUESTS FTLT COMMS-LINK WITH KEVIN MARQUES, CHIEF OF MILITARY AND CON-QUEST.

Before she knew what was happening, Tanya found herself being pushed into a swivel chair by the windowless window. The chair spun and Tanya had to grab a nearby side-table to keep from falling off, almost knocking over Marques's untouched mug of Fava coffee in the process.

Hastily standing up and walking to the next room, Marques positioned himself at his desk and smoothed his hair before pressing a green button that opened the comms-link.

A short, plump woman flashed up on the screen, a captain of some sort, Tanya thought, judging by the stars on her arm.

"Captain Singer," Marques barked, clearing his throat.

Tanya smirked to herself. It wasn't much of an achievement, being able to correctly guess a person's rank from their uniform, but it was still oddly satisfying when she got it right.

"To what do I owe this unex-pec-ted pleasure?" Marques hissed, his sarcasm was tangible.

"Chief Marques," the woman on the screen replied curtly nodding. Her pupils flashed an indignant shade of yellow before subsiding back into black and Tanya instantly recognised that this woman had Terineti blood in her, her eyes were too sensitive to be a normal human's eyes. This would be interesting, she thought, Marques hated what he called quasi-modes almost as much as Tanya hated Marques.

"What have you got for me, Captain?" asked Marques, already bored with the conversation. He began fiddling with the Newton's cradle on his desk. "Did you retrieve any useful information from the *Siltis*?"

"We are not entirely sure, Chief Marques," Singer replied, her eyes flinching in time to the swinging beads. "We picked up the signature for a ship, a light cargo vessel called the Zephyra. We have reason to believe this might have been the same ship that infiltrated *IGC 0765*."

"You have reason to believe it?" Marques sneered. "Well, it's a relief to see that your seventy grand a year salary isn't a complete waste of Gate resources." While he sounded sarcastic there was a smile of enjoyment on his face as he forced the Newton's cradle to start off again with a little more force. His enjoyment appeared to grow with the twitches of Captain Singer's eyes in time to the cradle's movements.

"Chief Marques," Captain Singer began cautiously, but Marques cut her off stopping the Newton's cradle.

"Tell me, Singer," he mocked her, "exactly what you expect me to do with this little titbit of information. Surely you don't expect me to go speak to my superiors and request that we pour more funds into your already over-budget mission?" Marques trailed off, looking over at Tanya, as if he had just realised she was in the room.

"Over-budget, Chief Marques?" Singer questioned politely. "I find that very difficult to believe. We have been most careful in our economics. I am sure you would find our accounts in impeccable order, do you require me to send them to you?" Singer asked with all sincerity. She would never dare to be condescending to a superior, and never to a Chief.

Neither Marques nor Singer noticed as Tanya rolled her eyes disdainfully at the pair of them. If they'd only bothered to ask, Tanya could have, but would likely not have, told them that most of the money that Marques thought was going into the military missions had been cut since his latest, very poor, performance appraisal and was now being poured into the Security and Defence department of the Gate. The department, incidentally, that was run by Tanya's employer, Clive Wassell.

"You have a rich and colourful history involving Stationmaster Vels Imleros, don't you, Singer?" Marques taunted, carefully avoiding Singer's question. "That wouldn't have anything to do with this sudden desire to track a ship that might possibly be connected to *IGC 0765*, would it?" Captain Singer's pupils flashed red, it only lasted an instant, but that instant was enough of an indication that Marques had hit a nerve. His lip curled. It was almost enough to make Tanya feel sorry for the Terineti. Almost, but not quite.

"I assure you, Chief Marques," said Singer, all emotion suddenly sucked out of her voice, "my loyalties are, and always have been, with the Gate. Any personal feelings I may or may not have towards anyone who may come between me and the Gate are inconsequential. You have nothing to worry about on that score. And as for funds," Singer grimaced, "We do not need more money, we have enough resources and fuel to last us a very long time. I merely need to know whether you wish us to pursue this possible lead."

"And why should I put my entire career in the hands of a good for nothing lizard?" Marques demanded. "Do you realise what will happen if you turn out to be wrong and the ship is just some smuggler trading vessel?"

"Chief Marques, I believe we should be more concerned about what happens if we turn out to be right," Singer replied, ignoring the slur against her. "Just imagine what your superiors would think if you intentionally allowed a group of Federation criminals to go free."

"Yes," Marques mused, "I see what you mean," He was suddenly unsure of himself. At forty three years old, Marques was the youngest Senior Associate by far and, as such, hadn't quite perfected the cold poker face that each of the others used when talking to their inferiors. Tanya could almost read every thought in his internal struggle to work out the best course of action.

"Might it be prudent, Chief Marques, that we send additional resources to backup the *Sanitarian*," Singer filled in the silence, "If this does turn out to be a Federation covert ops vessel, we should try and capture it in one piece." Marques looked up towards Tanya again and appeared to be lost in thought, he briefly looked at the door control switch to his office wondering if he could close the door without making his intention for privacy obvious. "Sir, what should we do?" Singer broke the chain of thought.

"We don't need any more ships, you should be enough. The great lizard captain with her lizard second in command. Go pursue your little ship. Apprehend them and bring them to me. I want to have a little chat with them." Tanya suppressed a shudder, the way Marques said little chat made her skin crawl. "Oh, and Singer, before you go, if you deem it absolutely necessary to dispose of the criminals, be a good girl and tidy up after yourself. Thank you."

Marques threw his finger down on the receiver key cutting off Singer as she began. "Yes Sir, but,"

He rubbed the sweat from the back of his neck and glanced at a photograph on his desk. It showed a tall, relatively handsome young gentleman with a crew-cut under his commander hat. The man had Marques's dark skin and high cheekbones and Tanya recognised him as Marques's second eldest son, Theo. Marques had gotten Theo a commission as a Lieutenant three years ago and, since then, Theo had been rapidly scaling the ranks, he was expecting another promotion, to Captain, by Christmas.

But, Tanya knew, if Marques failed another performance appraisal, and making a wrong decision here would definitely hurt his already slim chances of passing, then his entire family would be disgraced. Theo would be decommissioned, or at least shunned, and Marques would be retired.

Tanya, feeling Marques's eyes on her, pulled out a nail file and pretended to manicure her immaculate nails. If she were to actually let on that she understood the entire conversation she'd probably be hurt badly, to make sure she didn't talk, or she'd be retired. It wasn't very common, but unexplained disappearances did sometimes happen to mouthy Gate workers. No one particularly liked it, but the entire safety of the Republic depended on keeping information from the Federation and, if removing a few loose tongued individuals was deemed necessary by the Senior Associates, it was presumably the best option available. Although it made Tanya squirm when she thought about it too long, she knew the Gate, even Mr Wassell and Marques, must have the best interests of the Republic citizens at heart, so who was she to assume she knew better?

Marques let out a sigh of frustration and, getting Tanya's attention, said, "I seem to have acquired a lot of tension from that conversation. Do you think you can give a tense man a back massage?"

Tanya smiled at him. "For you, Mr Marques, of course."

"Between you and me, your employer is going to get the shock of his life when I get the credit for retrieving those blasted criminals, especially if they turn out to be Federation." Marques told her.

Chapter XIX

It was Tetriana's late shift tonight to captain the ship, but to her surprise she found Captain Singer already occupying the position that, on this night every week since she had started working on the *Sanitarian*, she looked forward to. Singer stood to greet her and then sat down again.

"I'll take the late shift tonight. Have the night off," Singer murmured preoccupied by different readings on the console built into the arm of the chair. Tetriana raised an eyebrow, the concept of having a night off was unthinkable to her, but she couldn't argue with her superior officer, so she turned on her heels and headed out of the bridge towards her quarters.

Her quarters were as any normal military quarters, all standard plastic furniture and accessories. As a command officer, and indeed a captain, she was entitled to a larger room with more personalisation, something she had refused during the setup of her quarters. The room was a uniform grey throughout, only broken by the spaces where doors were and where a console was set into the wall. The door made the distinctive sound of the movement buffers designed to protect the door as it opened. She marched into the room and neatly placed her overcoat into her closet before she walked across her room and through an exit that led into her ensuite. This was an all-grey bathroom, which had no discerning features, apart from a small mirror above the sink.

In the corner of the mirror was a small picture of a beautiful young Terineti with sleek long hair. The woman in the picture had a striking resemblance to Tetriana but clearly was not. At the sight of the portrait, her hair changed to a milky white colour. Every time she looked at this image, she wished it could just disappear. An unvocalised wish that would be followed by a pang of pain as she imagined one day not seeing the picture in its place. She shrugged, suppressing any feelings towards the image, and set about getting ready for bed. After completing her military routine as she had done every night for as long as she could remember, she slid beneath the covers and pulled them up to her chest and closed her eyes.

When Tetriana opened her eyes, she was looking out of the eyes of her younger self. Nothing in the image was in focus except for the sharp image of her clean-shaven father and a beautiful woman standing before him, who she recognised instantly as her mother. There was a clear air of annoyance between the two of them. Tetriana started to walk forward through a stunning blue stone archway covered in golden Republican emblems. Moving closer, she could start making out what her mother and father were quarrelling about. Whisps of white interrupted the clear image and the voices sounded like they were being heard through an old-world technology.

"We can't tell her," her father exclaimed, "If they were to find out that she knew anything, you know what they would do to her!" he continued aggressively, in his strong, commanding voice, up close to Tetriana's mother, waving his arms frantically.

"But she has the right to know," the woman whispered, through gritted teeth, with the distinct sting of disapproval.

Tetriana's father looked towards the woman as her skin and hair changed to a purple colour. "What if she hasn't even got it? What if she isn't like us, Gabriella?" he whined.

"Well I am telling her, like it or not," Gabriella made to turn around. Tetriana felt like she was being pulled out of her younger self before looking down and seeing the back of a young girls head. A feeling of suction with no source begun behind her before surrounding her and the image begun to fade.

The younger Tetriana made to run forward towards the Terineti woman. "Mummy," she cried.

Growing distant Tetriana heard her father growl, "I can't let you do that." Tetriana switched her gaze to her father just as he revealed a gun from his military coat sleeve.

A beeping broke the old-world sounding audio, Tetriana lurched forward. The image that met her was clear, and her quarrelling parents were gone. Without looking around she knew the sound to be from the computer panel opposite. Her hair, having turned silver in the night, slowly changed back to a blue as she got changed into freshly ironed and straightened clothing for another day of work. She made her bed the way she had been taught since she started in the army at the age of five, just after her mother's death.

She marched to the bridge, taking the same route she had taken since starting aboard the *Sanitarian*. As soon as she arrived, Captain Singer greeted her and nodded towards the conference room. They entered the room, and Tetriana noticed other commanding officers sitting round the table. The seat on the right-hand side of Singer's had been left vacant for her. As the two Captains entered, the rest of the command staff stood to greet them. Singer and Tetriana took up their two seats synchronously triggering the rest of the people around the room to sit back down.

Singer gave a loud cough, clearing both her throat and the muttering from round the table in one swift move. "We have been given an updated set of orders," she announced, her smile that of someone looped in on a devious plan. Tetriana had seen this smile on numerous occasions, and she knew its connotations. "A search and capture, with a kill option if they refuse to be captured," She stood up and looked across the table, her smile growing to a grin, "which no doubt will be the case. But that won't be a problem, the scans of the ship we are going after show we won't even need half our weapons online, so," she turned to address an engineering officer sitting several seats down, "continue as normal with the weapons maintenance, just leave enough weapons for me to take them out if we need to." The man she was addressing nodded and, as if this was her sign, she turned to the person opposite her on the table. "We will need to find this vessel quickly," she paused, "My superior has informed me we are not the only organisation after them. If we fail to capture the vessel." Singer paused, although Director Marques had not explicitly told her the Gate were considering using Assassins, she was not naive enough to think they wouldn't. More importantly, she knew what it would mean to fail because a captain does not fail twice in the Gate. She continued, "private government operatives have been instructed to take over, with their own methods. The reputation of the Republic Military relies upon your tracking them down. Do you think you can do that?"

"Just give me the last known whereabouts and maybe a signal they use specifically," the woman started enthusiastically before being cut off.

"I like the eagerness, but a simple nod would have sufficed," Singer snapped, the woman she was addressing nodded and sank into the back of her seat. "Right, as a standard last week of the month, all other commands are as normal," she glanced round the room as if checking her commands had been understood, "Tetriana, please wait behind. The rest of you are excused." The room clicked into one synchronised noise as everyone left with a nod. The door made a slight whoosh as it closed, leaving the last two occupants in silence. Singer made her way to an observation window on the furthest side of the room while Tetriana stayed in her seat.

"Let us talk freely for a moment." Singer said, staring out into deep space. As if this was a command, Tetriana's hair moved slowly into a sympathetic yellow as she sat back and waited for her captain to continue the conversation. Oddly, Tetriana, who disliked the woman standing ahead of her, couldn't explain this sudden feeling of sympathy.

"As I know you are already aware, I," Singer started then paused, taking a deep breath, "I am having personal problems, and," she turned to face Tetriana lowering her tone, "that colour does not suit you."

Tetriana shook her head down to her neck as if she was shivering and as she did her hair changed to a flat blue. When she was done, she sighed and stood up. "Of course I have noticed, and do not worry, another outburst like the one on the *IGC 0765* will not happen again," she said, keeping her gaze steady, directly at, but more through, Singer's eyes.

"Of course, of course, but that is not why I have asked you to stay behind," Singer said, walking shakily back to her seat and sitting down, talking directly to Tetriana. "I'm going to put your name forward for promotion to captain of a vessel." Tetriana looked at her in shock, she never expected that to come from the person it just had. "And not just any vessel, this vessel," Singer continued, raising her hands, and gesturing openly around her.

Tetriana continued to stare at her captain in disbelief and then spoke with suspicion, "Why?"

"I am planning on taking shore leave after this mission and the ship will need someone of your calibre to command it," Singer said, lowering her arms, shocked that Tetriana's reaction wasn't one of excitement and gratitude.

"Captain, speaking freely, you know as well as I do that, when we accepted the jobs, we were given no shore leave, no holidays, no time off of any sort. We work until we," she paused and slightly raised her shoulders, "disappear." Tetriana shifted her posture towards the door, her hair appearing to turn translucent blue. "Captain, we have not always agreed on much. But we both know what would happen to you during your shore leave, should you take it." Tetriana said, catching Singer off guard with the concern. Directly, but still sheepishly Tetriana continued, "Permission to be excused?"

"Permission granted," Singer barked, her tone as if the pair had not just had a personal conversation.

That was all Tetriana was waiting for. She nodded to her conflicted captain and turned to walk out of the door.

Just as the door opened, Singer called after her, recapturing her composure and adjusting her expression back to one of command. "We will be making a routine stop to restock and drop some crewmembers off so I will need you on the bridge today."

Tetriana paused and gave a quick, "Yes, Captain," before continuing out of the room.

Chapter XX

I T WAS A NEW EXPERIENCE for Elios to be able to walk down a long, narrow passage without fearing for his life every time he rounded a corner. He wasn't complaining, at least not about that. He liked feeling safe. He liked sleeping in a real bed, with real sheets and real pillows. He liked being warm and not having to worry about where his next fix of **The Drug** was coming from. He liked receiving three meals a day, no charge. But, even as he wolfed down his fourth helping of potato salad and ice cream, ignoring the odd looks exchanged by various *Elismere* crewmembers, he'd suspected the situation was too good to be true.

Ever since the Outer Slums had been created, there had been a general agreement among slum dwellers that, if there was a problem, you could bet your bottom credit that a spacer had caused it. When business was slow, it wasn't uncommon for a drug dealer to curse the "damned spacers" for coming to the slums and stealing all the jobs. If a baby cried for milk at four in the morning, the disgruntled mother would, more often than not, blame the noise from overhead spacer vessels for waking the infant up. Most of Elios's mother's more violent clients had been spacers. And, if slum folklore was to be believed, it had been a spacer who, long before Elios had been born, had drunkenly crashed his spaceship, creating what would become the Outer Slums.

So, it was fair to say that Elios had been inclined to dislike spacers even before spending the past few days in their near constant company. But, having got to know them, he had concluded that, despite clearly having no intention of poaching an honest drug dealer's clients or taking jobs off of slum dwellers, spacers certainly lived up to their reputation in their arrogance. Elios decided that they were weird. He found how tall they were to be rather disconcerting.

Being spacers, as far as Elios was concerned, was more than enough justification to dislike his new companions. In fact, it was probably a good thing that the slender crewman who'd returned Elios's gear had confiscated the switchblade. The crewman said this was for everyone's safety. Otherwise, Elios thought, things could have gotten very messy on several occasions.

Elios almost didn't notice the small group of elf-like crewmembers heading towards him. He'd been distracted imagining how he could have used his knife to cause some serious harm to a particularly infuriating crewmember who had laughed at his mix-up regarding the acronym STD. Elios still felt the raw embarrassment that he didn't know STD stood for Sonic Transmission Device to spacers.

It was the group's shrill laughter that brought the approaching crewmembers to his attention, and Elios hastily retreated into the nearest room to avoid them, dropping his bowl of remaining potato salad and ice cream.

"Hey." A voice behind Elios made him jump and the thief spun round angrily, reaching for the switchblade that wasn't there. He glared sulkily at the spacer standing in front of him. These guys were everywhere, watching him, he thought. The spacer just grinned back. Elios vaguely recognised him, it was the quiet man who'd let him out of the cell. Jenny's brother, he finally remembered.

"Andy, right?" Elios guessed, glancing around the room they were standing in. It appeared to be some kind of geek den. Ultra-modern computers and screens and other high-tech gadgets lined the walls, and floating just behind the spacer's head was a glowing blue globe. "What's that?"

"It's Adrian, actually," the spacer grinned. "And this," Adrian turned, almost reverently, towards the sphere, "is Earth. The planet on which humanity started."

"No kiddin'," said Elios, hopping up onto one of the computer panels to get a closer look. "Humanity must've started out tiny."

"No, Elios, you misunderstand." Adrian said, in the tone of a teacher trying to help, "Get down from there before you break something," he continued, waving Elios off of the computer panel, "this is a holographic image of Earth."

"Earth's hollow?" Elios scoffed, sliding down the panel so that he was sitting on the edge, his legs dangling over the side. "Yeah, right! Next you'll be asking me to believe there're tiny little people living inside," He gestured scornfully towards the globe, "that. I may be a slum rat, spacer, but I ain't thick."

"I never said you were." Adrian paused and then added, rather more quickly than was strictly necessary, "The Earth isn't hollow. A hologram is a visual construct composed of compressed light. This is a three-dimensional, scaled-down image of a planet thousands of light-years away. The actual Earth is about the same size as the planet you come from, and the humans living on it at the time were probably only marginally taller than you are."

"Huh," Elios huffed blankly. "Well, why's it called a hollow," he paused, unable to remember the word Adrian had used and opting for the much simpler, "thingy?"

"Hologram," Adrian told him gently. "As to why it's called that... I don't think either of us really wants an etymology lesson at this time in the morning, do you?"

"I s'pose not, I don't like insects anyway," agreed Elios. He hopped down from his perch and moved to see what the older man was doing. "Adrian?" he asked, more to break the silence than because he wanted to continue conversation with the spacer.

"Yes, Elios?"

"Where are all your buttons?"

This time it was Adrian's turn to be confused. "I'm sorry, what?"

"You know, buttons?" Elios prompted. "Big round things you press to make stuff work? I'd have thought a high-tech ship like this would have hundreds of 'em. But there're none. Just loads of screens and glowing stuff."

"Buttons have been obsolete for many hundreds of years, Elios. Nowadays, we only use buttons to turn on the computers or for hardwired manual interface." Adrian glanced at Elios's bemused face and added, "The technicians use buttons when they need to work on the computers directly but, for everything else, interfaces use touch panels."

"What's interface?" Elios wanted to know.

"It's how a human communicates with a computer," Adrian explained. "It could be a keyboard or a touch screen. EVI uses a vocal interface."

"What's EVI?"

"Hello, Elios," a female voice chimed from nowhere. "My name is EVI, and I am the *Elismere* Virtual Intelligence. I am pleased to meet you."

A stream of obscenities burst from Elios's mouth before he regained enough composure to choke out, "What the?"

"Don't worry, Elios," Adrian placed a hand on the younger man's shoulder. "She's the ship's computer. There's nothing to be afraid of."

"Nothing to b—" Elios was horrified. "Come out, lady, where I can see you!"

"You can already see me, Elios," the voice replied calmly. "As Adrian has told you, I am the ship's computer and my physical form is the ship I inhabit, namely this one. My core, that is, my processing unit and primary components, is located at the centre of the ship. I hear and see everything that happens within the *Elismere*, and I speak through miniaturised speaker systems throughout the ship. As a being however, I am not bound to any particular body and am fully capable of transferring between any hardware capable of supporting my system. If you wish, I could project a hologram for you to speak to?"

"N-no," Elios said hurriedly, backing away from the wall he was facing. "I've had enough holo, grams?" he turned to Adrian, who nodded encouragingly, "for one day." He finished the sentence proudly, but his expression suddenly darkened, and he added, "What was that you said about seeing stuff?"

"I use micro-cameras to monitor every section of the ship simultaneously. For example, as well as speaking to you, I am having conversations with thirteen other crewmembers."

"What about the crewmembers who aren't talking to you? Can you see them?"

"I can," the computer confirmed.

"What about me?" Elios insisted. "Before I knew you existed, were you watching me?"

"I'd assume so," said the computer. "However, I am programmed with many privacy protocols and therefore I seal any information that my databanks deem to be useless or private information, which includes everything a crewmember might feel uncomfortable about sharing with an observer."

Elios took a moment to process the implications of what the computer had just told him before deciding it was all too scary for his liking. "Look, lady," he growled. "I don't care whether your kooky virtu—, virty—, pretendy intelligence makes you forget stuff, I don't appreciate being spied on, and I've got a good mind to turn you off."

"Elios," EVI said gently. "I do not have an off switch."

"You have a core," Elios retorted. "I could smash it."

"No, you couldn't," EVI replied. "You'd be immobilised before you could reach it."

"Besides, Elios," Adrian interjected, "even if you could turn off a VI," he said, adding air quotes, "which is literally impossible," at least without the right knowledge, but he wasn't going to tell Elios that. Besides, turning off a VI was considered akin to murder in the Federation. "EVI manages all of the little things on this ship that we spacers, and, to an even greater extent, you planet-bound citizens, take for granted. Life support, artificial gravity, heating," he shrugged, before continuing, "yeah, they'd last for a bit, but space is a big place and, without EVI to perform the hyper equations which allow the *Elismere* to access hyper without exploding we'd run out of everything but power before we reached the nearest star system."

"Not food?" Elios asked aghast.

"That'd be one of the first things to go," Adrian told him solemnly. "But don't worry, you probably wouldn't die of starvation. If our life support systems crashed, the ship would slowly run out of oxygen but it'd be the cold that killed us." He nodded at one of the bulkheads. "On the other side of the *Elismere's* hull is a frozen, dark abyss which is lethal to all but a few very weird creatures."

There was a pause.

"Well, crud."

"Don't worry," Adrian laughed at the young thief's appalled face. "We've come a long way as a species since we left Earth, and even the first generation of space launches tried to have backups. We're safe as safe can be. But I'd advise you not to threaten one of the few crewmembers, and EVI is a crewmember, with both the authority and ability to catapult you out of an airlock."

"Very funny!" Elios grumbled uncertainly, then added, just to make sure, "Look I'm sorry, kooky computer-lady. I wasn't really planning on turning you off."

"That's quite all right, Elios," the computer replied. "But, please, kooky computer-lady is very clunky. Feel free to call me EVI."

"Duly noted, kooky com— I mean, EVI," Elios saluted the ceiling sarcastically. "Now, go away and stop spying on me."

"Don't they teach you manners in the slums?" Adrian asked absent-mindedly, his attention mainly focused on the glowing facsimile of the Earth sphere.

"Only what to avoid if you don't wanna get shot," said the thief.

"You might want to apply some of that knowledge if you're planning on remaining around my sister for any amount of time." Adrian grinned and then added, "Now, why don't you go pester the captain for a bit, huh? I'm sure he'd more than appreciate the company. You could tell him I sent you."

"Captain Jack's asleep," Elios answered insolently. Adrian opened his mouth to reply, but before he could make a sound he was interrupted by a scream from elsewhere on board.

"I didn't do it," said Elios, a little too quickly.

"Would Elios Bennett please come to the second deck dining room immediately to collect his unruly monkey?" Even over a loudspeaker, Jenny's voice was laced with danger. Adrian raised an eyebrow.

"What?" Elios demanded. "I didn't do it. It's Moncello who's causing trouble."

"You brought him aboard."

"You kept us aboard!"

"We kept you alive."

"You kidnapped us!"

"You were stealing from us."

"We were," Elios stopped and frowned. "I mean, um," He trailed off, lowering his eyes.

"You'd better go," Adrian advised the younger man, "Jen sounds pretty irritated." Elios's shoulders hunched.

"Listen, spacer," he growled to hide his discomfort, "I ain't going anywhere near your sister until she's calmed down enough to not use my full name!" Adrian looked at him for a moment, almost feeling sorry for him.

"Three, two..." Adrian counted appearing to expect something.

"If Elios Bennett doesn't appear in the second deck dining room within the next five minutes, Moncello won't be the only primate to be shot today."

"Ah, there we are."

There was silence.

"That bitc—," Elios exclaimed.

"Yes, but she does happen to be my sister," Adrian's voice hardened.

"She shot my monkey!"

"I expect she lowered her stun setting before doing so."

"Is that supposed to make me feel better?"

"You probably have about four minutes to get to the dining room," Adrian replied, green eyes suddenly amused. "I'd advise you run."

Elios swore.

Adrian merely blinked and raised a prompting eyebrow.

"Your sister's a psychopath," Elios grumbled.

Adrian shrugged. "Three minutes forty seconds."

"Elios." At EVI's voice, Elios spun round guiltily.

"What now?"

"I think it would be wise for you to retrieve Moncello from the dining room floor," the VI told him. "And perhaps help to clean up the mess of wires, orange peel, tiramisu and smashed china that your pet created?"

"I thought I told you to leave me —" Elios cut himself off, picturing his frozen corpse floating through space following Adrian's previous cautions. "Fine," he mumbled, feeling very much like a reprimanded child,

"I'm going." But as he left the room he couldn't resist adding, "What kind of upper-class twit eats Tiramisu, anyway? It's a poncy food!"

Adrian watched him leave before allowing himself to grin. "Things are going to be a lot less peaceful around here from now on, aren't they, EVI?"

"Empirical evidence would certainly suggest that you're right, Adrian," the VI replied, her tone clearly amused.

"How long until we reach the planet EVI?" Adrian continued, "Do I have enough time to finish up here?"

"It will be several hours yet," the VI replied, "More than enough time for you."

Chapter XXI

A s Tetriana entered the bridge she heard the distinctive voice of Captain Singer in the process of barking at a crewmember for not reporting something.

"Is there a problem, Captain?" Tetriana approached Singer.

"There is a ship sitting on the other side of the planet that fits all the descriptions of our target, but," Captain Singer's voice started to become raised, "someone didn't think it IMPORTANT ENOUGH TO TELL ME." She finished, gave a sigh, and screamed the words, "BATTLE STATIONS!"

She occupied her chair on the bridge and straightened up her posture. "Jump so that we come out, give them the standard disabling shots but don't destroy the vessel. Our mission is to take them alive if at all possible and only kill as a last resort." Everyone seemed to understand instantly what to do and rushed to get their jobs done.

The ship jolted as it made the short distance jump, a risky manoeuvre that only the most skilled Republic pilots could do and returned to normal space alongside its' target.

Chapter XXII

REPUBLIC SPACE

THE *SANITARIAN* SHOT OUT of hyper within barely ten kilometres of the Elismere. The shockwaves from the battlecruiser's crash transition to normal space sent the smaller vessel spinning out of her parking orbit and Glen was sent flying across the bridge as the artificial gravity desperately attempted to compensate for the sudden change in velocity. His head crashed into a panel on the opposite side of the bridge and he went limp, the impact knocking him unconscious.

As they had been watching the sensor overlay, Jen and Emily had had just enough time to activate their personal tractor fields before the *Sanitarian* came rocketing into normal space, just ahead and to the starboard of their position. Strands of focused plasma shot from the military vessel, burning across the *Elismere's* flight path as she fired a series of shots. In the instant that Jen and Emily had to fasten themselves in they increased the strength of the ships shields. The ship vibrated as the shields absorbed the energy of the *Sanitarian's* salvos.

The *Sanitarian* slowed, powerful thruster banks spinning her into line with the *Elismere* as her shields dispersed the translucent shots. Jenny's fingers blurred slightly as they shot across the virtual interface, bringing the *Elismere's* stabilisers online to match the manoeuvre. Thrusters fired, halting her midway through her second spin. Her main drive caught her, ship gravity reasserting itself, and the sleek, almost organic ship swept around, rising to face the blocky prow of the *Sanitarian*.

"Jack, a light battlecruiser just dropped out of hyper right on top of us!" Emily reported, as her sensors caught up with what had just happened. "We had some warning from the proximity sensors, but Glen didn't have time to get his tractor field online. I think he's fine, but you should probably bring a medic up here to make sure."

"Adrian and I are both OK too, we'll grab Susan on the way up. What are we looking at?" Jack's voice was cool, with barely a thread of shock in it even now, and Emily smirked.

"Cracking the ID now. Whoever these people are, it is taking longer than normal to break the ID. They clearly don't want to be identified." She paused for a second as data scrolled across her screen. "*GBS Sanitarian*, Calypso Yards, *Corazon*-class capture ship. She was commissioned five years ago and then promptly vanished off the grid. Looks like that attention I talked about has caught up." She winked at Jen. "That trick of yours must have worked though, if they actually knew who they were going after, they would have sent the bigger guns. Her shields are quite a bit weaker than ours and she's woefully lacking in active weaponry for a ship her size. Scans show about a dozen plasma banks, a few particle batteries and some sort of matter-to-energy conversion system. That's all they have active. There're other weapons arrays too, but they're all powered down. Not accounting for anything they have well hidden."

The lift door slid open as Emily finished her gleeful report. Susan was the first out, moving quickly to Glen's side with a medkit as Adrian and Jack filed out behind her.

"Su, how is he?" Jack asked.

"It's just a concussion, he'll be fine with some rest," Susan replied. "I can give him something to let him keep going if you need him."

Jack shook his head. "No, get him to medical, from Em's report I think we'll be able to handle this."

"That's putting it lightly, Jack," Emily's voice was more amused than angry as Susan lifted Glen with deceptive ease, there were some advantages to growing up on a high-gravity world, and disappeared back into the lift. "They really should have done their homework." She finished, adjusting her red hair from her forehead.

"We're being scanned," Adrian remarked idly. "Baffles are holding steady. I'm activating the forward weapons systems." Jen blinked as an attention signal flared on her board.

"That's interesting, they're hailing us. From their initial actions, they didn't seem like they were here to do much in the way of talking." She shrugged. "Then again, I never could understand the military."

"What ID are we under?" Jack asked.

"The *Zephyra*," Jen responded. "Should I acknowledge?" Jack straightened his green-on-black 'uniform outfit and smiled slightly.

"It would be quite rude not to, considering their entrance," he smirked, black eyes glittering. "Get a lock on their weapons and bring our shields down to half strength. Show them that we are not here to fight." Emily shot Jack a look and he lifted his hand to her in a calming motion.

"On it," Adrian and Jenny replied in sync.

"Don't fire unless I give the order." He nodded to Emily. "Open channel."

"This is Captain Singer of the *GBS Sanitarian*. Stand down, Captain of the *Zephyra*, and prepare to be boarded." Singer spoke calmly, perched on her seat, looking directly towards the captain of the *Zephyra*. She made a deliberate movement with her arm to draw attention to her Captain's Stars.

"Nicomedes Velia, commanding the *Free Trader Zephyra*. By my rights under the Republic Trading Charter, Article Seventeen, Section Three, you are bound by law to inform me of the reasons for your request," Jack responded coolly, meeting the gaze of the captain on the viewscreen before him without flinching.

Singer turned to the comms desk and swiped her hands across her neck to signal the line to be muted and the video to be paused. She turned to Tetriana and questioned, "What do you think, should a ship, such as ours, that does not technically exist, be bound by laws and charters?" She waited for Tetriana to nod and, when she did not, Singer commanded, "Pull up all information, weapons, shields, armour and drives. Now!"

"Captain, they seem to match the vessel that was scanned by *IGC 0765*. Just a simple cargo ship with low to minimal weaponry and defences," Tetriana replied formally. "In theory, they should not be mobile after our opening salvo." Tetriana continued typing away, "Mass displacement and scans confirms the weapons and shielding complement expected, and, they are carrying an unidentifiable cargo that makes up the remaining unknown mass."

Singer turned back to the comms desk and held her thumb up to signal the reactivation of the link.

"Captain Velia, I have scanned your vessel and I don't believe you are currently in the position to be quoting charters and regulations to a superior military ship. Now stand down and prepare to be boarded!" Singer said mockingly, sitting back, relaxed in her seat. Tetriana gave a quick glance to her Captain noticing the calm posture and her deep black pupils.

Jack smiled at Singer's mocking face. "Captain," he said, shaking his head slowly in mock sadness. "The *Corazon* class was retired from active service two years ago and for good reason. Your weapons are meagre, your shields are weak and your armour is about as effective as paper when confronted by modern shipboard weaponry. Not to mention the well-known design flaw. There are more ships than just the *Zephyra* in orbit, how do you know that I don't have friends among them? Are you sure you want to do this?"

Again, Singer closed the connection, she closed her eyes and sat for a couple of seconds. She pulled herself forward on her chair and sat upright, before reopening her connection. "Check your scans again please," She sighed, it wasn't the first time, she thought, that someone had misidentified the *Sanitarian*. While it was certainly a *Corazon* class ship, it's extensive retrofit meant it was nothing like its siblings. Even the design flaw that caused the ships obsolescence had been resolved. Indeed, Singer knew that the spectre of a design flaw had been overplayed in order for the gate to acquire the remaining stock. "My ship is a mid-class, retrofit of the *Corazon* class, that does not appear on any official databases making us non-existent and therefore you have no idea what we are capable of. We are answerable to no one. We are, for all intents and purposes, your worst nightmare!" She hissed with more than a hint of arrogance in her voice.

Jack snorted, the slight smile on his face turning icy cold. "Non-existent? If you were non-existent I wouldn't know when your ship was laid down, commissioned and when it vanished from Republic Navy records. You should have done your homework, Singer, you're not even close to my worst nightmare."

Singer turned to the comms desk and cut the connection once more. She sat up abruptly, forced herself off her chair and stormed over to the sensors console. She pushed against the ensign behind the console with her hip, knocking the person to the floor and started to work rapidly on the console. After about five minutes, she curled her lip on one side and let out a small grunt of amusement.

"Open the channel," the Captain mocked, then headed back to her seat. "Nicomedes, please tell me you did not just threaten me when half of your systems are non-operational. Compared to my vessel, size and weapons, I do believe the upper hand is on my side," She finished, with a satisfied grin on her face.

"You know," Jack replied, holding one side of his face in his hand with the air of a disappointed parent, "you should really get a new sensor specialist. Your current one missed a few things." Singer sat slightly up in her chair, her pupils flickered, red then black again, as Jack continued to speak. "But, I think you need to realise a few things. I did not threaten you." He continued, bringing the tips of his fingers in a flat hand to his chest, "Statements of fact are not threats." Singer straightened further, her pupils flashed crimson, taking longer to fade back to black this time. "You have disregarded the laws that your organisation is built upon, you are outgunned and outclassed. Is that quite simple enough for you to understand?" There was a momentary pause and Jack smiled sweetly. And in a friendly tone finished, "Bethany."

Singer made to stand up before hearing her name. She paused as the bridge of the *Sanitarian* fell silent only broken by some hushed muttering in the background. "How do you know my name?" she yelled, jumping from her seat as her eyes hardened on crimson, but, before Jack could reply, she continued, "Close that connection, NOW!" She and her crew were supposed to have been erased from existence. How could someone in a meagre trading vessel possible have that information?

In her mind she played through all the possible ways this ship could have known her name. Could they have intercepted messages? Unlikely, and even if they did, decrypting them would be impossible. Could they have retrieved data from the *IGC 0765* that had important information? The station shouldn't have had any information on them. Could it have been a lucky guess, she questioned. Could they be Federation, as she had worried, meaning they could be much more powerful than they were showing.

At this point, with the slightest risk this was a Federation spy ship, she knew what she had to do. In quick strides she marched to a small console off to the side of her seat and stood there, her eyes never flickering, her foot constantly tapping as she took in each individual deep breath. She started to slowly type on the console and whispered, "Open the connection." Looking up at the viewscreen, she slowly spoke. "I will give you ten seconds to either lower your shields and be boarded or make your final goodbyes." Tetriana closed the connection and turned to her captain, her hair now slightly red.

"Captain, that is against our orders," Tetriana said in a very official voice. "We were instructed to capture and only kill as a last resort. We still have the larger firepower."

Singer threw a sharp look at Tetriana. Beneath the harsh look she felt pity for her co-Terineti. While the Federation and Republic battles were well known by all staff, only ship captains are trusted to know what the Gate truly knew about the Federation. Singer understood what she had to do, and she could not let her subordinate know. "So? That doesn't matter to me. I vowed to remove any threat in space and that is what I am doing. If they have something as simple as my name imagine what else they could have," Singer said, feigning that this was about their hidden identities, her hand on the panel waiting to push the button.

"Then you are doing exactly what Nicomedes accused you of, you have disregarded the laws that our organisation is built upon," Tetriana said with a calm, sincere voice, "And worse than that you are allowing your emotions to cloud your judgment."

Hearing these accusations from her second in command, Singer snapped, "Either follow me, or get the hell off my bridge!" Tetriana turned on her heels and marched out from behind the security desk. She forcefully ripped the four stars from her left arm and dropped them on the ground.

"I now relieve myself from your command, and from your bridge, Captain." Tetriana turned once more on her heels and headed off the bridge.

As the doors to the bridge closed behind Tetriana, Singer whispered under her breath, "I wish I could tell you what is really going on here." Before she could dwell on it further, she reopened the connection. "Have you made up your mind yet?" Singer demanded.

"Do your worst, my dear," Jack said lightly, one hand tapping furiously on a keypad outside of the transmission's input. "But know that if you pull that trigger, the Republic will be tarnished forever." A message flashed on Jen's screen from Jack reading, Prepare to fire.

"Do you think anyone will care? You will be destroyed." Singer replied. It had been a poor bluff anyway, she thought, the only people who would look at this situation and take the side of a criminal vessel over the Republic military were already enemies of the Republic. And as such, there weren't many of them, since enemies of the Republic tended to disappear.

She moved her hands rapidly on the console. Beams of crackling plasma and compressed particles shot from firing ports dotted all across the *Sanitarian's* bow, orbs of utter blackness cutting down across the stars from the dorsal torpedo bays to thicken the muted storm of energy fire before it cut out, hard-wired safety protocols taking the beams offline before they overloaded.

The *Elismere* shuddered as the beams crashed onto her shields, the torpedoes shaking her further as they exploded against them in flashes of indescribable colour. A few lights flickered as the EM pulse battered against the *Elismere's* rad-shields with admirable futility, in the process scrambling the feed between the *Sanitarian* and her target. Singer turned her head.

"Sensors, report!" she barked. The Lieutenant at the station started to respond, but a voice resonated through the audio system, cutting him off.

"That, Captain Singer, was a mistake." Her head jerked up, shock painted clearly on her face, as the video feed cleared to show Jack standing completely unharmed in the middle of his untouched bridge. "And you have no idea what you just attacked, do you?" His eyes flared. "Say goodbye to your weapons." He nodded to someone out of the viewscreen's input. "Fire!"

Singer spoke over Jack in a worried tone, "Where are the rest of our weapons?"

Kolbe replied without hesitation, "Still offline for maintenance."

"Well get them back online, NOW!" Singer roared.

"That will take up to four hours," Kolbe stated in a matter-of-fact tone.

"Not quick enough, get it done now," Singer commanded.

Kolbe caught a glimpse of the console opened on her desk and saw a reading pointing out that the ship standing up to them was charging more weapons than it apparently had. "Captain, the target is raising weapons, they also appear to be charging three times as many weapons as our original scans picked up. Shields are at maximum." Kolbe began a full scan on the *Zephyra* as the ID briefly switched to Elismere. "Captain, they are using baffles, their ship is not what was reported." Just as quickly as Kolbe tried to send the data to Singer's console, all the new information disappeared.

Kolbe looked towards Singer as her Captains eyes turned blue and an expression of fear covered her face.

Tetriana stood in the lift with a strange feeling of emptiness running down her arm. She tried to shrug it off but could still feel the emptiness without her captain's stars. Her mind was set on what she had to do, she knew what Singer was thinking and she knew she had to do something. Her hair withered into a worried grey.

Panels hissed aside all across the *Elismere's* hull, revealing particle batteries and plasma arrays that until now had been hidden beneath layers of electronic and mechanical trickery. Chains of blinding, blue-white fire flickered between the two ships, hyper-accelerated ions piercing the *Sanitarian's* shields like paper and shattering them as the plasma banks opened fire. Streams of golden droplets washed over the *Sanitarian*, their beauty belied by their lethality as they reached out to every single weapons array in reach and blew them away. Shockwaves rocked the larger vessel as explosions hammered her from all sides, inertial fields strained desperately against the forces overloading them. The dorsal torpedo magazines detonated in a flash of dark fire, sending a fan of burning debris sweeping out from the front of the vessel and strands of cobalt light lanced into the *Sanitarian's* prow, each pinpoint hammer-blow burning out entire quadrants of hyper nodes. The vessel staggered, power flows fluctuating wildly out of control as the conduits they relied on cracked and shattered, spraying plasma through sections of the *Sanitarian's* interior. Alarms howled on the vessel's bridge, a ringing death cry accompanying panels falling offline as the systems they were linked to died.

Singer sat up in her chair as the impact of this full-on attack registered. She announced without blinking and at the top of her voice, "Damage report."

The ensign behind the sensors console announced, "Primary weapons are offline, life support has been damaged and there are several hull breaches."

Deeper in the *Sanitarian* Tetriana fell against the side of the lift as it came to a halt on the engineering floor, the jolt turning her hair to a deep crimson.

She marched through the metallic double doors of main engineering and continued to the fuel core. She turned on the spot until she noticed Tim standing on the second level working at a small solitary console.

The reddish-blue fuel core pulsed off to one side as Tetriana marched up a set of steps to reach Tim. She tapped him on the shoulder and whispered, "I have a job for you." He looked up to see her with slight pink streaks in her blue hair, he gave her a small look of confusion. "Please follow me," she requested, turning on the spot and marching towards the stairs.

Tim tapped the console he was working on until it went black, and then, without questioning, he followed Tetriana towards and down the stairs and out of the large, grey, metallic double doors. He noticed that Tetriana was not wearing her captain's stars and assumed that she had forgotten to put them on in the rush of the attack on the ship. Tetriana led Tim through many different corridors, some of which he had never seen. On their journey Tetriana filled Tim in on the situation on the bridge, They stopped outside a set of double doors marked with the words Transporter Room. As the doors opened Tetriana ushered him in.

Meanwhile on the bridge Singer sat back in her chair again, clasped her hands together and closed her eyes. When she reopened them, the pupils were pitch black. She stood up and moved towards the helm, and pushed the helmsman out of the way so she could type on the console. Moving back to her seat she said with a sigh, "Abandon ship." As she sat back in her seat, she exclaimed, "Activation code," she took a breath, "Singer beta," she then took one last deep breath, "active forty-two." She closed her eyes and pushed herself deeper into her chair. As was expected of a Gate ship, the bridge crew did not move from their stations with the announcement of Abandon Ship.

At that very moment in the Transporter Room, Tetriana ordered the person behind the command console to, "Leave us," while nodding her head towards the door. The person nodded back, tapped the console, and left the room. Tim stood looking in amazement at the hardware that was present. Most of the ships Tim had worked on didn't have a transporter room and, even if they did, he usually only left the ship by shuttle or through a docking port.

"Can you get that to get us to the *Zephyra*?" Tetriana asked, pointing at the console for the transporter.

Tim's eyes glowed with excitement as he walked towards the console, "What sort of system is it?"

"Gravity catapult system," Tetriana answered quickly.

"Easily, give me five minutes," he replied, reaching the console. Even though he hadn't had the chance to use one of these in real life, he was the only person in his class to ever manage to manually program a transporter to send a living animal onto the local moon without any damage and for it to land exactly where he wanted it, give or take a couple of meters. "Oh damn. Access security codes."

"My code is," Tetriana started with the air of importance, as she was the only one of the two that would have had any codes. That sense of importance was quickly destroyed by Tim interrupting her.

"I don't need codes. Your password system is primitive to say the least." Tim reached down under the console and started to do something. "Am I allowed to ask why I am doing this?"

There was a pause while they were both silent before she answered with, "I disagree with Captain Singer's tactics and I have to get over to the *Zephyra* to find out what they know."

It was obvious that Tim was not listening to the answer by the way he exclaimed, "Ok that's it, just need the go-ahead."

A mixed look of caution and worry appeared across Tetriana's face as her hair transited blue to grey, "You will know when you have the go-ahead."

Very little time passed, just enough time for Tim to think of asking what the go-ahead would be, before a metallic voice cried out, "Abandon ship. Abandon ship. Abandon ship."

"I'm guessing that's our cue?" Tim questioned, instinctively typing on the console. "Get on the pad."

Unfortunately for the rather brave, suicidal Captain Singer, she had failed to note the crucial importance of one surviving system. The communications array was still online. And the channel to the *Elismere* had remained open. The entire command crew heard Singer's preparatory words and their sensors noticed the rising energy patterns.

"Jack, we're getting a power surge!" Emily said from her station, her voice taut. "Their MatEC is going haywire."

Jack nodded.

"Thank you, Emily. Jen, they're all yours."

The Matter to Energy Converter, or MatEC, was used as a final line of defence by the Gate. In essence, the matter of the ship was converted to a steady stream of energy and fired towards the enemy vessel. Given the amount of energy that the mass of even a small ship could produce, neither party would survive and all trace matter would be destroyed. Only the ship captains of Gate ships knew the weapon existed built into the vessel, and as they were the only people with the access code. This resulted in the expectation that a Gate captain would give their life for the Tannhauser Gate, especially in order to protect its identity. Knowing that failure was not an option, and that this was likely a Federation ship, Singer saw no other alternative than to sacrifice her ship for the Gate.

"You are coming too," Tetriana commanded, and Tim looked up confused. "There is no point in staying here, there are not enough escape pods and for my plan to work I need your skillset."

Without questioning, Tim looked down and typed frantically, then ran towards the pad. A low drone started before the pair of them were safely and rapidly crushed into a very small space by high gravity, which as the name suggests, was then catapulted at high speed towards their destination.

Jenny smiled again, a dangerous smile more suited to a wolf than a human as targeting data streamed across one of her boards and her fingers twitched. The *Elismere* shuddered slightly, and two silver lances shot from recessed firing ports just ahead of her wings.

The particle beams punched effortlessly through the *Sanitarian's* desperately regenerating shields and the armour beneath them simply evaporated. The military vessel listed as her drive connections were cut and she lost main propulsion, staggering off-centre away from her attacker as all station-keeping ability failed. Plasma jetted from the *Elismere's* thrusters and she shot forward, driving two lances of unstoppable flame ahead of her into the *Sanitarian's* now all-too-fragile hull. Bright orange flared at two points on each side of the *Elismere's* bow, losing four bars of hypervelocity iridium that slammed into the *Sanitarian*. Kinetic force met matter, and the result blasted the entire nose of the *Sanitarian* apart.

The impact shockwave threw the *Sanitarian's* bridge crew from their seats and then the *Elismere's* vertical thrusters fired, sending her up over the top of her foe, particle beams deactivating as she did so before they cut the vessel completely in half. The *Sanitarian* rocked as further safety systems failed, secondary explosions tearing through her hull as atmosphere streamed from the ragged gaps in her hull in a sick parody of blood. Bodies and shattered shards of metal poured out into the blackness, borne upon that wild torrent of air, and the *Elismere's* thrusters fired again to cancel her momentum. For a moment she simply hung there, perfectly still in relation to her target, like a sword raised to strike. Then the particle beams fired. The sword fell.

The particle beams stabbed down, impaling the bridge of the *Sanitarian* at their convergence point before continuing to shear cleanly through the vessel's hull. The mass drivers fired again, the resulting detonation sending fissures splaying across the *Sanitarian's* structure, micro-fractures covering her in a pattern of deadly spider-webs. And the *Elismere* swivelled, her beams burning a smooth line through the cracking and bleeding chassis beneath her, cutting her almost completely in two before the next mass driver salvo fired. But this time, they had launched something far more deadly than simple bars of metal.

Antimatter power had been a Federation invention to start with, and one that they had never let completely out of their hands, for quite obvious reasons. They had played with the technology extensively before releasing it as a power source and one of their best researchers had pioneered a very different approach to its use. It was simple enough to make antimatter warheads for missiles, they had the space for containment generators. But creating mass driver shells, with antimatter cores, was a far more complex problem, one not solvable with the technology of the time. But that researcher had seen something that none of his fellows could. Electromagnetic containment was by far the easiest way to contain antimatter, but it wasn't the only way. It took him almost fifty years, and several asteroid research bases, but he finally managed to contain antimatter within an artificially created molecular structure whose electromagnetic fields held the antimatter at the centre of their pattern. And to release it, all that was needed was to break a single atom's connection to the rest of the structure. The physicist had taken his findings to the Federation Navy, and they had latched on to them with a gleeful ferocity that had been almost frightening. And that reaction had become all the more pronounced when the Navy realised that manufacturing mass driver shells with a core of this explosive, and a detonation device, would be laughably easy. The cost was a bit higher, but the increase in firepower was monumental.

Technically, these shells were available only to the military and the Federation maintained an iron grip on them. However, Glen had managed to acquire a few dozen for the *Elismere's* use. It might have had something to do with Glen's father being a Senator, but if it had, he wasn't telling. Regardless of how they had come into the hands of the *Elismere's* crew, it mattered very little to the few still alive on the atmosphere-spewing wreck that was the *Sanitarian*.

Two elongated needles shot from the *Elismere's* bow, each moving far slower than their solid iridium predecessors, digging deep into the core of their target and shaking the shattered vessel like a toy. The tiny computers inside them noticed that their final parameters had been met and promptly detonated. Exploding the shells.

Fierce white light erupted at the *Sanitarian's* heart, a ball of blinding heat and plasma that consumed everything in its path as it swept outwards. More explosions marred the fractured surface of the ship's once pristine hull, sending white-hot fragments of metal whipping out in all directions, some sparking on the *Elismere's* shields as they evaporated. Then another explosion, far larger, welled up from deep inside the *Sanitarian* as sympathetic detonation cut the reactor containment field power lines. Plasma exploded outwards as the *Sanitarian* came apart, her internal structure reduced to little more than fragments borne upon the edge of her own apocalypse.

Chapter XXIII

The *Elismere*, Republic Space

TETRIANA AND TIM sprung back into existence in an open metallic room. They both jumped back with surprise when they looked up and saw the black nothingness of space in front of them. Realising that they were not floating, it became obvious that the image they were seeing was being projected from the wall.

Tetriana turned to Tim and muttered, "This must be some kind of recreation room." As she looked up at him, the ends of her hair showing a worried orange.

Tetriana made to move towards Tim but was interrupted by the sound of a door opening behind her. She froze on the spot and looked towards the ground, letting her hair change to a red, listening intently for footsteps. When she was sure the interruption was where she needed it, she jolted her right arm releasing her gun into the centre of her hand.

She moved the gun between her chest and left arm, holding it against her body and closed her eyes. She pulled the trigger and lifted her head all in the same moment, reopening her eyes to face a shocked and fearful Tim. There was the soft thump of flesh on metal behind her.

Tetriana's hair returned to blue but this time with pink ends as she looked into Tim's eyes. She held the gun facing the ground, her arm fully stretched towards the floor before jolting her arm again to return it to where it had been before.

"What just happened?" Tim asked, his confident tone slightly breaking. His face bore an expression of confusion. In his mind he was trying to piece together the series of events that would lead him to standing on an enemy ship with someone he met only days before.

"Captain," she started, pausing as a jolt of pain travelled down her body at the thought of her Captain's fate. A wave of blue in her hair turning to a soft lilac, "Sorry, Singer," she continued, "allowed her emotions to get the better of her and I was not willing to let that get me killed. The command of this ship seemed to know more about us than we did them. I need to find out what they know, who they shared the knowledge with, and protect The Gate."

A cacophony of questions flooded Tim's mind and without thinking they all made their way to his mouth, "But why jump here, why not take an escape pod like everyone else? Why single me out to help you?"

"Look at my rank," She lifted her arm to reveal the missing stars, "I would not have been allowed on any escape pods," there was a brief pause as she inhaled deeply, "or even better, look out there, do you see any surviving pods? No, they were either destroyed by the attack or did not work in the first place. Our line of work has no escape." Another brief pause was punctuated by another deep breath, "And even if we had escaped in the pods we would have been deemed cowards and executed for leaving our posts. That is why I resigned from Singer's command so when I get back to someone who can help us they can see I disapproved of her methods." She finished looking out of the viewscreen at what had been her work and home. Tim watched as Tetriana's hair switched from blue, to Orange, with some of it staying a sickly mix of lilac and yellow. Putting her hands to her head she closed her eyes and forced her hair back to blue. She found it frustrating at how much concentration it was taking to control her hair.

As she opened her eyes something on the giant viewscreen caught her attention, she shuddered. A large piece of silver coloured metal floated past, the title *GBS Sanitarian* gilded in large letters and the edges of the fragment rough and broken telling the story of the destruction of the once powerful vessel.

Tim saw the reaction in Tetriana's eyes as her expression hardened, and in her hair as it changed to a soft green. He looked round to see pieces of the *Sanitarian* free floating in space. Within the debris was a tall backed chair with Captain Singers family insignia undamaged. The chair which once sat fastened to the floor of the bridge, was now freely moving through space.

He turned back to Tetriana just in time to see her hair turn deep red with patches phasing to magenta and back. A piece of fabric floated within the field of view, and without prompting, as if the screen knew Tetriana was watching the swatch the picture zoomed in. It appeared to be half of a uniform top. It was purple, and on what appeared to be an arm there were two-star pins and one circular pin. Printed just on the charred edges was the name "Kolby".

Unsure if he should look at Tetriana or avoid her gaze, Tim looked at the ground hoping she was planning something.

"Standard Republic recon and retreat," Tetriana snapped, looking Tim directly in the eyes when his gaze met hers. Her hair appeared to be shimmering like the magenta tails of a flame. Noticing the blank look on Tim's face, Tetriana rolled her eyes and took in a deep breath. Forcing her hair once again back to blue. "Standard Republic practice if you are found on an enemy ship. Find out as much as possible, destroy the ship, and report back. How would we take a ship like this down without being noticed?"

Tim jumped as she directed the question towards him. He didn't know how to answer. He was unsure how this new calm but clearly angry Tetriana would respond. "Eh, well," he started.

"WELL WHAT?" Tetriana shouted, her hair once again snapping back to fiery anger. She noticed Tim jump and breathed in deep again. With this deep breath her whole personality seemed to click and change completely, her hair became ice blue and her breathing slowed. "Sorry, Tim, I guess ranks are now unimportant." She said softly, in almost perfect control of every part of her being. "But please, still call me Captain," she continued. "What can we do to take down this vessel?"

"We could," he started again, uneasy around this even colder Tetriana. "Well, I could reprogram the ship's Virtual Intelligence with some form of self-destruct or just deactivate it." Tim approached the body of the man Tetriana had shot and patted him down, looking for some form of keycard. He found nothing approaching normal Republic identification, but on brushing back a sleeve on the body he found a glowing wristband. He recognised that this was definitely not Republic hardware. But could it provide a way out? He examined its functions for a few moments, and then tapped in a sequence causing the band to snap open.

"What are you doing?" Tetriana demanded.

"Hopefully getting us a way out of this room," Tim replied carefully, rising to his feet. "This man wasn't carrying a weapon, so I'm afraid I'm not going to be much use in a firefight."

Before he could continue, Tetriana let out a harsh bark and replied, "You will not need to be. I will deal with any obstacles that present themselves." She drew herself up to her full height and snapped her guns out into her hands. "Get us to the VI."

Tim nodded. A verbal reply didn't seem to be the best of ideas right now. He approached the door which, sensing the wristband in his hand, slid open.

From there the two moved quickly through the ship's corridors, meeting no resistance. The crew must have been at stations, more evidence that this was not a merchant vessel. But then, any ship with enough firepower to blow the *Sanitarian* out of space definitely wasn't a mere merchant vessel. The thought crossed his mind that it could be a Camelot Warrant ship, but that was ridiculous. There was precious little evidence that those agents of the Union Directorate even existed. Especially, he thought, if the rumours were true, there would be a lot less evidence of a firefight.

Unfortunately for the two boarders, the digression into rumours meant that Tim had failed to consider the fact that a ship this advanced would have an equally advanced Virtual Intelligence. One that would likely have already noticed them.

*

Up on the bridge, EVI was just making that fact known to the command crew. Jack's face twisted in a frown.

"We didn't get them all?"

149

"No." The VI sighed. "My scans indicate the use of a gravity catapult system just before the *Sanitarian* was destroyed. I initially dismissed it as part of the explosion. That analysis, it appears, was in error."

"Can you neutralise them with ship systems?" Jack asked. This wasn't common, but the *Elismere* had dealt with it before.

"I believe so, however one of them has hacked a wristband taken from Robert when he entered the viewing deck. I have already notified medical and am guiding them to him around the intruders. Given the technical skills of the one who hacked the wristband however, I cannot guarantee quick capture." Jenny was already standing as she finished. "Personal Touch recommended."

"On my way." Jenny replied, checking the charge on her pistol as she headed for the lift. "Have a security team meet me at the elevator."

*

Tetriana and Tim continued through the ship, heading inwards towards what Tim hoped would be a transit tube that could take them closer to the computer core. Given the complexity of the wristband, he was certain he could get the lift to move. He was less certain about being able to do so without an alarm going off, but he hadn't bothered to pass that fact on to Tetriana. In her current state of mind he doubted that she'd care about the possibility of their current mission being a one-way trip.

More empty corridors passed them by, leading, he hoped, to the bank of tubes that should be at the centre of the vessel. It was a basic design feature common to most ships. As he saw the bank on rounding a corner, he smiled, but Tetriana didn't.

Her arm reached out and yanked him back around the corridor, slamming his head against the bulkhead. He looked up at her, his expression a mix of confusion and anger.

"Hostiles in one of the elevators." She snapped. Hearing the alarm in her voice stomped out his anger in an instant, as well as his confusion. She'd probably just saved his life, or at least temporarily extended it. She snapped out her guns, the familiar shapes nestling into her hands like she'd been born with them.

"Stay here. Don't move. I do not want you to get in my way." A tone sounded down the corridor, and she went forward at a run for a better vantage point. The doors of the lift slid open as she crossed the final paces and she felt the distinctive ripple of sound that could mean only one thing pass behind her. Sonic pistol fire. Whoever fired it was fast.

Tetriana could appreciate a quick opponent, after all she did like a challenge. But right now it was just an annoyance that she could have done without. She flicked one of her guns around the corner she was behind and held down the trigger for several seconds. She wasn't really expecting any shots to hit, but it might warn the attackers enough to stand down. Suppression was about all she could hope for. With a swift movement she pulled the gun back from firing just as two ripples of sound sped through the space that it had occupied a moment ago. It was followed by six more.

These people were definitely not merchants, she thought, their shots were too accurate. This did not deter her, these people may be good but she was better. Up to now she had never met someone who could win against her in a gunfight.

"Captain, two at five metres!" Tim yelled from his vantage point further up the corridor. A pang of anger crossed her mind, she had told him to stay out of her way, but in the same moment she was thankful for the heads up. The thought passed in the same instant as she moved, flowing across the crossed corridors like a panther. She didn't even see the sights of her pistols, she'd not needed them for years, and the two guards dropped.

More ripples of sound cut the air around her, but she had trained for shipboard combat. She kept her body's movements desynchronised as she'd been taught causing all the shots to miss. Given the skill the security had shown so far though, she knew that trick wouldn't work twice. She needed to get the numbers down.

"One at," The call from further up the corridor was cut off with a strangled cry followed by a thump. A rush of thoughts poured across Tetriana's mind, carrying with it a flood of guilt, and something snapped. She hurled herself forward behind a hail of blue energy bolts, forcing the security staff to duck away from the suppressive fire. One didn't, though, and Tetriana's eyes narrowed as she recognised in the slim figure the look of a fellow predator. The woman twisted away from the energy fire directed at her, turning in place to present a smaller target profile as she adjusted her aim. Tetriana saw the woman's hand clench and threw herself into a forward roll, but she wasn't quite fast enough this time. The sonic bolt caught Tetriana's legs, and she stifled a gasp of pain as they hit the deck hard, preventing her from continuing into the upwards spring she'd planned.

As the world shattered into nothingness Tetriana felt more than a small amount of respect for this highly trained individual. She had to be some kind of officer to stand her ground like that and take Tetriana down. And like that Tetriana's world shattered into nothingness in a blast of sound.

Chapter XXIV

Tongues was back at his desk on The *Hope* listening to garbled and muffled words, he could make out a stream of sentences that came at him from the haze around him. "Tannhäuser was a poet. By next lesson, you are expected to have written an essay on the Tannhäuser Gate. Remember, we may not check up on all of you, but you can never be sure. On that note, the following children are to report directly to Medical and Discipline. Not you, Blue-46-04-1000, you're safe. Remember, someone somewhere wants you to do good things. By next lesson you are expected to have done good things. Remember, you're safe. Safe from the Tannhäuser Gate. Safe to do good things. By next lesson you are expected to be safe," He became aware of the harsh light of a new day-cycle slipping through a chink in his dreams and stabbing him in the brain.

He sounded his disapproval through something that was a mix between a grunt and a moan, but obediently forced his eyes open anyway. After all, being late for things only got you disciplined. His eyes were already open, and his brain almost awake, by the time he remembered that the light in room Blue-46-04-1000 had been broken for a while.

The ceiling he was now looking at, was not the ceiling he had become conscious to for so many years. That ceiling was not any ceiling on *Tomorrow's Hope*. It was too clean and sterile looking. And the light fitting that was pumping out the irritating glow was unlike any light fitting he recognised.

A blonde head leaned into his field of vision. The head wasn't any more recognisable than the ceiling. It was, however, noticeably that of an Adult.

Tongues swallowed as subtly as he could, and waited to be either told what was going on or hold back a flinch from pain.

"Good morning," the Adult said, with a fake smile, the smiling ones were always the worst, and the smiles were always fake, in Tongues's experience. "Do you speak English?" Her voice was peculiar, indeed, her strange accent rendered the words almost completely incomprehensible to Tongues.

"More proficiently than you do, without question," Tongues answered honestly. Constantly seeking the answer to words repeating in the mind does tend to lend itself to reading a lot of dictionaries.

The Adult's smile gave way to look of surprise. Tongues tensed mechanically, he wasn't awake enough yet to stop himself. He'd forgotten that Adults had a habit of hurting you if you did not say what they wanted.

"Right, well, that's a relief," the Adult replied in an unimpressed tone. "You've been mumbling about a poet, Tannhauser," the adult continued, watching him intently, "So do the words Tannhauser Gate mean anything to you?" She looked confused at the young boy as he winced when she said Tannhauser.

Tongues's insides somersaulted at the mention of the words he'd had stuck in his head for so long. The adult had wrongly pronounced them, he thought, but they were clearly the same. He had finally found another human being who seemed to understand that they were significant for some reason. "I think you mean Tann-hoiser," he blurted out. "The umlaut—-" he went to continue before being cut off by the world going black.

The Adult moved to the shimmering curtain that isolated her and the boy from the rest of the med bay. "Susan, is the child all right?" she announced, concerned as to why the boy had lost consciousness. She looked around the isolation area for the head of the med bay who turned out not to be present but there was a white-clothed assistant nearby, engrossed in whatever they were reading on their little handheld computer. The assistant looked up, tapped in a brief code and consulted the patient's notes.

"That depends on one's definition of all right, Jenny," they said. "He's currently undergoing treatment for a variety of conditions," the assistant began to scroll on their device, "mild case of rickets, scurvy and about a dozen other kinds of malnourishment. There's a continuous history of unhealed or poorly healed fractures going back at least ten years," they winced as if reading a particularly gruesome part of the medical records, "His left knee was completely destroyed when we picked him up, he's partially blind in his right eye, he has a grade two heart murmur and a faulty kidney." The assistant paused reading further on, "he has the only modern case I personally have ever seen of asthma."

Jenny looked up in confusion, asthma had been treatable for more than a couple of hundred years, there was no need for anyone to suffer with it now.

The assistant looked at Jenny as if expecting her to speak. Noticing Jenny was just expressing annoyance, they continued, "most of his muscles are un or underdeveloped. His weight is way too low for someone his age and build, and he even has the beginnings of something we can't find in the books, but which almost resembles the ancient earth disease leprosy. Whoever was looking after him made an effort to keep him alive and walking," they forced a cough, "but not much else."

They called up a tiny holographic list of the notes as she flicked through them. Jenny winced, growling something under her breath as she glanced back at the thin, pale shape on the pillow. A deep pang of sympathy passing through her.

"Beyond the body, though," she replied, turning back to the medic, "what about mentally? Is his mind all right?"

"It's not easy to carry out a psyche evaluation when he's asleep," the medic pointed out gently. "We'll take care of that once he's cogent. Either way, however, I'd imagine more than a little social ineptitude is to be expected if he is indeed one of the *Tomorrow's Hope* children. Have you read the records your brother pulled from the station?"

"Not all of them," replied Jenny darkly. "I found I had to stop after the phrase, theoretically endurable."

Jenny heard movement behind her and turned to see the figure jostling uneasy.

The unfamiliar ceiling appeared in Tongues' view once again breaking his slumber. Tongues raised his head a fraction. He was lying on a comfortable bed in a curtained-off space. The sterile white of the ceiling moved to a hazy washed out shimmer at the walls. The blonde-haired Adult was stood behind a chair next to him. The chair was a shock to Tongues, having never seen a piece of furniture in such a good condition before. The adult was dressed in some high-quality uniform, and there was some kind of gun on her hip.

This was unlike anywhere he knew on The *Hope*. His mind began to race, this had to be in the Adult's Area he thought. Unless, he considered, his dreams had been correct. He'd been dreaming before he woke up, and his dreams had flitted back and forth, from being on *Tomorrow's Hope*, in vaguely normal lectures, to being somewhere else. Somewhere safe. Somewhere off The *Hope*.

Memories jostled for position in his brain, trying to arrange themselves into either dream or reality. He began to question. Had he actually escaped? Had he really done it? Had Val really set him free? And was he now really safe? He struggled to even fully understand the concept of complete safety. To him it was entirely theoretical. Just words on a page. Defined as, protected from danger or risk, without possibility of harm, providing security and protection.

"Hi," said the Adult. Tongues winced, questioning, was she and Adult of The *Hope* or just an adult. "I'm sorry about before, I didn't realise." She paused, grappling with herself for a few moments. This was something Tongues had never seen any of the Adults on The *Hope* do. She reached out her hand in greeting. "It's hard to believe that you're scared of us, I guess. My name's Jenny, what's yours?"

He answered hesitantly, "Tongues," he froze, in case it was a trick question. He decided it was probably best to give his proper name if he was indeed still potentially on The *Hope*, "Blue-46-04-1000. I'm told I might have had another one once, but no-one has ever told me it."

Jenny forced another smile, and Tongues wasn't sure whether he was supposed to find it reassuring or frightening. "You probably have a lot of questions, and I am here to answer some of them. Firstly, you are indeed no longer on-board the *Tomorrow's Hope*. You are on another ship now, a considerably smaller one, called the *Elismere*, in Republic Space. Do you know about the Republic?"

"Loosely," Tongues answered, attempting to shrug. "I know they commissioned the *Tomorrow's Hope* Project and hand-selected us all, and as I understand it they're more or less the most dominant of the Interstellar Superpowers. They didn't strike me as particularly agreeable people from that description, but anywhere's better than The *Hope*."

"Right," Jenny nodded. "Well, the reason for the Republic's unpleasantness is, we think, that they've become little more than a puppet government for a supposed Secret Service Advisory Assembly named the Tannhauser Gate."

"Tann-hoiser," Tongues corrected, again, automatically, his conscious brain being overrun with signals. This was the furthest he'd ever come in his investigation into those words all in one go.

"Tann-hauser," Jenny repeated. "I know, I've had the words in my head a lot longer than you have."

"Yes, yes, yes, but you probably pay only as much attention to the language as is needed to shoot people," Tongues replied, waving a hand distractedly. Tongues thought, this person may not be an Adult, but given his experience of adults, he assumed there was no way one could have understood as much as him. "I can assure you, it's pronounced Tann—"

Jenny shrugged, cutting him off, she knew now wasn't the time to deal with correcting a child, "The Tannhauser Gate runs everything in the Republic, to varying degrees, and we're quite sure that it has at least half the other nations out there dancing to its tune through manipulation, bribery and God knows what else. The only people who seem to be completely free from their influence are the Anglesian Federation, and that's just because the Tannhauser Gate can't get in. They also appear to have no influence on the Bisolar Democratic Coalition, but that's a mix of them being too small to effectively infiltrate and also being a neutral power that no one wants to be the first to attack."

Jenny looked at Tongues to see if he was still paying attention, before continuing, "Nobody knows what they really want or what they're really doing with all the power they've amassed. But for some reason, there are a few people, like you and me, who were born with a little message in our heads that tells us that the Tannhauser Gate is important."

Tongues's head reeled. This was the kind of chance he'd been dreaming of for his entire short life. He now knew what Tannhäuser Gate meant. And he was with people who could help him find out more. He wasn't even entirely sure there were words to describe how he felt right now.

Struggling to decide on a response, he opted to correct Jenny before continuing, "It really is pronounced Tann–hoiser."

CHAPTER XXV

TIM AND TETRIANA, THE *ELISMERE*, REPUBLIC SPACE

TIM AWOKE IN WHAT he recognised as a cell. There was nothing special about this cell. Fairly standard for any ship brig. He looked towards the entrance almost instinctively. On a normal day, he would have been the one standing waiting for a criminal to come to after receiving a stun shot, but today he found himself in the criminal's position.

"I'm glad to see you're awake, Timothy." The man that met him was obviously part of the crew. Tim stood up immediately and looked at the figure addressing him. Judging by the way the man knew his name, Tim decided that he was either an acquaintance or an old enemy he had locked up.

"Please, it's just Tim." He said, stretching his back, "Friend or foe?"

The man that stood in the door raised an eyebrow and replied slowly. "A question fitting from either of us. Don't you think?" Came the response, in a quizzical tone. "Our computer system caught you trying to sabotage our ship and now you're in one of her cells." The man entered the room and behind him a particle field sprang up to stop Tim from escaping. "We know who you are, more by reputation than anything else." The man sat on the nearby bed, seemingly not caring for his safety around Tim, and with a swift hand offered a seat to him. "We know that you single-handedly managed to decrypt communications within the largest drug ring in this part of the galaxy." The man paused and dipped his head as if expecting Tim to respond.

"I did," he replied slowly but proudly, before his tone turned to one of panic. "How do you know so much about me?"

"Someone who has been working as long as you and done as much as you is bound to have a reputation on the net." The stranger countered calmly, his face then shifted to a forced look of confusion, "That was the odd thing, we could find information on you but not the woman."

Stopping the man from continuing, Tim interrupted, "I should have been the same. I was scrubbed."

The man rolled his eyes and loosely swatted his hand in the air while mumbling, "They were always bad with new recruits," clearing his tone and turning his eyes back on Tim he continued, "But that's not why I have come to you. We need you to decrypt some files created by an organisation known as the Tannhauser Gate. Do you think you could do that for us?"

Tim eyed the man from his seat, trying to work out why they needed secured files decrypted, and more importantly, why they would ask someone who had just attempted to destroy their ship. He was certain there was an ulterior motive. "Are you expecting me to ask, what's in it for me?"

"An excellent question, Tim. I can answer it in two parts. I think you will manage to get the answer to the first within minutes of getting to work. As for the second part, I," he started, pausing, then nodding, "we on this ship can offer you and the woman liberation from the government and in return you can help us finally show where the corruption lies." The man looked through the particle field to a cell on the opposite side of the corridor where Tetriana's limp body lay. "We did try and ask the woman to help, but that ended with one of my security staff sitting in the med bay having his arm reset." The man put his hand in front of his eyes and appeared to be observing his hand flexing and unflexing. Letting out a forced laugh and shaking his arm he looked back to Tim.

Tim let out a small smirk of amusement. "It's usually her policy to shoot people. The officer is lucky he got away with a broken arm."

"She tried to shoot and she failed. The form of energy her weapons use is now nullified by our security systems." Tim's captor remarked, raising both eyebrows, "I think it was her confusion in the lack of gunfire that allowed us to get control of her without having to call EVI into it." The man ended with a smile.

It wasn't clear to Tim if the smile was fake or real. "EVI?" Tim questioned.

A voice answered as if expecting this response, but not the voice he was expecting. "Hello Tim. My name is EVI, and I am the Virtual Intelligence aboard this vessel."

"Nice to meet you EVI." Tim responded, without so much as changing is expression. He was so used to dealing with VIs that hearing and responding to one was nothing extraordinary. Having access, he thought, even if only voice access to the VI could offer a means of escape. Hoping to keep his captor as long as possible he continued, "So what do you need me to decrypt?"

From a deep coat pocket, the visitor removed a small, hand-held computer and handed it to Tim. "The file and an operating system is all that is installed. I'm sure it will take you," The man was cut off as Tim handed the device back to him. "Now that was quick." He laughed "Your reputation isn't half as good as it should be."

"Your VI could have done that quicker than me, why did you need me to decrypt it?" Tim questioned. The file did not need human input to decrypt. He knew his captor was playing with him, but what was the game and how could he get the upper hand.

"I needed you to see the authenticity of the file," the man said, cooly, "Indeed, EVI has decrypted this file for us already," he continued, closing his eyes as if in pain, "are you satisfied the file is of republic origin and authentic?"

Proving the authenticity of communications was part of Tim's function when he was hunting drug rings. He knew the file was authentic, or more accurately, the file was signed by a republic trust server. Which could only be done using one of the keys from within the government. He also knew by the signature that key came from the same body that recently recruited him. All he couldn't work out, is how this individual, or crew, had managed to fake the signature.

"What game are you playing?" Tim demanded, his demeanour more becoming of when he worked in law enforcement.

"No games. You've seen the file. You've decrypted it yourself. All there is left now, is for you to read it."

Tim decided that in his current situation it was probably better that he read the file. It was probably just junk designed to look like authentic data and in the worst case he could destroy the tablet with a couple of swift commands.

Tim accepted the tablet back and started to read the information he had managed to decrypt. Almost immediately his's expression went from one of confusion to one of disgust and hatred. The device he was reading was informing him of a lab report from a ship known as *Tomorrow's Hope*.

It started:

Day one: Subject Red-13-J2-1000 administered with test drug 20101028. Awaiting biological response.

Day two: Subject shows little or no response bar minor abdominal pain. Experiment Manager Dr Saint-John recommends doubling dosages every two days.

...

Day seven: Subject evidencing extreme pain, theorised to be a result of chemical mixing with growth hormone. At subject's age, growth hormone should have been expected to hinder. NB: SUBJECT AGED 13 AT TIME OF ADMINISTRATION

...

Day twenty-three: Subject's organs display evidence of rejection. Subject is complaining of lack of sleep due to pain. Subject witnessed vomiting blood and as-yet unidentified viscous red liquid on regular basis.

...

Day forty-five: Subject's body commencing shutdown. Experimental Manager has recommended cancelling experimental procedure when subject's body becomes incapable of normal functioning.

…

Day one hundred and twenty-two: Subject's body has undergone biological death, consistent with external evidence of test drug's full capabilities in the human body. Subject revived successfully. Experiment Manager recommends submitting for a period of treatment before return to normal schedule. Subject will be resubmitted into experimentation schedule when health is deemed to have returned to practicable levels.

"They are just kids? This has got to be a hoax!" Tim started to frantically work on the computer and within seconds seemed to freeze up. What he had just found was what he was looking for, but the information was not what he wanted to see. Breaking the audit chain and signatures he could see that a Tannhauser Gate computer had produced the report and judging by timestamps with signatures, it was no forgery. "Does," he paused, "Tetriana know about this?"

"Tetri," the man began, "Oh, your colleague," he paused and looked towards Tetriana, "No, she probably wouldn't have believed it anyway. Just as you didn't. That's why we were hoping you would tell her for us?"

Tim felt the question didn't really need an answer and so just stood up and walked to the entrance. Without a command the particle field disabled itself and Tim walked straight through. He was moving on autopilot and hadn't even considered that his captor just let him walk out.

Crossing the corridor felt like a lifetime. How would he tell her? Would she believe him? More importantly, how would she react either way? As he neared the entrance to the cell that Tetriana still lay unconscious in, he debated if this was the right thing to do. Again, without interaction, the particle field disengaged itself and after he had entered the room it reengaged itself. Hearing his own voice before he thought of what he would say, he announced, "EVI, are you able to wake her up?"

There was a short pause before Tetriana's hair turned red, and then out of nowhere she lunged for Tim. It didn't take her long to realise that she was pinning him to the ground. She jumped off him and backed away. With every step her hair went a lighter shade of red.

"What are you doing in here?" she demanded. Tim was happy to hear that commanding tone again, just as a reminder that she was all right.

"I have something I think you might want to read and might actually change your mind about our hosts." he stretched out his arm, offering the computer to his colleague, who snatched it with the ferocity of a starving hyena. Without warning she retracted her arm is if to throw the device before Tim jumped at her and pleaded, "No! just read it!"

She gave a look of confusion to Tim, he had never spoken to her like that. Actually, no one of a lesser rank had. Bringing the device to reading level she analysed the text for some time, showing the same disgust Tim had earlier. On completion she snapped back to an emotionless face and insisted, "It is not true. It is fake!"

"I wish it wasn't, I have checked all the files' attributes and core information." He replied, with a tone like a pleading partner, "It is true and it was sent by a Gate science vessel." Tetriana looked straight at Tim. There was no wavering in his eyes, no show of a lie whatsoever.

"How could something like that go on within the Republic? It is not possible!" she spat and then shouted, "If the Republic government knew."

"They do know, the files are signed by the government, and the Tannhauser Gate." Tim said, cutting her off mid flow.

"You are not Tim, you are an impostor, I want to see your captain, immediately!" Tetriana said, her hair matching her temper.

As if on cue, and before Tim could respond, a voice came from outside the cell, "Jack Claramae, Captain of the Federation Trading Vessel *Elismere*," the man who had given Tim the tablet said. "May I enter without the threat of attack?"

Tetriana clenched her fists and turned to the doorway. "Depends on what you have to do with the *Zephyra*?" Tetriana hissed with bile in every word.

Jack seemed to ponder something for a second and then shrugged, spreading his hands out in the universal gesture of trust. "We," he paused, "well, we are the *Zephyra*. Or to be more precise, the *Zephyra* is the *Elismere*. And I can assure you, that is indeed your colleague Timothy,"

Tetriana stepped towards the doorway with one eyebrow raised, then in one swift movement drew the gun concealed in her right arm. "Explain!"

Jack raised his own eyebrow in response to her, but didn't step back. "Explain what?" he asked with a soft tone, with an underlying current of command a match to Tetriana's own.

There was a noticeable pause before her response. Her back straightened to a position of attention and the red in her hair, whilst still obvious, seemed to calm in sudden realisation. Only someone of a higher rank than her could bring about this change in her attitude and she couldn't explain how an apparent civilian had prompted this reaction.

Jack tilted his head slightly to one side, eyes studying the Terineti before him for a few moments as a few more pieces of an intricate puzzle fell into place. And when he next spoke, the undercurrent of command was more pronounced. "What do you need explained?"

"Why a trading vessel would need the ability to change ship ID, Sir?" Tetriana began, as if responding to an admiral, "And why we are being held captive on this ship, sir." The gun in her right hand lowered and then snapped back into the recess in her arm as she stood to attention.

"You're being held due to your attempt to sabotage this ship and kill its crew. As for changing our transponder code, you of all people should know how important it is to appear as something else. Or simply not appear at all." The last statement was said with a point to it, clearly aimed at the apparent non-existence of Tetriana's records.

"I work for an organisation designated to protect this section of space, and to carry out our jobs, we are required to be non-existent."

"Ah." Jack nodded. "And would this organisation of yours happen to call itself the Tannhauser Gate?"

"My captain," Tetriana began, crimson spread along her hair, flowing out from the root towards the tips, "whom you killed!" She took a step forward, closing the distance between herself and the doorway, "was not allowed to let us know who we were working for, at least not by name." She took a deep breath, then sighed. "One of their many names may have been the Tannhauser Gate. They were secretive," She paused, as if contemplating if she should be saying this, "Off the books," again she paused, "But you will never find out about the—" Her words juddered to a halt, hair flashing through a light green into blue as she fought for control. She stared at the symbol that had materialised out of the air by Jack's right hand, which was none other than the very symbol Captain Singer used to prove her authority.

He lowered his hand, the hologram flashing out of existence. "Will you listen now?" he asked, all gentleness in his tone gone, nothing but command behind his words, the one thing Tetriana could never expect from a civilian.

Tetriana stepped back from the door, moving back to sit on the edge of the room's bed. "Listening, Captain."

Chapter XXVI

Tongues opened his eyes with a start becoming instantly aware that the unfamiliar ceiling was becoming more familiar.

"Don't worry about Jenny; she's not usually so direct with people," a kind voice informed him. He looked up. There was a different adult in the seat near him now. An older woman, with darker hair. "She's just stressed right now, with four extra passengers on the ship."

"Who —" Tongues started.

"My name's Susan. I run the medical bay."

He froze, gulped and then stuttered "As in Medical and Discipline?" Susan smiled gently.

"I should hope not. We don't go in for discipline in my med bay, beyond that required to keep staff professional and patients safe. I'm a healer, not a hurter. It's my job to make sure you're as comfortable as you can be."

Tongues blinked at that, and lay back to let everything sink in.

It was almost impossible to feel anything, his brain had become overloaded. He would never be on the *Tomorrow's Hope* again. He'd never be disciplined like before. He'd never be given sudden, unexplained and above all painful medical tests. And he'd found some people, completely by accident, who would be willing to help him with the Tannhäuser Gate.

Without warning a flood of pain hit. He realised he would also never see Val again and that hurt. It was like the insides that had been threatening to burst from him with excitement at the thought of freedom had now suddenly contracted into a tiny knot. Like they'd undergone Val's point widening trick in reverse.

Suddenly, he was sure of what he had to do. He had to get up, out of this medical bay, and he had to find out what he could about his new keepers. Importantly, he thought, he had to start solving the mystery of Tannhäuser Gate. Trying to piece what he had learned together so far in his head he listed. They were a gate of the judicial assembly kind, but what were they judging? Why had they formed? What did they want? And most importantly, how and why had a message about them reached him, but apparently not anyone else on The *Hope*? In his mind every second he wasted was a second Val's decision to send him in her place was wasted.

He struggled to get up but found that his muscles weren't responding properly. Most of them seemed to be still asleep, and his left leg felt unused and unfamiliar.

"Hey, hey, don't move so much," Susan urged him, reaching out to steady him as he almost fell. "You're not ready to leave the bed yet. You're still recovering from more than twenty different medical procedures. I'll tell you when you can be up and about, OK?"

"No," Tongues objected. "I've already wasted so much time! I need to start doing, things,"

He looked down, dumbly, at the tube leading under the skin of his arm. He hadn't noticed it before, but now there was an odd pulsing sensation, like it was injecting him with something. Tongues had been injected with all sorts of stuff over the years, and he wondered dimly whether this was going to make him as ill as some of the other things had.

He collapsed back onto the pillow, suddenly too tired to bear his own weight. The ceiling began to swim out of view.

"Oh, for pity's sake," he muttered, as unconsciousness took him again.

CHAPTER XXVII

"AND THAT'S EVERYTHING we can tell you." Jack finished. He had, over the period of the conversation, moved from outside the doorway to sitting on a chair opposite Tetriana. Although he didn't show it, he was worried. Tetriana was young, and apparently devoted. Having almost her entire worldview systematically dismantled in the course of less than an afternoon was going to affect her. And he couldn't know how she would react to that.

The half-Terineti in front of him had sat through the entire briefing in perfect silence, listening intently and clearly watching for anything that might give it away as a lie.

Now she raised her head, forcing her gaze away from her almost, but not quite, shaking hands. Her expression was an intricate tapestry of controlled shock creating shades of blue and yellow slashing back and forth across her hair, their clashes outlined only by the occasional, quickly vanished, bloom of bright green. But even then, her voice was steady when she spoke.

"As much as I might want to believe you, Captain, how can I know that you are not just making this all up?" Jack met her eyes, his strange black on black iris and pupil staring across the space between them.

"You can't." He shrugged, almost helplessly. "But there are a few things I can say that might help. For example, we could have just killed you after we caught you aboard our vessel." He raised his hand, palm up. "We didn't. Even when we knew that you were here to try and kill us all and destroy or take control of our vessel. But if you want proof Tetriana, if you want to see what I've told you, then all I ask is that you trust me, even if it's only for a little while. Come with us, both you and Timothy, and we'll show you the truth you're looking for."

Tetriana paused, turning her head slightly so that her light-blue eyes met Tim's, where he was sitting slightly off to the side, watching the conversation. An eyebrow twitched, and he nodded.

"Very well, Captain," she said finally. "But if I am going to work with you, I would like better quarters."

"Easily done." Jack rose and his hand flashed up in a Republic Military salute. "Welcome aboard."

Tetriana was on her feet in a flash, snapping to attention in a blur of unconscious movement to return the salute. Her right foot slammed down, ringing on the deck. She did not like how she felt manipulated by Jack. She felt it was clear the salute was to test her reflexes. For now though, her best chances of staying alive was to continue with these strangers.

"Thank you, Captain!"

Chapter XXVIII

The next time Tongues awoke, it was to the sound of a door opening nearby, and footsteps approaching him. He opened his eyes, squinted at the light, mumbled something half-coherent in which he accused the ceiling of being a villain and rolled his head to the side.

There was a man there, about the same age as the medical woman he'd been talking to earlier. At a guess, he'd have said somewhere around forty. But then, the Adults on *Tomorrow's Hope* had all seemed to show age less than the children. Probably something about being better looked after, and some sort of medical treatment, Tongues vaguely remembered Val saying. With his warped sense of aging, he realised the man could have been any age. He was dressed in another uniform like the woman earlier. Black and green, which Tongues was dimly aware were the colours of some sort of organisation or a place.

He hoped he didn't have to speak to this one as well. All of this speaking to strangers was making him uneasy. And he was unsure if his tiredness was down to the medications or social exhaustion.

"Hello there," said the man. Tongues couldn't work out his tone, but he guessed it was supposed to be friendly since, hello there, was usually an informal greeting. Of course, he could be being ironic. "Tongues, isn't it?" the man smiled. Tongues thought, another smiler, great. Although this one looked like he was more used to it. "That's an unusual name."

Tongues wasn't sure whether that was meant to be an attack or a test or something else, but after a moment's hesitation he decided going on the defensive was his best bet.

"Names are meant to be unusual," he snapped. "Their whole purpose is to make it easier to identify one individual among many, and thus they become entirely ineffectual as soon as they become common enough to count as," he attempted air quotes, "usual."

"An excellent point," the man replied, without dropping the smile. Tongues noted that this one also had a gun on his belt. "My name's Jack Claramae, Tongues. I'm the captain of this ship."

"Captain," Tongues repeated. "That implies importance and authority, does it not? I assume you're in charge around here then?"

"More or less," the man shrugged. "Insofar as I am the one who pulls rank whenever people step out of line, and it's me that takes the responsibility every time we make a mistake. You could think of me as being the father if this ship was a family."

"Father means even less to me than captaincy, Jack," Tongues replied pointedly. The captain dipped his head.

"My apologies." Jack said with a sense of guilt.

Tongues sighed. "If you're in charge, you can tell me what I'm doing here."

"We rescued you from the station you'd found your way onto, after we intercepted a message from it. We could tell from your bioscan that you had the same genetic markers as my crew, and your conversations with Susan and Jenny have firmly suggested that you have the same trigger as two of them. That makes you quite special. You've been touched."

"In many, many ways I would rather forget, with an excruciating variety of implements," Tongues agreed.

"It's rather more complicated than that, I'm afraid. Jen has done her best to explain, as has Susan, and that you recognise the words so clearly is only further proof that you have the same trigger in your head. Something that makes you push and search for a meaning to the phrase Tannhauser Gate."

"It's pronounced Tann-hoiser," Tongues groaned exasperatedly. The captain shrugged.

"Be that as it may, that organisation is what this crew is dedicated to looking into, and we believe you are supposed to help us."

Tongues's guardedness and fear were gone, "So you'll let me stay and help?"

"We will see what help you can give. But yes, for now you will be staying with us," the captain agreed. "But you'll have to listen to the crew, and do as we say while you're on the ship. At some point soon we'll be heading home. Home to the Federation, out of the Republic for now, and then we'll decide what to do from there."

"Can I meet the other," he paused, "uh," he tried again "touched people? The others with the words in their head? I've already met one, the tetchy woman that was in here earlier."

"Jenny," Jack nodded automatically. "When you're allowed out of the medical bay, I'm sure we can introduce you to Adrian." Jack smiled, apparently considering his next words, "and Elios. He's not a crewmember, but he is on board for now and he does have the same trigger. We do have another one present right now. But I'm not sure she'd be ready to accept visitors of your temperament."

Tongues raised an eyebrow.

***

Due to the irregular sleep cycles, Tongues was unsure how long it had been since Captain Jack visited to let him know about the others. What he was sure about was how nervous he had been feeling at the prospect of being allowed to leave the medical area and explore the rest of the ship. It was, he learned, considerably smaller than *Tomorrow's Hope*, although still large enough to make him feel small and nervous whenever he walked through it, past the larger and more competent humans that inhabited it.

On his first tentative exploratory trip, he had found an edge. A wall beyond which there was no more ship. Just the vast expanse of the nothingness of space. Tongues had never even thought before about the idea that a person could stand, touching a wall, and on the other side of that wall there could be no more air or warmth. Of course, *Tomorrow's Hope* had outer walls. He understood that ships couldn't just go on forever. But the outer hull of *Tomorrow's Hope* had been so far away to walk to, even if he'd had authority to do so, he wouldn't know where to go.

Susan had given him some sort of bracelet, that Tongues thought looked like a modern-day equivalent to a manacle. The device allowed him to gain access to approved areas of the ship while preventing his unwanted entrance to the remainder. This was, so Susan said, for safety reasons. She also told him that he had implants in his body when they picked him up, and that at least one of them controlled his access to areas of the *Tomorrow's Hope*. Tongues stopped listening when she started listing the other functions of the implants. This was probably for the best.

Up to now, the only outer edge he could remember ever seen for himself was the dark void that got him off the *Tomorrow's Hope*. Considering this, tongues thought it funny that he had indeed seen an edge to the ship, even if it was an edge within the ship. His thought process drifted from ships' edges to his new favourite word, Rubicon. Not long before he left The *Hope*, he had learned the word to mean a point of no return. And he saw his leaving The *Hope* as his Rubicon.

After his first trip out of medical, he had been a bit less bold with his exploration, ensuring that he never travelled far enough to panic about getting lost. Susan did teach him how to get the bracelet to direct him back. But he worried the bracelet would take him to more adults, or worse, a one-way airlock. Recently he had been spending time in the silence of the reading room.

When Susan told him there was a reading room and library, Tongues could not hide his excitement. Prompting her to equate him to an over excited puppy. His excitement didn't lesson when she informed him that most ships had reading rooms. The library had been his favourite area of *Tomorrow's Hope*. In fact, it had been the only area of that ship he'd actually enjoyed, at least until he met Val.

Now, on one of his short forays into the unexplored regions of the ship, he came across Elios, the man who, he'd been told, shared the same internal message as him. The trigger as Captain Jack had called it. Elios was considerably shorter than everyone Tongues had seen on-board, closer in height to Tongues himself, but much stockier. Tongues had noted that, within the crew there were two clear groups, most of the crew were tall and slender built whereas there were a few, like Susan, who seemed shorter than most.

Tongues was nervous meeting a non-crewmember. He was very aware of his own physical inadequacies and Elios's build reminded him of Police, back on The *Hope*. Although, he didn't remember Police smelling of sweat.

This room, whatever it was, had a drinks machine in it. Elios was frowning at a cup as it gradually filled, one arm crossing his body to drum its fingers on his ribcage while the other hand idly combed the fur of the creature clinging to the first arm. The creature regarded Tongues with an amusingly familiar expression.

"Hey," said the older man, after a couple of seconds of awkward staring. Tongues continued to stare for another second while he worked out how best to start a conversation with a person who could be a potential source of information about the meaning of the Tannhäuser Gate.

"I like your," Tongues started, getting stuck thinking of the word for the pet before awkwardly settling on, "thing," he said, catching the eye of the animal on Elios's arm. Elios's mouth curled slightly in a way that didn't look friendly.

"What the hell, thing?" he demanded.

Tongues looked at him, glanced left and right, and raised an eyebrow. "Simian," he tried, seeing the expression in Elios' face harden. "I mean, Monkey?" he finished.

"Yeah. Thanks," Elios muttered, rolling his eyes. This must have been another one of those know-it-alls, he thought. Turning back to his drink now more impatient with it.

Tongues briefly considered bailing out of this conversation at that. He concluded that Elios must be better read than the rest of the crew and found his poor use of English insulting and so decided to try again, "You have a particularly distinctive stature and constitution," he noted. "I presume the aforementioned phenomenon has an explanation?"

Elios suddenly spread out his arms, palms upwards, startling the monkey. "Mate, I'm pretty sure none of those words even have a meaning."

Tongues, now confused at Elios' use of language, decided he clearly wasn't so well read and would probably find the definitions interesting. "Of course they have meanings," he smiled. "One's stature is one's natural height. One's constitution, similarly, is one's physical make-up, that is, one's build. So, by distinctive stature I am referring to you being shorter than average." He continued with all sincerity, "would you like me to explain phenomenon as well?"

Elios observed him with half-lowered eyebrows. "Perhaps one would have more luck if one limited one's syllables the first time around," he suggested in a mock posh spacer tone. Almost as an afterthought, he added, "And I wouldn't look so small if we were on the friggin' ground. I mean, I've never had to duck a doorway, fair enough, but this thing was obviously built for spacers." He gestured vaguely to their surroundings before picking up his cup and turning to leave.

"Spacers," repeated Tongues, noticing Elios appeared to be leaving. "I've not heard that word before."

"Spacers, those who live in space, horrid people," Elios said, turning back to Tongues. "The longer you stay out here, the more you change. Especially if you're still growing anyway. All the stations and ships have some sort of man-made gravity and air and whatever, but it's not quite the same as a proper planet." He waved his fingers through the air in illustration. "You get taller and, like," he gestured vaguely, "thinner."

"More streamlined," Tongues smiled, trying to be conversational.

Elios shrugged, "Sure, let's go with that. Doesn't seem to make them weaker, mind. But that's probably, like, steroids or something." He glanced at Tongues over the rim of his cup. "You ought to know this crap. You grew up on a ship yourself, didn't you?"

"Well," Tongues began. "Technically, yes, but my ship was constantly travelling at superluminal velocities for virtually all of that time. You, on the other hand, grew up on the surface of what was, to all extents and purposes, a vast, naturally occurring, spacefaring, orbital satellite. If anybody within this particular room should be called a spacer, it really should be you."

Elios's hand shook suddenly, spilling his drink, and he cursed. "Are you mocking me?" he demanded, shaking droplets from his sleeve. Tongues raised an eyebrow. "Forget I said it," Elios snapped, turning on his heel and striding across the room towards another door at the opposite end, dropping the cup indignantly onto the silvery counter top as he went. "Spacers," he muttered under his breath as the door closed behind him.

Tongues stared for a moment, and then shook himself and marched back out the way he had come.

Chapter XXIX

Elios sat cross-legged on the floor holding a small metal cup of tea. After a few uncomfortable interactions with the crew, he had asked out loud for a place to get away from everyone, and his wrist band answered. The band had suggested the maint. shaft. Elios had no idea what a maint. shaft was but was happy for the solitude it provided. He assumed that the secluded nature of this area meant it wasn't being surveilled in the same way his quarters must have been. Little did he know that EVI had segmented a small area of a maintenance shaft with the permission of Captain Jack.

One thing did cause Elios to distrust this place. The absence of dirt, grime or even common dust made Elios nervous, it was unnatural to live in a world of disinfectant, but the maintenance shaft was quiet and offered as much privacy as you could get on this ship, so overall Elios liked it.

Catching sight of his distorted reflection on the uneven surface of a bulkhead, Elios could see that he looked terrible. He hadn't slept all night. His addiction keeping him awake. Susan, the *Elismere's* medic, had given him some sort of concoction to delay the withdrawals but they still came eventually, the shakes and soon the sweating and then. Elios had warned Captain Jack what would happen after the shakes but, obviously, the captain had chosen to ignore him. Elios huffed irritably, shaking his head, and took a sip of tea. The shakes were so bad now a large glob of tea landed on his chest.

Elios glanced down at the glowing band on his wrist. It was a necessary evil, he thought. The only way he was allowed out of his quarters was if he had agreed to wear one of the spacers tracking devices. Every time Elios tried to get into the hold, where **The Drug** was kept, the door would check his wrist band, see it was him, and not budge. No amount of swearing or kicking could convince the door otherwise. It was for his own good, Captain Jack had explained. If Elios ever wanted to be free of his addiction, he would have to take it only when the sweating started. Captain Jack had described this step as a necessary evil. Even Captain Jack couldn't prevent him from using **The Drug** when he got to that state.

"But I thought **The Drug** was highly addictive," Elios had protested, when the captain explained the plan.

"Highly addictive, yes," Captain Jack had replied. "But that's not the same as hopeless, with a lot of work, we can help you through this. That's what you want, isn't it? To stop using **The Drug** entirely?"

At the time in a moment of clarity, Elios had agreed, now he wasn't so sure. Yes, it would be amazing not to have to endure the side effects that came with **The Drug**, but if he was just given a fix whenever he needed it, then surely everything would be fine? Captain Jack had insisted that open access to **The Drug** could only cause an even higher dependency and severe damage to Elios's internal organs. More damage than before the crew had picked him up.

Elios closed his eyes tight shut and grimaced as pain shot across his chest like a three-second heartburn. Surely this was worse for his body than a few leaves every couple of days, he protested to himself. He exhaled slowly as the pain diminished, but the tightness wouldn't go entirely until he was actually in the process of using **The Drug**. And then, of course, it would all start again. It hardly seemed worth it.

Elios jumped, startled by a soft squeak. It was Moncello. The small space monkey swung down from the support girders using his eight-inch tail as an extra limb. Elios tried to smile and reached out his hand to stroke Moncello's soft, now clean, furry back.

"Hey," he whispered. Moncello cocked his head on one side and stared up at Elios curiously. Elios held out a monkey nut, fully aware that Moncello really wanted a leaf or two of **The Drug**. Moncello glared reproachfully at the offending legume, but he still grabbed it and started gnawing with his little, sharp teeth. "Soon as I start sweating, they'll give me **The Drug** and I'll save some for you," Elios promised, scooping up Moncello and placing him on his shoulder.

"Hello there." Startled, Elios spun round in the direction of the voice. It was Captain Jack, peering in from the door that Elios was sure only he knew about.

"What do you want?" Elios snapped. Moncello sprang from his shoulder, he didn't like it when Elios raised his voice, and scurried away back up to the conduits above. Elios watched him go and clenched his fists so tightly that his nails dug into his palms. He let out a small sigh, trying to relax himself, and glanced sheepishly up at the captain. "I," he stuttered before sighing again, "I'm sorry, Captain." he continued, but the captain cut him off.

"It's perfectly understandable under the circumstances," Captain Jack smiled kindly. "May I come in?"

"Do what you like," Elios shrugged, indifferently. "It's your ship." The captain, who had only asked out of politeness, entered the maintenance shaft and stood, hunched slightly to look down at Elios. He, like most of the crew, was too tall to stand up straight when speaking to Elios. Elios considered this one way in which he was superior to the crew. Apart from Tongues and Moncello, Elios was the smallest on board, he was the smallest adult on board by far. All of the crew were in their fifties at least, but none of them looked much older than Elios, who was only twenty-two. This was a badge of honour to Elios, he believed this showed he didn't have a comfy upbringing and had experienced real life.

"What are you doing hiding in here?" the captain asked, not accusingly, more as if he were genuinely interested. He leaned against one of the protruding bulkheads and placed a hand on knee trying to balance himself in a way he could keep eye contact with Elios.

"Keeping out of the way," Elios answered, keeping his voice in check and willing himself not to snap. "I've already annoyed Adrian, snapped at Tongues and upset Tetriana with some chopsticks and a mace. All that in one day! I mean, why do you have a mace on board?" Jack grinned but didn't answer. Elios shook his head, managing to half-smile back at him. Jack was suddenly serious.

"Look, I know it's difficult for you being here," he said quietly. Elios scoffed. Difficult was an understatement. "You have to adjust to a new place and socialise with people who view the universe very differently to you."

"And then you take away **The Drug**," Elios muttered, accusingly. Captain Jack's jaw tightened as he slightly adjusted his head in the way of a disapproving teacher.

"You've been clean for eight days now, Elios," he said quietly. "And, thanks to Emily's medicine, you haven't even started sweating, yet."

"True," Elios had to admit, drawing out the word as if trying to find some flaw in Jack's statement. Normally even going without **The Drug** for five days would have sent him over the edge. Another wave of pain tore at him. The captain watched him sympathetically. "You don't know what I'm going through," Elios told him, staring into his cup.

"I do." He said, raising his eyebrows revealing a caring smile.

"Then why won't you help me?" Elios shouted. Suddenly he stopped and looked down, surprised. He was standing closer to the captain, fist poised, not really sure how he'd got there. Breathing heavily, Elios let his arm drop. The captain blinked at him. Elios backed away, ashamed and afraid. "I'm sorry, Captain, I'd better go." And Elios turned and ran out of the maintenance shaft.

Jack let him go, unsure of what had just happened. Maybe Elios was further gone than he showed signs of. As Jack left the maintenance shaft, he momentarily contemplated letting Elios have some of **The Drug**, but decided against it. Elios would be fine, he just needed some time alone to cool down.

Chapter XXX

AFTER ALL THAT HAD happened since Tetriana left the *Sanitarian* she needed to think. After their first conversation Jack had been kind enough to show her where the gym was and give her access to the equipment she wanted to use. As her guns had been disabled by the ship, her equipment of choice was her hands, and her training of choice was fighting. If there was one thing Tetriana could do without much thought, it was fighting. She stood on the spot, stretching every muscle she could before doing drills of sprinting and jumping, which would be impossible for a planet-based person to carry out. And this was just her warm-up.

"Computer, fight options!" Tetriana demanded, not even fazed by the work she had already done.

"It is customary to refer to VIs by their name," EVI responded, her pleasant tone not matched to the rebut.

"That may be true in the Federation, but we are in the Republic, and you are a machine, nothing more." Tetriana retorted, an undertone of disdain. Never before had a computer chastised her, and a computer should never talk back to a flesh and blood person, she thought. "Now, do the job you are programmed to!"

"I must really insist, if we are to have a mutually respectful relationship then courtesy would be advisable." The VIs tone still unchanged, like a well-trained head teacher reprimanding a child.

Tetriana gritted her teeth, deciding that it was not worth the fight at this point, but she would have to take it up with Jack later, "Fine, EVI."

She started, her tone the same dismissive tone she would use to talk to any computer. She sighed, and tried again semi sarcastically, "EVI, what fighting options are there?"

"There are nine levels of fighting. One being easy, nine being most diffi-cult." The VI answered, with what Tetriana was sure was a mocking tone. Tetriana hated the idea of being mocked by a computer. Republic VIs would never be allowed to mock real people. In fact, Republic VIs would rarely have the capability to mock. The Republic did use VIs and very few basic AIs but they were both heavily restricted so as to keep them in check.

"Level nine, and remove the safety and security precautions."

"To remove safety and security precautions command privileges are re-quired." The VIs voice stated matter of factly.

Tetriana sighed. She hadn't fought against a holograph with precaution active since she was twelve, and the thought of doing so now was insulting to her. But she wasn't likely to convince the hosts of the ship to allow her to disable the precautions. "Give me six to fight, and don't hold back on the skill."

"Understood." At once, six faceless black figures came into being, stand-ing in a circle around Tetriana.

The figures came to life and began to fight. Two came at her. one from the front and one from behind. Before they had reached her, Tetriana had begun to plot their demise. She grabbed one hand of each of the figures and, using their own bodies, she destroyed the two hard-light beings. The remaining four rearranged themselves around their target, as if learning from the death of two of their own. A third decided to make its move and, unlike the last, it had chosen to go for a low attack. In one swift move, Tetriana kicked the being in the chin sending its head and neck backwards, but this didn't even slow it down.

"Oh! Nice move, EVI, sacrifice the easy ones to find my style." She landed another blow into her opponent's chest. "But it will not work." With these words, Tetriana sent the being hurtling backwards where it hit the wall and without warning vanished.

It was Tetriana's turn to move around the room. She ducked and dodged one of the figures until she managed to get into a position where she was directly facing the remaining three foes. After several seconds of standing, eyeing each other up, a fourth finally decided to make a move and came at Tetriana. She tried to meet it with a one-hit knockout but was forced onto the defensive. This didn't matter to her, it made the time more enjoyable, and made it last longer. After some well-placed blows, Tetriana sent the being hurtling backwards.

The door that Tetriana had entered by hissed once more announcing someone's arrival. A rather emaciated, young boy entered the room just as the flying black figure hit another causing both to vanish. Tetriana shot the new visitor a look so cold it seemed to freeze him to the spot. This short pause was enough for the remaining figure to make its move on her and to successfully throw a punch. Before the thing's fist could meet her skin, Tetriana grabbed the fist and hurled the faceless figure across the room. The creature stood up not far away from the boy. Tetriana and her final foe locked into a bout of fighting. After several minutes of intense fighting she plunged her hand in towards it's chest and straight through. The being dissolved between Tetriana and the young boy, leaving Tetriana looking down at the boy with her fist less than a hair's width from his nose and a look of fear on his face.

Tongues stared, cross-eyed, at the large, tightly clenched fist that remained immobile in front of his face. For a while, he did nothing else. Slowly it occurred to him to take a deep breath and edge backwards, flattening himself against the wall so as to gain a little more space between him and the fist.

With the extra space, he was able to glance over the fist and up into the face of its owner. It was a face unlike any other he had seen. All minimalist precision and ruthless efficiency. The cold, blue eyes gave the impression that the woman, was quietly and calmly calculating whether it would be worth wasting energy to speak to him.

Indeed, he was right, Tetriana had recognised this boy when she first spotted him. He matched the description of the test subject she was hunting not long before she was taken by her captors. It was clear to Tetriana that these people had also taken the boy captive, but now looking at him, she was unsure why. Given all the hassle this one child had caused, she was left asking if she could bring herself to speak to him.

The woman was intimidating, in a way the Adults and the B4 children had never managed to be. It wasn't her motives, or what she would necessarily do to him, that froze the saliva in his throat when he tried to swallow. It was what she could do. This was an adult with ability. This was an adult who could be useful, who could get things done. Elios had been intimidating enough with his lifetime of real-world living skills, Tongues thought, but this woman must have had training and this intimidated him more.

Tongues tried to unstick his mind, and as seemed to generally be the case, Tongues's brain eventually answered with what was probably the wrong answer.

"What in the name of all that is holy do you think you're doing?" he demanded. The woman scowled, over her outstretched fist that she had not yet decided to retract.

"I am training. Or trying to, except the VI here does not seem to go up to my level. If I had wanted tactically unskilled weaklings who politely attacked one by one, that would have been what I asked for. However, I was about to ask you the same question, Cadet."

"Cadet?" repeated Tongues, raising a confused eyebrow to mask his fear. "Do you think they would let someone of my disposition sign up for service?" Tongues said, sarcastically, before he could stop himself. "I happen to be a common civilian. You are military, I understand that makes it your job to protect and serve me." He could hear each word come out but did not know how to stop it. Like some kind of psychosis where he could watch himself but not control himself.

The woman straightened up, folding her hands behind her back, although she did retain her accusing look. Tongues noticed with some alarm that her hair was not the same colour as it had been originally. He was sure it was some shade of purple when he walked in and it was definitely now red.

"My loyalty," the woman informed him, "according to my oath, is to the Republic and the safety of her people. I am only currently operating on this ship due to," she paused, appearing to consider her next words carefully, "unusual developments."

"Right," agreed Tongues, trying very hard to force his body to stop shaking. "Well, by birth and breeding, I am one of the Republic's people, and I doubt they disowned those onboard when they flung *Tomorrow's Hope* into the Great Unknown."

The woman's irritated stare lessened abruptly. "So you were the subject from the *Tomorrow's Hope* project?" she asked, as Tongues confirmed her belief.

The woman's scowl returned, but she turned away from him. "Unless you have training of your own you wish to do, I suggest that you leave this room and do not bother me again until I am finished," she told him. Tongues decided that now would be a good time to finally give in to the urge to flee. As he did so, he could hear the woman's voice before the closing door cut it off, "EVI. Increase opponent number. Increase opponent skill. Recommence."

Chapter XXXI

Moncello had taken it upon himself to explore his new spaceship home. His investigation took him eventually to the reading room within which Tongues was endeavouring to stay out of everyone else's way. The boy was quietly scribbling away in a notebook he had acquired from Adrian, writing words that would likely never be read. He shot a cautious glance towards the monkey as it hopped his way up onto the table and regarded the human with his head cocked. Tongues hesitated.

"Um," Tongues began, "hello," Moncello blinked. Tongues sighed. "Even you're taking all this crap in your stride," he muttered nodding at his tablemate. "And you're a monkey." Moncello padded closer to the boy and sat in front of him. Tongues looked at him for a few seconds, and then looked down, his shoulders slumping slightly. "But then," he continued, still apparently speaking to the primate, "you don't have some inexplicable message floating around your head. And for some reason others on this ship think it makes me special."

Moncello's eyes regarded him with vacant attention. Tongues looked back up at him, exhaled at length and brushed the smooth red hair from his eyes. He wasn't used to smooth hair. It seemed to get in his way all the time without the dirt to keep it in place.

"I don't know how to be special," he said quietly. Moncello made a vaguely concerned clicking squeak. Tongues hesitated, reached out tentatively, and stroked the space monkey's head. "Do you know how I survived *Tomorrow's Hope* for so long?" he asked. Moncello gave no reaction.

Tongues sighed. "Of course not," he said. "You don't even know what that is." He moved his hand, stroking the monkey's fur.

"I wasn't disciplined as much as everyone else," he said. "Wasn't disciplined, wasn't bullied, was barely noticed. I don't think I could've taken it. I'd have been one of the weak ones that just stopped turning up to lessons and was eventually forgotten. It happened occasionally. Nobody liked it much."

"I got lucky," he scowled, sarcastic bile seeping into his tone, "by not being interesting enough to die. They had no reason to bully me because I gave them no material to work with. I rarely got disciplined because it took a while before the Adults remembered I was even there. I survived," he spat, word by word, "by being excessively dull. If I was special, I wouldn't be here." Moncello started to shrink away, his expression going from vacant concern to confused worry. Tongues removed his hand and gazed at the animal. "And they don't make self-help books for stuff like this," he added, more softly. "I checked."

The door opened. Both boy and monkey whipped their heads around to see who was entering.

"Moncello?" exclaimed Elios, stepping inside. The monkey scampered happily to him. Elios looked up at Tongues.

"I," Tongues hesitated, "sorry," he gabbled. Elios frowned slightly and raised an eyebrow.

"Moncello's old enough to look after himself," he replied. "Pretty sure talking to him ain't a crime. And if it was, it wouldn't be his first anyway." With that Elios turned and exited monkey in tow.

Tongues laughed, thinking to himself, I've hit it off with a single person on-board this ship, and it's a self-reliant space monkey, before continuing with his scribbling.

Chapter XXXII

A Republic Service Station

THE *ELISMERE* CREW were pretty sure that right now nobody was directly after them. It would take a while for the Gate to discover and process the destruction of the Sanitarian, and even longer to work out that the *Elismere* had escaped intact. As no additional outbound transmissions were detected during the battle and there were no other ships about, as far as anyone on-board could tell, the only reliable witnesses to the event were all conveniently aboard the *Elismere* herself.

This state of being off the radar was one that the *Elismere's* crew was not expecting to see again, not for a long time. Now they had gained confirmation of a pursuit and a respite from it, at the same time. A mix of Federation research and Tetriana unintentionally supporting, had given the *Elismere's* command confidence in this earned grace period. Tetriana had accidentally let slip that the Sanitarian was in stealth mode, and the *Elismere* crew already knew that even the Gate cannot track a Gate ship in stealth mode. The Gate believed that, if they could track it, someone else would be able to intercept the tracking. Therefore, it would be some time before anyone would now be after them. But they knew this would be temporary, as their days of covert operation were effectively over.

That was why they had decided that, before the indefinite period of fleeing and hiding that would likely follow, it made sense to make the most of this one last period of anonymity, and the advantages it offered them. There was an *R3* service station near their current location, like a vast, decorative metal wheel eternally spinning around its own axle.

The ship docked and the crew disembarked without anyone attempting to capture or arrest them. They allowed themselves a little extra burst of optimism. It might not have been much cause, but the crew knew, in times like these, you had to grab all the happiness you could.

The crew broke off into groups and made their way to different sections of the station for their own purposes. There were far better places in the galaxy to get anything you could get here, stations like this so far away from normal civilisations were designed to pander to the needs of people who were too far away from anywhere to have any alternatives besides going hungry and insane and running out of fuel.

At least some of the crew intended to wrap up some business or trade dealings knowing they would likely not pass this way again. There were certain goods and services which some of them intended to buy. And it was a common thing for more than one to relax in a local café with a latté.

As the crew headed off in their own planned directions, those new to the *Elismere* began to group together.

Tongues had no first-hand experience of economics whatsoever, and had never heard of an *R3* station. But after some comforting from Susan that this station was self-enclosed and he could not get lost, he decided to go out on his own. The alternative was to follow Tetriana or Elios, both of which terrified him more than being on his own.

Elios had never been off-world and it hadn't really occurred to him before that places like this presumably existed. He tried to waste as little time as possible thinking about spacers and the little sheltered societies they ran. On reflection, he was starting to think that maybe wandering alone through a bunch of strange space-farers would be easier than spending time trying to put up with Tongues know-it-all use of language. His only other choice was the ever-unnerving presence of Tetriana, whom Elios doubted was ever anything except highly strung.

Before disembarking Jack had tried telling Elios that theft was next to impossible on the *R3* stations due to the enhanced security systems, but he was taken aback when all Elios appeared to take away was the term next to impossible. Ultimately Jack had decided that Tongues and Elios could not be trusted on their own. He didn't want a diplomatic incident where Elios would use Tongues as a distraction in order to steal from a stall.

Jack had also tried to convince Tetriana that all communication with the Gate would be blocked, but her incessant asking how the block would work made him realise she was not buying the deception.

Finally, realising he could not trust a single member of the group, he asked Susan to join him to chaperone the party.

"We used to stop off at places like this on the longer, more remote patrols," Tim was telling Tetriana, in an attempt to distract her from the bickering of Tongues and Elios while Jack and Susan defused the situation as best they could. "Not to mention the number of times we'd get called out to sort a disturbance at one of them or catch some high-class criminal operating from one. Good places to do shady business without arousing suspicion. Lots of people coming and going all the time, no one really paying that much attention to what they're doing so long as they keep buying and don't," He tailed off, clearly distracted by something, "don't cause trouble," he continued, Tetriana followed his gaze curiously.

"Speaking of which," Tim muttered, gazing surreptitiously at a handsome man seated at a table in a nearby eating area. The man had dark hair, beard and suit. Something niggling at the back of Tim's mind told him that he was also dark in his intent.

"Do you know him?" Tetriana asked. Tim found it hard to tell if she was actually interested, but he was glad that she was at least paying attention to him rather than reacting to Tongues and Elios. He also promised himself that at some point he would find a Terineti expert and brush up on how to read their emotions. Years of patrolling an area of space mostly void of Terineti had left him unable to remember what it meant when Tetriana's hair turned pink at the tips as it was doing now.

"I've definitely seen him before somewhere," Tim replied, returning his gaze to the man he recognised. "I'm sure I know someone that's tried to catch him. Someone in one of the other warden departments." He screwed his face up in thought, "I just can't remember which one."

"I could capture and interrogate him for you," Tetriana suggested. Tim glanced around.

"That." he paused, "Would be a bad idea,"

While Tim and Tetriana were engrossed in their discussion, Susan was busy buying drinks and Jack was distracted looking at someone else over the other side of the large, bustling room. Tongues and Elios, it seemed, had used this opportunity to rekindle their argument. As a result of something Tongues had said, Elios finally had enough and grabbed Tongues by the collar, lifting him off the floor with surprising ease. Tongues shrieked, attracting the attention of several people seated nearby. A Terineti couple, who just happened to be passing at the time, dropped the tray they were holding causing both Jack and Susan to drag the squabbling pair apart.

"You know if you weren't able to resort to violence, I'd win!" Tongues spat tearfully.

"Yeah, well, welcome to real life, ya know-it-all," he retaliated. "There always is more to it than words."

"Elios," Jack hissed.

At the same time Susan barked, "Tongues!" Elios and Tongues glowered at each other with almost identical hurt expressions.

"Sorry, Captain," Elios said, slowly and just a little sarcastically.

"Sorry, Doctor," Tongues begrudgingly mimicked.

"Good boys," Susan nodded, softening slightly. "Now, since neither of you have been on a service station before, I realised that you would probably never have encountered Synthia's."

"What?" said Tongues.

"Huh?" said Elios.

"Exactly. They're one of the largest drinks companies in the galaxy, and there's a branch in pretty-much every service station in the Republic. They pride themselves on being able to synthesise hot drinks that taste as good as they would if they were made from natural ingredients. They don't quite manage it, of course, but, well, you should try some. See what food and drink tends to be like outside of spaceships or slums." She handed them each a disposable cup filled with frothy, strong-smelling liquid.

Elios judged it suspiciously. It smelled a little like coffee, but not like any coffee he'd ever smelled before. He took a sip.

"No bad," he nodded. "A bit too sweet, maybe, but I've drank a lot worse."

"Drunk," Tongues corrected, before downing most of his own and almost immediately half-spitting, half-regurgitating it back into the cup. Elios made sure not to let his joy of what he only assumed was karma show.

"OK," Susan nodded sympathetically as she took the cup from Tongues and patted him on the shoulder. "It looks like Tongues's body reacts badly to synthesised lattés. Good to know for the future."

Jack sighed and glanced back to the part of the room he'd been monitoring earlier, but he couldn't see the people he'd been looking at any more. He frowned, and turned back to the group.

"I don't suppose you recognise that guy over there?" Tim asked him, pointing out the handsome man in the dark suit. Jack shook his head.

"Doesn't fire a neuron," he replied. "Friend of yours?"

"No," Tim answered. "But I think he may be the enemy of a friend of mine."

"Hmm," Jack grunted, catching sight of a tall, limber man moving through the crowd not far from the man Tim had pointed out. He was headed vaguely towards them. Jack thought quickly. "OK," he whispered quietly enough that only Tim and Tetriana could hear him. "There's a man, white shirt, brown trousers, tan coat, headed roughly towards us at about your one o'clock. Make anything of him?"

Tim and Tetriana turned trying to appear like tourists looking around and spotted the man.

"Not really," Tim admitted. "Looks a little out-of-place though. Why?"

"Not long ago, he was across the other end of the room, talking to another man and a woman. I think I saw the woman glance deliberately in our direction. We made eye contact, briefly." He paused, gesticulating in a juxtaposed way to the conversation, clearly trying to hide the true nature to any onlooker. "You ever get the impression someone was sizing you up?"

"All the time," Tim replied quietly. "It happens as a warden. You think he's security? Or government? He's got no uniform."

"The Gate employs special operatives," Tetriana supplied. "They are said to be hand-picked and privately contracted. They were often the alternative if the military option ever failed."

"Have you ever known them to do so?" Tim asked.

"I have never known the military option to fail, if that is what you are asking." Tetriana replied curtly, prompting a shocked eyebrow raise from Jack. "And it has never been my place to speculate about failure."

"Hate to point out how we got here. But if you had to speculate about special operatives?" Tim prompted. Tetriana sighed towards him, a little irked.

"I have heard loose talk that they are significantly less professional. They clean up all their problems by killing and destroying everything linked to the problem in question. It is said that they are stationed all over the galaxy and perform missions of the most covert nature, answering directly to the highest most rungs of the Gate, not the government."

"The assassin network," Jack said, ominously. "I've heard similar tales myself. I think I've even seen some of their work. I think I've personally known some of their problems."

"What's the matter?" Susan asked, anxiously moving closer to the trio. Jack nodded sideways to the approaching man so as not to draw attention.

"Nothing yet. But things might be about to get much, much worse. Tetriana, do you think the Gate had assassins set up to follow us if you failed?"

"Captain Singer was fighting with our superiors in the Gate. She did not give any details, but it is possible her failings to find you were being highlighted further up the chain." Tetriana pondered aloud. "But, if the Gate had assassins already assigned, they were planning for us to fail." Her tone was now one of annoyance again, the idea the Gate would not have complete faith in Singer and her crew, was never something she had previously had to contemplate.

"Could they have found us already?" Tim asked, now growing more scared. "Could he be one of them?"

"It is possible," Tetriana admitted. "If they had better resources with which to track you than Captain Singer had."

"I think they probably do," Jack said, exchanging a look with Susan.

"However," Tetriana continued, "the fact that we have seen him means these men are unlikely to be Gate trained operatives. When the Gate wishes to be secretive, it succeeds. When it does not wish to be secretive, it does not send special contractors, it sends people like myself. For now, I think we can assume safety."

Jack nodded, breathing heavily but with a sense of relief. Susan turned back to check on Tongues and Elios. Tim scratched his cheek and opened his mouth to say something to Tetriana.

A woman sitting alone at a table near the approaching man pushed her chair out, stood up and made to barge past the man. The man's head did not waver from facing directly forwards, but his arm shot out straight to the side, catching the woman in the face so that her head was snapped to the side. There was a blur of movement as he placed a second hand on the side of her face, he appeared to guide her back to her seat. The woman's head lolled oddly as she slumped limply into the chair.

Tim and Jack swore simultaneously. Tetriana blinked. The rest of the tables and servers either didn't notice or didn't want to get involved in whatever was happening.

"Susan, get these four back to the *Elismere* and arrange to have her leave immediately. I'll contact the crew and get them back here. Everyone try to look natural," Jack ordered immediately, and Susan, Tim and Tetriana lost no time in turning to walk back the way they had come, Susan urging Elios and Tongues along in front of her, urgently silencing their protests.

Although no one noticed him talking, the tan-coated man spoke carefully into a hidden communication device without even moving his lips enough to be picked up.

"They've seen me. They're on their way. Expect the ship on the move within five. All of them in one shot, as expected."

Chapter XXXIII

THE *ELISMERE* SHIP herself seemed on edge as she undocked from the *R3* and made her first jump. She could outrun and outmanoeuvre almost any ship out of almost any catalogue, but assassins of this calibre did not tend to use ships that could be found in any catalogue. They were colloquially known as *Ninjas*. Super-fast, highly advanced ships, with the kind of weapons even the best loophole lawyer could only get by illegal means. With cloaking technology so ingenious the only way to tell where they were was to look in the direction from which you were being shot. By which time it was almost always too late. Those who knew of their existence kept their mouths shut, and those who didn't keep quiet were branded mad and often disappeared.

Nothing conventional could outrun a *Ninja*, and no ship had ever been known to survive a fight with one. It was simply suicide. The only hope was to confuse them and even that would only hold them off for a while. The ship came out of FTL, executed a dangerously imprecise 320° turn and jumped again. Everybody on-board at least flinched. Jenny shook her head for a moment to clear it before launching herself back into a series of rapid navigational calculations. Elios staggered comically into a wall, and Tongues simply yielded to the unfamiliar sensation and collapsed sprawling on the floor. Tim didn't seem to notice much. He was busy running something on a hand-held warden-issue computer.

"I don't believe it!" he yelled, frustrated, when the thing in his hand bleeped. Those not otherwise occupied turned to him. "That guy on the rest station," he hissed. "The one I recognised. It's Jarett Pastornak. Possibly the only person ever to anger the Galactic Police's Illegal Trading Department more than the Federation!"

"You obviously don't have our full record," one of the crew muttered half chuckling. Tetriana, however, was clearly more interested.

"What does he trade in?" she asked.

"People," Tim paused, his face growing queasy, "Girls, mostly," he said with distaste handing Tetriana the full report. A sudden heavy chill fell over the room as several of the surrounding crewmembers went very quiet. There was the slight judder of another FTL jump sequence.

"I say we go back," insisted Tetriana. "He is a sitting duck. We have someone with the authority to arrest him. For all we know, no one will have a chance like this again for years." Nobody answered.

"Why," Tongues stuttered, "why girls?" he finally asked, his brow furrowing as he tried to keep up. Again, nobody answered, this time for a different reason.

It was Elios who eventually replied, shaking slightly with the visible effort of containing his own anger. "How could you not know," he spat the words with a kind of knowing disgust, staring down at Tongues, "you aren't possibly so much a know-it-all and not know the basics!" He hissed, appearing to try and coax Tongues on.

Tongues stared, blankly, then frowned. Behind him, a couple of crewmembers winced. Even Tetriana's face twitched a little as the boy's expression changed, his mind drawing connections that he'd never had reason to draw before. His mouth opened, but nothing was said. He gestured slightly, as if to protest or object, but found no words. Disgust, horror, rage and despair battled on his face for control of his expression. Finally, he threw his head back and screamed a volley of obscenities into the sky.

"We must go back," he spat, and purposefully fled the room.

"Thank God," Jenny muttered once the door had closed behind him. Tetriana shot a look at the back of her head and left, Tim following. There was silence, broken only by occasional grunts of discomfort as the manoeuvres continued.

"Tom Childe's aunt was taken by slavers," Adrian noted eventually, his hands almost blurring across controls as he constantly adjusted the *Elismere's* ECM in an attempt to keep her invisible to even her own sensors, and hopefully those of the *Ninja's* in pursuit.

"Who's Tom Childe?" Elios asked.

"Someone whose aunt did not deserve to be taken by slavers," Adrian replied.

Tetriana and Tim found Tongues sat in a corner, rocking slowly back and forth, clutching Moncello, who for his part at least looked slightly more sympathetic than usual. They exchanged glances and approached him slowly. He sniffed.

"Val sometimes had trouble walking," he said, just on the verge of audibility. "I mean, she was bruised all over, so I never thought anything of it, but," he sniffed again, tears now slowly wandering down his face. "They were trying to make her less happy. They tried everything. Everything." Tetriana and Tim exchanged a pained look. Tongues looked up at them. "What did they do to her?" he whispered. Neither could answer, not through lack of knowledge. "What did they do to her?" he wailed. Tetriana's hair slowly faded into a deep orange colour. Tim stepped forwards and gently embraced him. Moncello gratefully slipped free and scampered off to find Elios.

Eventually, Elios walked in. There were occasional grunts of concentration from behind him as the crew tried to stay one step ahead of an enemy that had already apparently prepared for the next three steps.

"The cap says the crew would like to go back, but they're all needed to keep us alive right now," he said, with a half-shrug.

"I understand," Tim said, obviously dejected, but hiding it well.

"Good," replied Elios, producing his transporter.

"What are you doing?" Tetriana asked.

"I told you. The crew want to go back, but they're all busy. So we're going instea—" The entire ship shuddered, cutting Elios off. Alarms were howling as she dropped out of FTL well before she should have.

Jenny's voice came over the intercom. "All hands, brace for evasive action!" Sudden motion threw the four across the small hold they were standing in as the *Elismere* spun faster than her gravitics could handle, and she jerked as her shields took a glancing hit and died.

Jenny peeked at her sensor boards and swore vilely as she threw the *Elismere* into another series of wild manoeuvres, crackling beams of light lancing through her flight path as she spun through multiple axes to avoid them. "Adrian, find out how they pulled us out of FTL. I know it's possible, but I want a defence against it," she reeled off, eyes never leaving her console as the *Ninja* came into view in their forward display. It was a hazy, inconsistent shape visible at all only because it had just expended so much energy in hauling another vessel out of FTL. "Glen! Weapons!"

"Still offline due to that uncontrolled downsync. And even if we had them, they have a defensive field that makes our energy weapons useless."

"The next one we run into, I want them in pieces," Jen growled. "Salvage rights bypass technological restrictions." A waterfall diagram built on her display, showing the estimated charging cycle of the *Ninja's* weaponry as analysed by EVI. She tapped her comm again. "Brace for jump, this might be bumpy."

"Jen," Adrian said worriedly, "what are you doi—" Adrian started before being ruthlessly cut off by his sister.

"Dealing with this problem. Just pray our calculations are correct." A warning flashed up on one of her screens and her hands danced over the keys below it, sending another message to every screen on the bridge:

FTL SAFETY PROTOCOLS DISABLED

Jen's eyes narrowed on the scrolling meter showing the distance between the *Elismere* and the rapidly approaching *Ninja* as the waterfall diagram at the side of her display peaked. They were only alive now because these assassins could generally afford to wait for a guaranteed kill shot. That and the fact the earlier attack hadn't killed anyone. Which was likely just to tire her out. With a bit of luck, the *Ninja's* tactical complacency would last long enough for Jenny to take advantage of it. It wasn't much, but it was the only chance the *Elismere* and her entire crew had.

Jenny flung the *Elismere* up onto a wingtip, spinning up out of the line of fire as particle beams and mass drivers spat death, a distraction while the

Ninja's main weapon recharged. The fire hissed at the edge of her frantically rebuilding shields for a heart-stopping moment, but then she was out of arc and on top of her foe. The *Ninja* fired. Jenny hit the jump drive.

The *Elismere* vanished in an indescribable surge of colour unrecognisable to the human eye as she flashed into FTL. Unfortunately for the *Ninja*, she was just a little too close.

The prow section of the *Ninja's* hull warped, metal seeming to flow inwards like a fluid. A fluid that was rapidly leaking, crumpling into nothingness as the edge of the *Elismere's* drive field pulled it out of synch with the rest of the universe. It crumpled further, solid metal screaming a silent protest through the emptiness of space. Armour and personnel suddenly pulled into hyper as alarms screamed throughout the vessel. Blast doors coming apart even as they slammed desperately shut against the encroaching vacuum. Atmosphere poured in torrents from the front of the *Ninja* vessel, the outward deluge of gases sending bodies bouncing down the corridors into open space. For a second, everything seemed suspended in this tortured vision of Hell.

And then the hyper field's effect vanished, and the ship's overpowered structural integrity field pulled the section of hyper that had been its hull back into normal space. The resulting eruption of energy was so violent that it scarcely could have been called an explosion.

"OK, what the hell was that?!" Elios shouted at the first crewmember through the door.

"Not entirely sure myself," the crewmember replied, brusquely. "At a guess, the assassins can somehow disrupt hyper, gravity manipulation maybe, or some sort of quantum flux, long enough to pull us out of FTL for a bit. We've corrected the issue and returned to our evasive pattern."

"So they're still after us?" Tongues swallowed nervously.

"Not exactly. From what I can work out, Jenny just made the transition to hyper through their ship."

"Ouch," Tim winced. He knew the theory of what happened to unstabilised solid matter when it got too close to a hyper jump. He wasn't sure he was entirely comfortable with the thought of doing it in practice.

"So they're not still after us?" Elios concluded hopefully.

"Not those ones," Tetriana replied, in a gruff but somehow oddly off-hand manner.

"Assassins never work alone," the crewmember explained.

"Oh good," Elios smiled, with a barb of sarcasm so sharp it could have shattered glass. Tongues whimpered.

"Doesn't change our plan in any way, though," Tim announced. "As I understand things, Mr Bennett, your device, at its maximum range, will be enough to get us safely inside the station somewhere we won't be seen?"

"EVI's programmed the nav systems to drop us out just in range of the bathrooms," the crewmember supplied helpfully. "You'll be setting off from up against the wall of the hold through here." She led them through a door in the far wall. "Jack would like you to take Tongues, he understands it is dangerous, but he will be safer with you, off the ship. This is our fight, not yours."

"All right," Tim said, stopping mid-word to steady himself after another particularly dangerous evasive manoeuvre by the ship. "It's a pity we have no time to make a better plan, but we can pull this off. You ready?"

"Confirmed," Tetriana nodded, her gaze set and steely. Her hair stable on blue for the first time since leaving the Gate.

"Yeah, sure," Elios shrugged. "Let's go give the universe's scumbag count a much-needed lowering."

Tongues nodded with a confidence he didn't feel.

"Good," Tim nodded. "We'll deal with the slaver while your people deal with the assassins. What's your name, again?"

"Adena," the crewmember replied. Tim nodded again.

"Goodbye, Adena," he said. "Please try not to break too many laws while I'm gone. And," he paused, "try to come back in one piece." The ship shuddered as it dropped into real space. Elios activated the transporter. Tim took an instant to wonder how he was going to get off the station assuming the *Elismere* was destroyed in the interim, before the arm linked with Elios's dragged him out of the ship and out of conventional existence.

"Capture team transported, Captain," Adena reported from the cargo hold. "We're clear."

"Got it Adena, now get to your station," Jack responded before opening up a shipwide broadcast channel. "All hands, the capture team is away. I know our prayers go with them." His voice changed, hardening into the voice of a captain protecting his own. "They'll deal with Pastornak. Now we need to deal with the potential of other *Ninjas*. We have basic scans on some of their tech and we're working on a defence system against their hyper disruptor. Activate all combat systems." He closed the channel and nodded to Jenny. "Find us somewhere to dance."

"With pleasure," she smiled thinly. "I know just the place." Jenny tapped her board and the *Elismere* boosted away from the *R3* station. There was a blinking flicker of light, and she vanished like a soap bubble in the breeze.

Chapter XXXIV

Republic Service Station

Elios, Tetriana, Tim and Tongues bounced into existence in the middle of a bathroom floor. The experience was uncomfortably like driving a wheeled vehicle over a sheet of corrugated iron. Tim and Tetriana both pulled unsavoury faces. Tongues stumbled, just about managed to keep his feet and clutched his own temple. While Elios appeared to be unphased by the experience.

Tetriana continued a conversation started on the *Elismere*, "I still do not understand why we are bringing Tongues along." She looked pointedly at Tim.

As if ignoring Tetriana, Tongues exclaimed, "Ouch! What sort of needlessly under engineered transportation system did we just take?" He thought back to his exit off of *Tomorrow's Hope* and found this jump to somehow be worse.

"I don't think there is more than one kind," Elios sighed. Tongues responded by throwing up at his feet. "Oh come on," Elios muttered. "There was a sink right there."

"You heard Adena, Tetriana. He will be safer here with us than on that ship," Tim replied, finally getting his composure before turning his attention to Tongues and Elios, "Gentlemen," he interrupted. "We don't know exactly how long we have. The very fact Pastornak is here means he's likely in the middle of a deal. If we catch him in the middle of that, he'll have a hard time wriggling out of it. I happen to have the means to record him, but first we need to find him."

Remarkably, nobody reacted to a group of mismatched travellers emerging from a corridor they had not previously entered. Tetriana and Tim sent looks to the other two and headed off. Tongues swallowed nervously and hesitantly set off in a third direction. Elios walked off in a fourth without so much as a shrug.

Chapter XXXV

THE TENSION WITHIN the ship was so intense that it could have been cut with a knife as she sped through hyper, EVI overseeing the execution of the course that she'd helped Jenny plot, but as Jennifer followed Adrian through the corridors to the weapon bay, the tension around them ratcheted higher still. They stepped through the doors and nodded to the two technicians working as the ship shuddered out of and back in to Hyper.

"Rick, Samantha," Jen said curtly. The two looked around, saw the looks on their superiors' faces and immediately locked down their stations and filed out. Samantha turned as she exited.

"Jen, Adrian, you and the Captain know that we'd follow you into Hell itself. I just hope you know what you're about to do here." She tapped a stud on the control panel and the door slid shut with the firm *thunk* of a good seal. Jenny looked at her brother and sighed.

"So do we, Sam." Then she straightened and walked to the main control panel, Adrian beside her. "All right Adrian, let's do this, before I lose my nerve."

"Got it, sis." Adrian's hands flashed over the panel before him, bringing down the false layers that lay between the standard user interface and Elismere's Virtual Interface core to bring up her full weapons' loadout. Very few of the crew had seen this list, and there was a reason for that. Text scrolled across the screen.

Twelve Grade four, four particle beam batteries [Enabled]

Twenty Grade four, five point defence laser arrays [Enabled]

Twelve Grade four, five plasma repeaters [Enabled]

Ten internal missile racks (various warheads ranging Grade three to zero) [Enabled]

Six Grade four/five mass accelerators (various armaments) [Enabled]

Two Grade five, five particle projectors [Enabled]

One Grade X Planck string displacement system [Disabled]

Adrian tapped several more keys, isolating the last system on the list. "EVI, bring the String Displacement System online, Technical Code Six-Four-One-Gamma-Sanchez," he said.

"Secondary confirmation from cleared command crew required to activate SDS targeting and firing modules," EVI responded coolly and Jennifer cleared her throat.

"Activate the disabled SDS modules, Helm Code Three-Nine-Two-Iris-Theta," she said harshly.

"Majority command codes accepted, bringing SDS arrays to full readiness." EVI's tone was unhurried, as if totally unaware of the gravity of what she had just said, and Jen's composure cracked a bit as Adrian's hand came up on to her shoulder.

"Are you OK, Jen?" he asked gently and she grabbed his hand with hers, her grip incredibly tight around his wrist.

"I think you know I'm not." Her voice trembled slightly as she spoke, tears sparkling in her eyes. "I know we've known for over a decade that, eventually, it would come to something like this. But," Her voice trailed off.

"But it's different now that it's actually happening, isn't it?" She nodded jerkily as he spoke. "Jen, look at me." She looked around and the siblings' grass-green eyes locked.

Jen's posture slumped slightly, and then suddenly straightened, strength pouring from her brother into her. He smiled slightly, then pulled her into a quick hug. When they broke apart, they were moving again as one. Adrian brought up the defensive barriers that sat around the Elismere's molecular-circuitry heart and returned the control panel to normal functionality as Jen wiped her eyes and unsealed the door.

Adrian joined her. "You OK?"

"Yeah."

"All right then—-,"

"—let's do this."

Chapter XXXVI

Republic Service Station

Pastornak was sitting at a small table, idly nursing a half-empty disposable cup of something hot and marshmallowy. Elios took in the handsome, tanned slaver from an inconspicuous position a few tables away, pretending to search for a misplaced friend. The silver-haired man he was talking to was clearly older but, equally, Pastornak was clearly the superior in the relationship. The old man had the constant air of self-reassuring confidence of someone who knows that if things go wrong they have the weapons and skills to get out. Pastornak had no such aura. He didn't need confidence. He never needed to reassure himself of anything.

With much smiling and a touch of well-acted backslapping, the two got up. The older man adjusting his black suit with just a hint of awkwardness, and they both moved off. Elios muttered something about having caught sight of Daryl, being the first name he could think of, and moved after them, catching the door they had gone through and slipping through it.

Both men were naturally cautious, but Elios knew ways to get near to someone without being seen or heard. Had he wanted to, he was pretty sure he could have pick-pocketed at least one of them and got away with it. As it was, he just needed to be close enough to check whether or not this was the conversation they were looking for.

"Don't worry about the experience issue," Pastornak was pitching to the older man. "I assure you, despite her age I have heard no complaints. And I would hear them if they were there." Elios's lip curled in disgusted anger.

Suddenly, all thoughts of what he was supposed to be doing seemed to be temporarily mislaid.

"Then what is the downside?" the old man hissed. "I know you, Jarett. You wouldn't be selling her if there wasn't a problem." Pastornak shrugged.

"Well, of course. Nothing major, but she upsets the other girls by talking in her sleep."

"Talking in her sleep? That's it?"

"Well, yes," Jarett shrugged again, like it really didn't matter. "But it's a bit disconcerting, apparently. She only ever talks about one thing. The Tannhauser Gate, would you believe? Otherwise, a perfect model."

Elios had to physically strangle the disbelieving retort that was trying to force its way up his throat.

CHAPTER XXXVII

JENNY HAD INDEED found a place to dance. The location was one of the myriad uninhabited systems scattered throughout Republic space. A young, F-class star orbited by a radiation-blasted rock and two gas giants. But far more important was that this system was also one of the many places that the *Elismere's* crew had, almost twenty years ago in this case, added to their network of boltholes. A series of solar arrays scattered across one of the gas giant's rings fed power to a small thruster unit and gravitational repulsor that had been installed on one of the more sizeable asteroids. The thrusters held the asteroid in place in the ring system whilst the repulsor created a small field of clear space, just large enough for a ship that knew exactly where it was going to drop safely out of hyper. The *Elismere's* crew, unlike that of the *Ninja* pursuing them, knew that position down to the metre.

Many minutes had passed since Adrian and Jennifer had left to bring their weapon of last resort online, and now both were back on the bridge. Jen brought the *Elismere* out of FTL in a textbook zero-velocity down-synch, dropping them into normal space with barely a ripple of movement, and a probe fired out of a concealed tube in the ship's spine, taking up position so that it could feed its parent data on everything around her. Then Glen flicked a switch on his panel, temporarily disabling power core transfer to all ship systems. The *Elismere* couldn't do this for long without draining her capacitor banks, and it wouldn't hide them for more than a few seconds from the level of sensors a *Ninja* had. But that would be enough.

Chapter XXXVIII

T HE *NINJA* INTERIOR appeared misleadingly simple but was unexpectedly brilliant and was in this way reasonably similar to its own crew. The bridge was smaller than that of the Elismere, and looked less technical, but looks could be misleading.

Seven assassins stood or sat at their small white consoles, checking built-in display screens and tapping at built-in touch screens. The scene, you'd think, would have looked more at home in a scientific research laboratory. Research laboratories, however, are often not quite so deadly.

Another similarity between these particular assassins and their ships was that neither existed. There were no records of anyone on the ship anywhere in the universe. They had no addresses, no homeworlds and no names. They knew each other only by what they were.

Captain was an imposing man, standing a little under six feet tall and not all that much across the shoulders. His expression was one of permanent detachment, although it was unclear whether this was due to years of intense training or the fact that there was a deep scar running through the facial muscles to the left of his mouth.

Currently talking to him through the upper screen on his console was a woman he knew only as Commander. The small, wiry-framed woman had a similarly detached expression, but in her case there was just a hint of superior contempt hidden underneath. Of the two, a casual onlooker would have immediately assumed Commander would lose a straight fight.

It depended on the person's intelligence how long it took them to realise that she wasn't the one with the scar.

"What happened to the other?" Captain asked, referring presumably to the first *Ninja* which had disappeared from their systems.

"Immaterial," replied Commander. "You have instructions. Carry them out."

Captain would never show it, but he felt a little confused. If he hadn't known better, he would have interpreted the situation as implying that the other *Ninja* had been destroyed. Except that it was impossible to destroy a *Ninja*. Especially if you were a lightly armed cargo vessel.

"They've jumped again," announced a lean oriental man diagonally left of Captain, who was currently referred to as Tracker.

"Follow," replied Captain with a nod. "Gunnery, prepare a kill-shot."

The strong, silent form of Gunnery nodded once and tapped in a few commands on his lower console, readying the blast that would quickly and cleanly eliminate the cargo ship. Captain flicked a switch and the image of Commander's stern face disappeared, instantly replaced with a display of the *Ninja's* progress through hyper.

CHAPTER XXXIX

THE *NINJA* BURST out of FTL, its hyper field clearing it a path into the ring belt as it followed its prey into normal space. The hyper field dropped automatically, no longer needed, as the shields spun up. and things suddenly went very wrong. The *Ninja's* crew were not prepared for the situation the *Elismere* had thrown them into and had come out under full combat power, teeth bared before they even opened their eyes. As such, the hail of micrometeorites that smashed into them in the fractional moment between the ship's hyper field going down and their shields coming online were moving at approximately five percent of light speed. Shards of ice ranging in mass from tens of grams to several kilos smashed into the *Ninja's* armoured hull at almost fifteen thousand kilometres per second, shattering sensor domes, exposed weapons and, most importantly, many of the primary emitters for the ship's absurdly effective cloak. The ship rocked for a few seconds as the barrage hammered against its hull and Helmsman slammed it into an emergency stop as more rocks continued to shatter against its shields. And for a few priceless seconds, the *Ninja's* crew were more focused on what was happening to them then on paying attention to their target.

Power flooded back into the *Elismere's* systems as Glen deactivated the power-feed shunt and Jennifer twirled the *Elismere* like a dancer, spinning her around to line her sensors up on the battered *Ninja*. There was no trace of her previous fear in her face as she, Adrian and Jack all hit the same key on each of their consoles.

The String Displacement System was an experimental device that the *Elismere's* crew had obtained, for once, through straight-up piracy. The first, and to the crew's knowledge only working prototype of the system had been en route to a military testing ground with a laughably small escort for something as important as it was. One of Emily's contacts had acquired the transport's flight path and the *Elismere* had intercepted her in deep space. It had taken years to fully integrate the weapon into the *Elismere's* systems, and even longer to actually work out what it did, but it had been worth it.

The SDS worked on a level below atomic, isolating and removing the strings that held a particular section of reality together. In simple English, as Jack had demanded, the SDS displaced the section of reality on which it was targeted. To do so had required a targeting system that went beyond the cutting edge, able to penetrate all but the most advanced of cloaks, and the weapon's designer had surpassed himself in that. He had done a slightly worse job in dealing with the energy consumption problem, but there was really nothing more he could have done about that. Firing the SDS from the capacitor supply of the *Elismere* would drain her to the dregs, even with a power grid as advanced as her's, which was why it was designed to pull power from an array of capacitors that were effectively Grade X in their own right.

"Acquiring coordinates of hostile containment field generators." EVI's voice filled the bridge. "Generator locations estimated. Coordinates locked." On the viewscreen, the *Ninja* started to recover, sensor systems locking on to its quarry.

"EVI," Jack straightened in his chair as he spoke. "Command code Zero-Four-Nine-Seven-Omega-Cerys-Delta. Fire."

"Voiceprint accepted."

Even with the batteries supplying most of the energy for the shot, the lights all across the *Elismere* dimmed slightly as the SDS fired. But unlike most weapons, there was no visible beam of light, and no showy fireworks as the terrifying power of human science tore the fabric of creation asunder. There was only that sudden dimming of lights, and a huge pulse of energy from the *Ninja* as her reactor containment systems simply ceased to exist.

An overpowering white light exploded from every window and seam of the *Ninja* on the *Elismere's* screen and the unchained fury of matter-antimatter annihilation tore it apart.

Light vomited across the stars as the *Ninja* exploded, and the *Elismere* dove into the heart of the detonation. Her shields streamed fire holding strong against the explosion that sought to sunder their power, and she rocked from prow to stern as she passed through the shockwave. Grav beams lanced out, latching onto the larger pieces of debris around her and holding them steady as Adrian focused the *Elismere's* normal sensors, searching for salvageable technology. The scanners locked on to several sections of the hull, locating the telltale signatures of active technology and the tractors pulled them swiftly into the small holds beneath the *Elismere's* wings designed for salvage operations. The silence on the bridge was almost audible as Jenny closed the ports, swung them around into the area of clear space created by the repulsor and took them back into hyper.

Jack finally broke the silence, "Adrian, shipwide channel."

"Channel open," the younger man replied and Jack nodded in silent thanks.

"This is the Captain. I know you have a lot of questions and I will have answers for you the moment I have the chance to give them. But for now I have to ask you to trust me again. We need to get back to our capture team so that they have a way off that station and I need every one of you at your best in case there's another *Ninja* out there." He paused. "Even if there is, I doubt it'll come after us after we just blew two of its comrades into space-dust, but we can't risk being complacent, not with Gate assassins. Once we have the capture group back, we'll head for Leta and there I promise you that you will have your explanation. Carry on."

He nodded to Adrian again and turned to the members of his staff who hadn't known what was coming. "Emily, Glen, I think Jen, Adrian and myself owe you that explanation now." He sighed. "You know the military transport we intercepted a few years ago, the one that prompted our first redesign?"

"The one that my contacts found for us, you mean?" Emily questioned sharply and Jack nodded.

"Yes." He paused. "Let's just say that there was more on that transport than our current power source. I don't fully understand how it works, for that matter I don't think anyone but the person who built it could do that. But its effects," he stopped looking for the right phrasing, "its effects are quite simple when you strip away the technobabble around them."

"And what exactly are those effects?" Glen asked, his voice soft. "From what we just saw, I have a feeling they breach at least one interstellar treaty."

"They do," Jack said quietly, not even trying to avoid the strike. "Specifically certain clauses of the Ishatof-Kellerman Accords and most of the Treaty for Interstellar Sanctity."

"Which clauses?"

"Those pertaining to the targeted destabilisation of reality."

Glen swore fluently. "No wonder you chose a dead system, you could have destroyed us," he half-spat and then shook himself. "Sorry. That was uncalled for."

"But not unnecessary, given the effects involved." Adrian replied, taking up the thread of the explanation. "Believe me, that weapon scares me far more than anything else. Almost every part of its construction would classify as Grade X even now and regardless of its small, relatively speaking, area of effect, it's probably one of the most powerful weapons I've ever had the tentative pleasure of knowing about. There's not a shield it can't breach, nor armour it can't bypass, and it has a sensor system to match that power. It's tightly focused, only able to target one vessel, but in the last twenty years it's gone straight through everything I've attempted to fool it with, both active and passive." He shook his head. "But you asked what its effects were," he sighed. "I believe you know string theory, how everything in the universe is made up of tiny, vibrating strings even smaller than an atom. This device removes those strings, and the matter that they make up goes with them."

"But that's impossible! Permanently removing mass from the universe contradicts conser-," Adrian shook his head as Emily spoke and she stopped, cocking her head in confusion.

"It doesn't do that, not exactly. Think of it as an incredibly powerful, weaponised version of a long-ranged teleport with one hell of a targeting system. I don't think anyone but the person who designed it actually knew exactly how it worked. I certainly don't. All I know is what it does, and that its use will be detected, instantaneously, by any subspace scanner array within five light-years. That's one of the main reasons we had to go to a dead system, so we could use it without fear of detection. Regardless of the fact that it's been twenty-five years, I can't imagine that the military wouldn't still love to get it back. This was their only prototype and the scientist who built it committed suicide when they lost it. And as of yet, no one else can understand the equations behind this device. It's like trying to understand the hyper equations and not even a VI can help with these, EVI's tried."

"I still maintain that I could eventually crack them if I was to allocate the cycles to do so," EVI retorted.

"Hush you," Adrian replied with a smile. "Even if you could crack them, what good would they be to us?"

"As I have told you before, we cannot know that without knowing how they work," EVI said primly, and Jen laughed.

"You know, she does have you ther-," Adrian glared at her and she held up her palms in a placating gesture. "All right, all right, it's a sore spot. We can work on that." She stuck her tongue out at her brother, evoking a laugh from the rest of the crew as he shook his head resignedly. Jen opened her mouth to continue but a sharp tone cut her off and her amusement suddenly vanished behind a professional façade.

"I think we need to continue this conversation later, we're coming up on the station." Jack nodded.

"All right. Glen, tell Su to stand by for possible wounded. Adrian, keep our ECM on full. Ems, keep an eye on the sensors. If you see even a ripple."

"Got it," Emily responded easily, linking her display to the *Elismere's* sensor arrays.

"Medical is on standby for incoming casualties." Glen quipped.

"Stealth systems online, jump muffler online and prepped for immediate activation." Adrian chirped in.

"Transition into normal space in one minute. Adrian, get the muffler synced." Jen continued.

"Already done, Jen. Glen, divert auxiliary power to the stealth systems, we may well need it." Adrian replied.

"Redirecting power flows now, stand by." Glen chimed in.

"All hands, this is the captain, hyper drive deactivation in thirty seconds." Jack concluded, nodding to those around him.

Chapter XL

"WHAT?" TIM EXCLAIMED in disbelief at what Elios had just told the group about Pastornak's visit. "That is—" he paused unable to find the word, before trying "the odds there are—" and pausing again.

"Astronomical?" suggested Tongues flatly, trying to help. "Exorbitant? Unreasonable?" He was excited to know that another person had the same trigger as him

"This changes everything. It is not about Pastornak anymore. We have got to get that girl." Tetriana interrupted Tongues, partly hoping to stop him listing words. Either this girl had accidentally learned of the Gate or was one of those with the trigger, either way Tetriana needed to get her out of of Pasternak's control. It was at this point that Tetriana realised the mist and gate that appeared in her nightly nightmare, and the constant fights in her dreams were about none other than the Tannhauser Gate. Before she could process this another voice appeared.

"Are we really suggesting stealing a girl from under the nose of the most notorious slave dealer of all time?" Elios asked, with a raised eyebrow. "Just, you know, for clarification?"

"We don't need to steal her," Tim reasoned. "We just need to set up a buy for her. Record the conversation as we do so and kill two birds with one stone."

Elios stifled a sarcastic snort. "He won't sell her to you, Lance-Corporal," he said, mockingly adding his title.

"Why not?" demanded Tim, confused. "I have more than enough money to pay for a deal without background checks. I have forty-one years' worth of saved-up money sitting right now in an account I won't be able to access again once the paperwork for my death goes through. I might as well use it while I can. I have worked for long enough to know every trick used to identify people and how to avoid being identified, so what is the problem?" He finished, rather taken aback.

"Posture," replied Elios. "You hold yourself like a cop. Heck, you move yourself like a cop, too. An undercover cop, maybe, but people like me and people like Pastornak can still tell." Everyone was quiet for a while.

"What about me?" Tetriana asked. Elios looked at her.

"No, actually. You hold yourself more like a retired soldier. You could maybe get him to talk, if you were unarmed."

"Retired?" repeated Tetriana indignantly, and her hair shifted colour rapidly as she fought her obvious irritation. With the wonders of modern technology, many well-off Republicans still looked her age when they retired, but more important to Tetriana was the implication that she looked like someone who would ever retire from the military.

"Yes, Cap," Elios sighed. "Retired. Because active soldiers don't buy personal slaves." He paused just long enough to let that sink in before dropping the punchline, "They rent them."

Tim placed a quelling hand on Tetriana's arm with the reflexes of a terrified cobra as Elios continued thoughtfully.

"But the girl would be on his ship, and he wouldn't take a military figure in there alone. It'd be too suspicious," Elios continued, apparently taking up the position of Tim's new criminal psychology expert.

"Wh—" Tongues tried, before spitting out, "what if she had a kid?" Elios turned to him.

He wants to help, Elios thought, worried that it was going to get Tongues killed.

"That works for me," Tim nodded. "You two go in there and get the girl. We'll stay out here in case you need us. I know Pastornak by reputation, and he'll have set up his ship's defences so that only his own men can use any weapons, so don't get in a fight whatever you do." Tim turned from

Tetriana and Tongues towards Elios, "can you teach me exactly how that transporter works? I might need to use it to get us all out of here in a hurry."

Elios hesitated, it was the only piece of technology he really owned, and he didn't want Tim to break it. Slowly he nodded. Tetriana gave a curt, affirmative nod. Tongues forced a smile and nod and tried very hard not to shake. Tim took a deep breath and tried equally hard not to dwell on how many ways this could go wrong.

"So, Ms Tella," Pastornak began as he walked his new buyer to the unassuming, red-hulled ship he had arrived in.

"Captain," Tetriana insisted.

"Captain Tella," Pastornak corrected himself with a charming smile. "Of course. Discharged or not. You must forgive me. I'm unused to all the attention of two potential buyers at once. May I ask what you and the young man have planned for the purchase?" He shot a friendly wink at Tongues, who couldn't bring himself to fake a smile. Tetriana maintained her steely gaze.

"We have our purposes," she answered. Pastornak nodded delightfully.

They were ushered into a med-sized room filled with armed thugs. Tongues's eyes nearly doubled in diameter. Tetriana barely acknowledged them.

"I have the purchase right here," Pastornak smiled, crossing to the other side of the room and opening a small metal door. He removed his jacket and hung it on a hook projecting from the wall next to him. Underneath, he had slung across his right shoulder something amusingly and ominously similar to an ammunition belt. There was a dial at the shoulder with a graded scale around the edge, and at the hip end was a holster in which a ceramic-coated gun was held. From the back of this gun, a pipe snaked into a hole that threaded it into the ammunition belt itself.

This was a preferred weapon of many slave-traders, as it allowed you to control and punish rebellious products without necessarily damaging them permanently. It fired tiny, spiked, roughly spherical projectiles, which stuck into the target's skin and held there. Once connected to a target, these projectiles would administer an electric shock of a level of severity controlled by the shoulder dial. It could be used to hurt, torture, paralyse or kill depending on situation. From what Tetriana could see it was currently set to some point in the middle of the range.

Pastornak returned, leading what he had referred to as the purchase by the arm. He wasn't exactly rough, but he was just a little bit too firm for Tetriana's liking.

"This is Nubia," he smiled. Tongues quivering slightly. Tetriana's expression hardened a little.

Nubia looked to be somewhere in her late teens. She was small in stature and slim in frame, with long blonde hair and fairly pale skin that gave her a slightly washed-out look. Her hair had been painstakingly brushed and someone had recently given her a very careful make-up application. The overall effect was to make her look like an oversized China doll. She looked like she would break if dropped.

The worst bit for Tongues and Tetriana, however, was her expression. She didn't have one. Her face was completely indifferent to everything around her. This was her world, and she had long ago learned to accept it all without question.

"Would you be paying cash?" Pastornak inquired.

Tongues threw himself at the slaver, screaming in a frenzy of rage. Everyone in the room reacted in the same instant.

Pastornak moved his arm fluidly, his weapon now aiming not at the girl but at Tongues and fired. The thugs, having all identified who they knew as Ms Tella as the main threat, turned to fire at her. Unfortunately, the space where Tetriana had been an instant before was now empty.

The nearest thug was hit twice before he'd had time to process anything. The first blow to the abdomen caused him to double over instinctively. The second blow snapped his head back, blood spattering from his face. He was too distracted to prevent Tetriana relieving him of his weapon. By this point, some of the other thugs had noticed her and had time to aim. She jerked her body as they fired, the bullets missing and not by luck. She raised her arm sideways without looking and shot the thug beside her, spinning to grab a pistol from his belt. She dodged into roughly the centre of the room and raised both weapons at the lights.

Tongues was knocked back by an unidentified projectile and startled by the pain of the shock, but it was a pain he could ignore in his anger. He'd had worse in discipline sessions on-board *Tomorrow's Hope*. He threw himself again at Pastornak, who wasn't expecting a second assault.

As the last light went out, Tetriana adopted a stance she'd been trained for long ago, crouching in the middle of the room with her arms crossed, both pistols aimed outwards at approximately heart level. The thugs, unable to see, were forced to fire at where they thought she was. Tetriana, however, knew how not to be where people thought you were. She fired, again and again, adjusting position every shot without even having to consciously think about it. The shots and the shouting around her were blocked out by a professional efficiency. All that existed was her body, and her weapons, and the optimum positions required to kill all the guards in as short a time as possible.

Pastornak was unprepared, but Tongues wasn't a fighter. Blows were raining down at random from all four limbs, but none of them hurt much. Pastornak stumbled back and fell over, ironically saving them both from the maelstrom of bullets above. His own hand was knocked as he tried to adjust his shoulder dial, and the setting was knocked down to zero. Pastornak grunted in irritation and managed to push the mad ball of fury far enough away to get in a good punch.

Tetriana noted there were noticeably fewer noises from the remaining thugs. This didn't much matter, considering her techniques worked on any number of adversaries. The last few might take a little longer to kill, but that was all.

Pastornak cursed as Tongues flew backwards. He had hit the kid pretty hard in the chest, and it felt like he might have broken a finger. He jammed his right hand into his armpit to dull the sharp pain and reached up to twist the shoulder dial as far as it could go.

He only realised the painful irony of what had happened when it was far too late. Upon punching Tongues, he had transferred the little spiked projectile onto his own fist. The pain in his hand wasn't because he'd broken anything but because he had some tiny spikes through his skin. And he had just jammed it into his armpit. Which was adjacent to his chest.

His scream turned into a gurgle midway through as the maximum charge of energy the device could deliver seared through his chest cavity. Muscles around his chest contracted uncontrollably.

Pastornak hit the ground, twitching rapidly and sporadically as Tetriana's guns both ran out of bullets and she felled the last thug with a jab to the face. Tongues crawled over to the dead man and looked him in the eye. He could not tell if Pastornak was still alive and whether or not he could see him. Probably not, he figured, given the expression and the dull look to his eyes. He hoped the slaver could at least hear him.

"You, Jarett," he said in a shaking voice, "are an evolutionary failure." He tried to go on but was prevented by the smell of burning flesh.

There was a terrified whimper from the corner. Tetriana and Tongues both snapped their heads around. The girl could just be made out in the darkness. She wasn't expressionless now.

Tetriana knelt down and tried to give her a reassuring smile. "It is OK," she said. "We will not hurt you. You will be safe with us." The girl shrank as far away as she could and babbled something. "Pardon?" Tetriana said, backing off a little. Another babble. No identifiable words. Tetriana hesitated.

A spew of words that Tetriana would have sworn had never actually existed in any language came from behind her. She turned and saw Tongues standing up carefully and walking forwards. The girl replied in another spew of similarly incomprehensible words. The indecipherable conversation yammered back and forth for a bit. Tongues stepped forwards slowly and reached down. The girl reached up, hesitated and, on the third attempt, took his hand, still terrified but now willing to co-operate.

"It's a sort of Russian like language," Tongues explained to Tetriana. "Not very close to proper Russian, but enough that you can work it out. She's going to come with us. I'm explaining things on the way." He winced. "That's assuming my chest doesn't kill me. Nice gun work, by the way."

They ran into Tim and Elios coming from the other direction as they left the ship. Neither looked particularly calm.

"Station Security is on its way down," Tim exclaimed breathlessly. "They picked up Pastornak taking you inside, and they have apparently reason to believe a firefight took place." Tim panted before finishing, "What the hell happened?"

"A firefight took place," Tetriana answered bluntly.

A door on the far wall was promptly opened revealing two lines of security guards. Tetriana scooped the protesting girl into her arms, and they ran for the door furthest from that one.

"Stay close! Head for the far end of the docking ports." Tim yelled. The point in question was another docking park further down this edge of the station. Tim and Elios reached the door and opened it. Tetriana followed close behind, ignoring the bastardised-Russian protests from the girl over her shoulder who had now taken up punching Tetriana's back. Tongues was still quite a way behind, clutching his chest as he ran, and gave a frightened yelp. Tetriana made a sound somewhere between a sigh and a grunt.

"Hold her," she instructed, shoving the girl, who had now gone rigid and stopped protesting, into Tim's arms before running back. She had her arms ready to encompass Tongues by the time she reached him and was already executing a narrow turn as she swept him into an impromptu hold. Someone let off a shot, and Tongues yelped again. Tetriana gritted her teeth and put on a new burst of speed, reaching the door as Elios prepared to slam it shut.

They got out into a corridor lined on one side with windows out into space. They pelted down it as the guards filed out and ran after them. Luckily, they couldn't run more than two abreast in this particular corridor. Unluckily, the front two guards were both armed. As of yet, they didn't seem to be firing much more than warning shots. This would change, both Tim and Tetriana knew. It was only a question of when.

"Wait, guys!" Elios shouted as they ran. "There's a ship!" Three heads whipped around to gaze out of the window, eyes scouring the blackness for anything moving.

The *Elismere* slid out of hyper with barely a ripple, her stealth systems at full power. She decelerated smoothly towards the station in front of her and Adrian opened a comm link to their capture team.

"Tetriana, this is Adrian. What is your status?"

"It is the *Elismere*!" Tetriana confirmed.

"They're too far out," Tim announced, irritated. "At that speed, they won't reach us before the guards do. Not to mention the fact we won't even reach the hangar in time. *Elismere*, Prepare for immediate return," Tim shouted over a series of gunshots. "Just keep flying at that velocity for a few more seconds."

Jack leant forward in his chair. "I thought this was going to be quick and clean. What the hell is going on over there?" Jack demanded.

"Things became complicated," Tim said carefully. "I'll explain when I am not in immediate danger of death." Jack brought his hand up to hold his face and sighed heavily.

"Fine," he replied curtly. "I'm guessing from the gunshots that you aren't in a position to board normally, yes?"

"That seems very likely," came the reply. "I am dealing with it. Hopefully we won't appear inside a wall or something."

"Elios," Tim commanded, slowing down to come alongside him, "Give me the transporter and take the girl."

"Tim, they're flying towards us at a couple of thousand kilometres per second!" Elios protested. "By the time you switch it on you'd be dumping us into empty space!"

"Not if I get the maths right," Tim insisted, his calculating eyes focusing on the ship out of the windows as they blurred past. "And it's closer to five thousand." Elios handed Tim the transporter as Tim handed Elios the girl.

"Tim, we've locked on to your signal. Get to an observation deck!"

"We are kind of on one," Tim relayed. "But I am not sure we have time to say anything else," he said with a tone of concentration. "Done!" Static obliterated the transmission for a second and an alarm sounded.

"Captain, the capture team is aboard and they have a companion," Emily reported from her station and Jack nodded.

"Security to cargo hold C. Jen, get us the hell out of here."

"We're already gone." Jen's fingers danced across her display, compensating for the station's proximity as a streak of light shot from one of the *Elismere's* wings, curving around towards the station. And as the low power charge Jen had launched exploded over her target's outer ring in a muffled flash of light, she vanished into the maelstrom of hyper as every computer aboard the station simultaneously reset.

Chapter XLI

APPEARING INSIDE A MOVING ship with the transporter was possibly even less comfortable than leaving one. Thankfully, they had indeed avoided the possibility of appearing inside a wall and had instead appeared inside a cargo bay.

"Hmm," said Tim in a displeased voice. "I was aiming for the bridge." No-one in the group knew if his tone was one of humour or genuine annoyance at himself. The idea that Tim could have killed turned Elios cold.

Elios set the girl down gently and she immediately ran to the corner of the room and stared out at the rest of it in incomprehension. Tetriana dropped Tongues, who immediately sat down on the floor and tried to regulate his breathing. There was the recognisable judder of the *Elismere* leaping back into hyper.

Two armed security guards burst in and looked around. The girl in the corner squealed and tried to press herself further into it.

"It's OK," Tim assured the guards. "There's no one hostile here. We left Pastornak behind."

"We also left him dead," Tetriana added. "Feel free to wait outside until I am done here." The guards looked confused, but they left.

"Right," Tetriana said to Tongues. "Before we do anything else, I want to tell you that what you did back there was incredibly dangerous, really rather stupid and could have got at least three people killed." Tongues shrank away a little and gazed up at her for a second with an expression of fear and shame before regaining some sort of composure.

"I'm sorry, OK?" he replied, not looking at her. "I won't do it again."

"Well the next time we come across a high profile criminal I'll remember not to have a teenager as part of the team," Tim smirked, in an attempt to lighten the mood brought about by Tongues's tone. Tetriana sighed.

"I am going to report back to the command crew," she said. "There are a lot of things they are going to want to know. The girl does not speak English, we are going to need a translator. Tongues, you've been able to communicate a little, I'll ask the crew to find a proper translator."

The girl watched them leave and her gaze switched to the boy sitting in the middle of the floor. He could speak her language, or at least get close enough that she could understand him. That made him the one possible source of answers in this new incomprehensible world she had been thrown into, where people could change location in the blink of an eye and a single woman could kill a room full of armed men.

The boy sagged a little once the two adults had left and looked somehow depressed. The other man, who was leaning against the wall saying nothing, seemed to consider going over to him, but hesitated. She swallowed gently.

"Are you all right?" she asked, eventually, in her non-English language. The boy looked up.

"Fine. Why would not I be?" He responded. In his free time searching for the word Tannhäuser he had come across an ancient earth language known as Russian. During the time he thought Tannhäuser may have been a Russian word, he ended up learning some of the archaic language.

"You look sad," she answered simply. The boy shrugged.

"What be your name?" he asked her. "Do not tell me it actually is Nubia. That's an old only friend-conversation word for slave. What are you in real life called?"

"Svetlana Rukovodjashhij," she answered. "My mum often called me Svet."

"I am Tongues," the boy said. "I don't have a last name."

"Where are we?" Svet asked. "Who are these people?"

"We're safe," Tongues replied. "We're among, friends, of a sort. This is a spaceship, the *Elismere*. A lot of the people on-board are like you, they know the importance of the Tannhäuser Gate."

"What is the Tannhäuser Gate?"

"A group of people who make decisions about things. They've been hiding things from everyone. The crew of this ship is trying to find out exactly what."

"What happens to us?"

"We," Tongues hesitated. "We're just, sort-of, along for the ride right now. I don't really know what's going on, but it's better than where I came from." Svet thought about that.

"I think it will probably be better than where I came from too," she guessed. "There can't be that many places worse." Tongues gave her a weak smile and stood up. The two of them looked at each other awkwardly.

"If what they told me about your past life is true, this will be much better," Tongues said at last. "You're not a slave now. You won't have to," He couldn't finish. Svet looked down thoughtfully as she worked out what he was talking about and let it sink in.

"I think I will like that," she supposed. Tongues smiled at her again. He looked a little unsure.

"You're just as scared and confused as I am," she concluded. "You don't know what we're doing here because you don't want to think about it too much, do you?"

Tongues made a move as if to hug her, but hesitated. Svet flinched a little. Tongues bit his lip and slowly dropped his arms again. He went to speak, but again stopped. He thought for a bit, and then glanced over at Elios.

"I think we're all like that," he said. Svet realised she was smiling. It felt good to smile. It didn't seem to be something she did often. Perhaps she just kept forgetting.

"So, what happens now?" she asked. Tongues looked her up and down.

"Firstly, I think we need to get you out of those clothes," he said. Svet's eyes widened in surprise, and she frowned, but slowly and obediently reached for her neckline. Tongues gave a look of confusion, then one of comprehension, then turned red and backed away.

"I meant change! Change those clothes! Find some new ones. Someone will have some somewhere. They got some for me. I don't think those ones are very suitable from anyone's point of view." Svet relaxed and let out a breath, remaining only a little tense.

"Sorry," she said. "Can I wash as well? I don't like this." She gestured to her face. The makeup was slightly smudged from being slung across someone's back.

"I think so," Tongues replied. "This place does have a bathroom. Ask any member of the crew, which is basically everyone on-board that you don't yet recognise."

Svet nodded and walked to the door. It opened for her. She stopped short, staring at the doorframe and the space where the door had been blocking it. A security guard who had presumably decided to stay behind for this exact purpose stuck his head inside.

"You can go with him," Tongues told her. "He's perfectly safe, I promise." Svet looked back. She nodded tentatively and walked through the door as it opened again.

"That," said Elios, "was incredible." Tongues turned to him.

"What was?" he asked.

"That, thing. With the language. How quickly did you pick it up?"

"I just got the basics," Tongues shrugged. "I knew a lot of normal Russian anyway, because I thought Tannhäuser might have been a Russian word. It isn't, by the way. I think it's German. But I read some Russian dictionaries and so forth and I liked the sound of the words. By extrapolation, I'd imagine my accent is horrendous."

"Incredible," Elios repeated to himself, shaking his head. Tongues studied his expression, trying to work out if he was being ironic.

"Well, I guess I had to be decent at something," he said half-sarcastically, and headed off to check the library for books on teaching people English.

Back on the bridge, Tetriana marched in to find Jen sat back in her piloting couch, stretching like a cat before sighing contentedly.

"I've got us on course for Leta," she said. "Should be there in about twenty-seven hours." She shook her head at Tetriana as she opened her mouth. "No. We can go over what happened when we reach Leta. For now, get some rest. We all need it."

Tetriana frowned disapprovingly, but reasoned that, if the *Elismere* crew needed rest, that probably rendered them unfit to discuss important matters anyway. She nodded once, stomped her foot, and marched back the way she had come.

Chapter XLII

"Captain!" barked Commander into her blank communication screen. "Captain! Report!" Nothing. She checked her direct readouts from the *Ninja's* again. Again, she found that there were none. One ship had apparently been destroyed, which was impossible enough in itself. The second, however, had apparently ceased to exist. No one had yet found any traces of it.

"Dammit," Commander hissed, resetting her screen. "Lightly armed cargoship my ass. What the hell are the Gate playing at?"

"Commander?" inquired her personal guard. She silenced the well-built man with a look.

The look said, we haven't been given an accurate description of the target. That is something for which the Gate will pay later. For now, we still have a job to do. Commander was good at communicating through looks.

A curly-haired, boyish blonde appeared on her communication screen. Ordinarily, Paperwork would have flashed Commander an annoying smile at this point. Clearly, he wasn't in the mood for smiling today.

"You got everything," Commander said. It wasn't exactly a question.

"Actually, I'm not sure I did," Paperwork replied. "The second ship,"

"It disappeared, yes," answered Commander.

"Ships don't do that, generally," noted Paperwork.

"This one did."

"How?"

"Irrelevant. Write up the report. Leave questions to me."

Paperwork disappeared from the screen again. Commander tapped in a code and called up a virtual representation of those parts of the assassin network she had access to or contact with.

"Target has been upgraded," she announced to Guard. "Send it out." she commanded.

The *Elismere*, Republic Space

Svet wandered uncertainly into the shiny room she'd been pointed towards by a smiling woman whom she couldn't understand. Mirrored surfaces seemed to feature heavily in the décor, as did the colour white. The logical conclusion was that this was a bathroom. She'd been in plenty of those in her time, but this one certainly seemed to be above average in terms of cleanliness for what she had seen.

Set in one wall was some strange metal and plastic creation within which a set of clothes sat innocently. Svet noticed a curtain that turned out to be concealing the shower.

She stepped carefully into the little cuboid space, searching for a way of turning it on. A spray of water started automatically, it was pleasantly warm water and she stumbled back out with a startled scream.

Slowly, timidly, she reached out with a single hand and held it in the path of where the water had come from. Another spray hit her, and she withdrew the arm. The water turned off. She'd seen one of these too, on an occasion a few years ago when she'd been provided to a client who had let her use his personal facilities. She'd assumed you had to be quite rich to get showers like this, and she began to wonder how wealthy her new captors were.

She held her arm in the shower again, idly watching the tiny rivulets of water meandering down her skin, gradually turning white as they picked up the make-up that had been used to painstakingly conceal the blue-green veins that showed through her flesh. After a while, more jets of water sprouted from the sides of the cubicle, creating an almost-pleasant tickling sensation.

With the purity of a carefully practised ceremony, Svet peeled off the clothes Pastornak had put her in and dropped them at the foot of the shower curtain, stepping into the cubicle. Some of the jets started spraying soap instead of water as she pulled the curtain back across and shut herself off from the world outside.

She stood for some time, eyes closed and head down, one hand idly winding strands of blonde hair around her fingers as it melted free from the set style it had been put into. White droplets cascading from her skin and black droplets cascading from her eyes, some of which may or may not have been from the shower.

After a while, she started to shake.

Tongues was seated at a computer terminal in one of the *Elismere's* reading rooms, clicking frantically and occasionally stopping to hammer in some fragment of rapid two fingered typing, staring with fascinated interest at the screen. It took him a while to register when the door opened, and someone walked slowly in.

"Hey, who," he began when he finally looked up. "Wow."

Svet was a very different picture underneath the China-doll façade. She had changed into a set of plain, but practical, clothes not entirely unlike those Tongues himself had been given, and with the make-up removed her face was now naturally flawed and wonderfully reassuringly human. It also revealed the damage of a crude burn below her left eye, which, if left untreated, could potentially lead to an eye infection. Her straggly, still damp hair seemed to have been tossed sporadically rather than brushed, with the result that it now tumbled down from her scalp, threatening, but not quite managing, to get in the way of her face.

"Hey, you," Tongues started before remembering himself and switching to her language. "You," and then he had to stop again as he realised, he didn't even know what he was going to say. Svet gave an unsure half smile and considered leaving again.

"No, wait," Tongues insisted, stumbling over his words slightly. "Come here. I was just looking for some stuff to help you." Svet bit her lip and gave him a wary look but nonetheless crossed the room to peer over his shoulder. The screen displayed the most recent webcomic he was reviewing. "Uh, yeah, sorry," Tongues apologised awkwardly. "I got kind of, distracted. A lot. A minute ago I was reading an article regarding correct predictions made by speculative fiction in the 21st Century," He realised Svet was staring at him with a politely blank expression and stopped. "But what I started by doing," he explained, apparently hoping to save the situation, "was looking up techniques for learning new languages. I thought you might like to be able to tell what, you know, what people were saying."

Svet just smiled a weirdly apologetic smile and nodded. Tongues liked her smile. It reminded him of Val's ability to always find something to enjoy about a world that mostly revolved around pain.

A sharp pang shot through his mind at the thought of Val, and he crashed back into the present.

"Anyway," he recovered, "this isn't going to be particularly easy since, as you can tell from my poor pronunciation, my knowledge of your language is almost entirely, um, hang on, extrapolated, entirely extrapolated from another language completely, Russian, for reference, a very old language that first emerged on the planet Earth in its pre-space-travel-capable stage of developing. Ment. Development. Sorry."

Svet didn't reply. It struck Tongues that she hadn't actually said anything since she'd come in. "Are you all right?" he asked. Svet met his gaze and tried to smile. She nodded.

"Yes," she assured him.

Tongues slept the sweet, simple sleep of the exhausted and unburdened. This was an unfamiliar experience for him, not that he cared right now. For as long as he could remember, sleep had been something he did to escape the harsh, burning reality of waking life on *Tomorrow's Hope*. Life on the Generation Ship had been straightforward but futile and unpleasant. The only surprises were of the expected, if painful kind. And then, when he'd escaped, he hadn't had much time to appreciate the world outside. When he wasn't being thrown around and generally hurt, he was hiding for his life, or transitioning in and out of consciousness, or trying very hard not to freak out at the new and unexpected surprises that were being tossed at him in all directions.

But now, he was at peace. *Tomorrow's Hope* was gone, and he no longer had to fear the Adults, or the B4-1000s, or the Medical and Discipline personnel. He'd had time to settle down and collect his thoughts. He'd even made what might tentatively be called friends. And, most importantly, he was making progress towards the secret of the Tannhäuser Gate with every second he spent in the company of this ship and its crew.

For the first time in years, Tongues's wiry body allowed itself to unwind.

In the next room along, Svetlana Rukovodjashhij curled up in the foetal position atop the sheets of her bed. She didn't like night. At night, there was nothing to distract her from the shadows in her own head. It was at night that the memories came.

Svetlana wasn't like other girls. She knew that from the little she'd picked up from her colleagues. All of Pastornak's workers were different to other people, it seemed, because Pastornak made sure they were, and punished them whenever they weren't, but Svet was worse than most of them. It meant that Pastornak had never had reason to punish her as much as the others, but it was a curse as much as it was a blessing.

Svet couldn't forget. Anything. If she wanted to, she could drag up memories of anything she'd seen, heard or done in the past. But when she wasn't distracted, when she was alone with only her thoughts, things started to drag themselves up of their own accord.

Svet swallowed gently, screwed her eyes shut and waited for sleep. Sleep always came eventually. Sleep didn't always make it better. Going to sleep in the state she always did, made for uncomfortable dreams.

It was at times like these, when she was waiting for sleep, that Svet would force herself to concentrate on the one thing in her head that wasn't a memory.

"Tangyeĭzer Vorota," she whispered to herself. "Tannhäuser Gate. Tannhäuser Gate. Tannhäuser Gate."

Eventually, still mumbling the words, sleep took her.

And the ship slid on through the timeless bands of hyper, wherein night and day were mere foreign concepts that had no place.

*Was there another Ninja lurking in the dark, or
something much worse waiting for the Elismere in their path?*

The End

—

For Now

Milton Keynes UK
Ingram Content Group UK Ltd.
UKHW050315041024
448978UK00020B/47/J

9 781068 753329